STEVE NALLON has been a writer and performer in the world of comedy for over forty years. Steve began his performing life with his own comedy act on the Northern Working Men's Club Circuit in Yorkshire back in the 1970s. After gaining a degree in Drama and English at the University of Birmingham, Steve became a founding member of the television series *Spitting Image*, where for over a decade he voiced many of the programme's most iconic characters, including Margaret Thatcher, Alan Bennett and The Queen Mum. Steve's acting work now ranges from theatre, film and television, to video games, puppetry and audio books. As a playwright and comedy writer, Steve has a considerable body of credits to his name, including plays and series for BBC radio, three one-man theatre shows and the satirical book *I, Margaret*, which he co-wrote with the novelist Tom Holt. Over the years, Steve has contributed to numerous periodicals such as *The New Statesman* and *Musical Stages*, and is a much sought-after speaker on the lecture circuit for his insightful and amusing talks.

Twitter: @SteveNallon

Praise for *Swidgers*

'*Grabs you from the beginning and doesn't let go. Steve is a master mimic and uses all his skills to create a powerful and dramatic tale of mystery!*' Rory Bremner, BAFTA winning writer and performer

'*A rambunctious riot of a book with a totally unpredictable plot – I never knew where I was going to be taken next! Granny is a joy of a character; delightfully irreverent with wicked one-liners.*'
Joseph Elliott, YA author of *The Good Hawk, The Broken Raven* and *The Burning Swift*

'*This brilliant story whizzes along and follows William's transformation from nervy kid at the back of the class to fully fledged adventure hero. We see this wonderful adventure through William's eyes and share the adrenalin rush from his perspective. This is a great story for YA readers and grown-ups who, like William, find themselves caught up in the whirlwind of life. I loved it!'* Sonia Beldom, author of the popular children's book series *Granny Franny's Big Red Bus*

'I loved it. As a former teacher, the parent teacher meetings struck a particular chord.' Geoff Northcott, comedian, writer and broadcaster

'Steve Nallon is an experienced and formidable talent and this departure into YA *fantasy may win him a whole new generation of fans.'* Jenny Lecoat, screenwriter, novelist and author of *Hedy's Girl* and the movie *Another Mother's Son*

'Steve Nallon has always been very good at everything he's done but this first novel could be his finest hour! From the very start, it is intriguing, innovative, snappy and witty. Nallon writes with a compelling sense of rhythm and just makes you want to keep reading and going further into his magical world. It really does gallop along. Granny is a great creation and a magnificent character in every sense: engaging, shocking, loveable, embarrassing, bright and very, very funny! It's all very impressive!' Alistair McGowan, BAFTA winning writer and performer

'The Time That Never Was is the marvellous story of a boy growing up with a very special power. He is a Swidger and Swidgers can see into people's timelines and perhaps alter them. But who, or what, is watching them? Exciting, often very funny and always gripping, this is a book about adventures in time – Past, Present and Future. And in the future? Well, the good news is that there is already a sequel on the way.' William Palmer, novelist and author of *The Contract, The India House, Four Last Things, The Good Republic, The Island Rescue*

'Beguiling, inventive and magical: Nallon has conjured up a perfect world and a perfect read. A dazzling piece of fiction.' Jonathan Maitland, author of the play *Dead Sheep* and presenter of ITV's current affairs series *Tonight*

What younger readers have said about *Swidgers*

The *Swidgers* book series has been enjoyed in book clubs and reading groups in schools in Manchester, London and Luton. And here's a selection of what young readers have thought:

'What struck me most about reading 'Swidgers' was just how funny it was. I didn't expect to laugh quite so much when reading a story about a lonely boy with special powers... 'Granny' was hilarious and meant that the book never became too dark, despite the more troubling tense chapters where we feared for the characters' lives. One of the things that makes the book so original is the mixture of fantasy, sci-fi, adventure and comedy, so you never know what to expect next... I found the book exciting, entertaining and very, very funny and wouldn't hesitate to recommend it to my friends.' Year 10

'I loved reading the story. It was creative and different from any other books I've read... I also found it very inspiring because I felt the message behind the story was to do with trust and friendship. When I was reading the book I was there because I could picture the events so clear. It was like I was watching a movie... It was a really good read and I would definitely buy the book. Thank you.' Year 8

'I liked the suspense at the beginning that makes you want to read on... I thought it progressed well and was clear what was happening. Furthermore, I thought the characters were well thought out and their characteristics and personalities were established at the beginning. Overall, despite being something I wouldn't usually choose to read, I enjoyed the book. I would recommend it to people between the ages of 11 and 14.' Year 9

'I think that the storyline of the book was great and that there were some great characters... A brilliant book... I really enjoyed the book and would definitely read the rest in the series.' Year 7

'It was a really good book with really imaginative twists. By using great metaphors the author helped me picture the scenes very effectively. It was a real page turner and I look forward to reading the next in the Swidgers!' Year 8

'I thoroughly enjoyed reading this book due to the amazing storyline, character, humour and general style of writing. The characters were well crafted, with every character being given unique appearances, behaviours and traits. This made the book all the more entertaining. A good example of this of this was Granny's character, with her bizarre quirky appearance and eccentric way of speech... I thought the storyline of the book was compelling and made the book hard to put down at times... perfect tension and abundance of carefully placed cliff-hangers which created a very engaging read... I loved the brilliant cliff-hanger at the end and can't wait to see what's next for William and Granny. Well done!' Year 10

'I feel that this is an excellent teenager book and if you are into mysteries and horror, this book is perfect for you.' Year 7

'I really enjoyed the book and I thought the main character was unusual and interesting. I really wanted to find out why he had the strange powers and discover his history. The story moved along really fast and made me want to read on. Overall, the plot was really good.' Year 8

'I found this book to be interesting and funny. I also found this book used a number of different emotions which drew me in to the story.' Year 7

'I personally enjoyed the book a lot, especially at the beginning of the story. I enjoyed that part because it gets you hyped for the rest of the story and does not fail to keep your attention. It leaves you wondering what is happening and does it in a way that keeps you reading... I'd recommend it to my friends as I think they'd like the mystery and adventure but also find it funny. It's a really original idea and I found it really entertaining. I'd definitely be interested in reading more books by the author.' Year 9

'I really like the concept. I thought that it was an original idea. My favourite character was Granny because I thought she was funny. The opening was really good and got me immediately interested... I really liked the story.' Year 8

A SWIDGER TIME ADVENTURE

The Time That Never Was
Book One in the Series

STEVE NALLON

Luath Press Limited

EDINBURGH

www.luath.co.uk

First published 2022

ISBN: 978-1-910022-61-0

The paper used in this book is recyclable. It is made
from low chlorine pulps produced in a low energy,
low emissions manner from renewable forests.

Printed and bound by
Clays Ltd., Bungay

Typeset in 10.5 point Sabon LT Pro by
Main Point Books, Edinburgh

Contents

For Doreen Mary

CHAPTER ONE

Saving the Man

LIKE LIGHTNING. SO sharp, fierce and bright it blinded. And it's that flash where I must begin my story. I couldn't tell at first where it came from… except I knew, somehow, it wasn't the sky…

I was there that Saturday because, for me, a busy street is better than my empty house. Why the house was empty, well, that can wait. It's not important anyhow. All that mattered that sunny morning was – *The Man*.

I should say to you straightaway that our kind usually do what we do and then move on. Yet that day, something made me keep on following. Even after my task was complete. And that one thought changed everything. My whole life. And yours, too.

This is what happened. I was standing outside the Crossed Keys pub. By the door. Well, they'd never let me into the bar. Not then. Too young. Besides, by the door is a good place to wait. So many people passing by, so many lives to change.

The High Street in Chipping Barnet is on a hill and the Crossed Keys pub is about halfway between the underground station at the bottom and the old church at the top. It's a steep walk up and people normally take it slowly but when I saw The Man, he'd already passed the Post Office. Getting faster and faster with every step. That pounding stride men have when they're late for something. Yes, it's the ones who rush who can be the worst.

I didn't know when the harm would come or what it would be. We never do. But I did know it was vital to stop *The Man* and *The Accident* coming together in *Time*. You see, that is what our kind do. We change Timepaths. We hinder. Block. Impede.

Or simply just get in your way. And it's those precious seconds that will save you from whatever danger is ahead. That is the gift our kind offer humans. Or try to.

Oh, but this guy – *The Man* – is quick. Only a few steps away now. I need to stop him before it happens.

But what delay to use?

Dropped wallet?

No, left that back at the empty house.

Shoelaces undone?

Not an option. Today I'm wearing slip-ons. And I'm only a boy, so can't ask for a light. Not that I smoke or ever would.

Oh no, he's about to pass me.

Yeah, there he goes.

But what's that he's carrying across his shoulders? A holdall? I hadn't noticed it before. Looks heavy. A tool bag, I think. I'm guessing he's on his way to work. Even on a Saturday morning.

Oh, but I should've stopped him by now.

Yes, I could just bump into him but the pavement's bursting with people and it's his Timepath alone I must alter, no one else's.

I walk close behind him, matching his every step. That tool bag of his has slipped a bit down his back and now I can see a wooden handle sticking out. A hammer, I suppose. No, too heavy. He'd feel me take it. And our kind must avoid being noticed. What else is there? Pieces of copper pipe. He's a plumber, I guess.

Wait… is that a metal file?

Yeah, that would work. He'd hear that when it hit the ground.

But do it quick, William, do it quick. Whatever is about to happen to The Man could happen any second.

I'm just a pace behind him. I fix my eyes on that metal file sticking out of his holdall. Tricky, but possible. Don't think he'll be able to tell it was me, not with so many distractions.

Just ahead there's someone in a pink rhino costume, collecting with a charity bucket. Hah! My plumber does a side-step to avoid it. But that's good because now I have a chance to reach inside.

Yeah, I was right, it's rough and scratchy. A workman's file. I carefully pull it away with my fingers and then gently let it drop to the pavement.

My idea was good. The Man should have heard it clang and so turned back to pick it up. Those seconds would have been enough. But that never happened because, right at the wrong moment, a car blasted its horn and the clang was drowned out.

Why do humans rush so much? Always battling against Time. Yes, there he goes, marching on.

I've said it's best if our kind don't draw too much attention to ourselves, but there are moments when we have no choice. Like right now.

'Hey, Mister!' I call. 'You've dropped something.'

My plumber half turns his head but still carries on walking, so I pick it up and shout, 'This metal file. It fell out your bag!'

Has he heard me? Yes, he's stopped.

At last, The Man's Timepath has been altered.

'Thanks, mate!'

Australian. I didn't expect that. Not sure why.

Of course, it would have been better if he had come to me – extra seconds always help – but no, he was one of those that just stood there so it was up to me to walk up the hill and hand the file over.

'Life of their own, these,' said the Aussie. 'Second one gone walkabout this week.'

I watched as my plumber put his metal file securely back in his bag.

'Cheers, kid,' he said. And with that, he was on his way up the hill again.

Well, that should have been it. Timeline changed. Task complete. Move on. Yet that day my eyes stayed on him and I saw what I hoped I would not see: he started to run.

Oh no, The Man was trying to make up the Time he'd lost. The precious seconds I'd just given him.

This sometimes happens. But you accept it. You've done what you had to do and should do no more. That's just the way things are. If The Man wishes to catch up with Time, then so be it. He doesn't know that today Time will not be his friend. Nor that those precious seconds I gave him would have saved his life –

Hang on a second… What was that? Save his life! Where did that thought come from? And how could I know? Because our kind never know.

This isn't right. Not right at all. We change Timepaths, but to feel what will happen next – the fate we're saving you from – impossible. Never had I had such thoughts before. Yet now I did. Somehow, I knew.

The Man is running to his death.

What to do? Turn and go? But how can I? I mean, this a human life at stake. Yet to run after him would go against everything I'd ever done before.

So, what would it be, up the hill or down? Scurry away or follow? Well, sometimes in life there never really is a choice.

As soon as I chased after him, I knew in that moment that my world would never be the same again. I couldn't tell you why. Just felt it inside. I could not yet know the battles I would live through or the horrors I would witness. Nor how I would become somebody I never expected to be. Perhaps you think I'm making too much of such a moment, but I tell you, I'm not, because, as my story will reveal – *just one thought can change everything*.

I'm tall for my age, not as fit like some of the lads at school, but I can run fast when I need to. As I do now.

Bit too quick. Nearly knock over a small boy. Oh, but he's too busy pretending to shoot his daddy with a toy pistol so doesn't see me. I have to swerve though, and when I do, I bump into the postman with his sack of letters. He does see me. And what a strange look I get.

As I dash and dart among the shoppers, I catch sight of my plumber. He's now nearing the top of the hill where there's a bend in the road and the street turns. Opposite is the old church, looking grey and tired. Along its wall are roadworks with men in yellow hats digging a deep trench. Good, it's blocked off that side, plus the temporary traffic lights are now on green, which means my plumber can't cross.

Yes, I'm right. My Man has had to stop by the coffee shop. *But wait, maybe this is where whatever it is will happen.*

I feel something… and it's getting stronger… stronger than anything I've sensed before. Oh no! Death is right there waiting for him. *But how will it happen?* No, no, I can't sense that yet…

Not that I can do anything about it because I'm still a bit of a distance from The Man. Plus there's a crowd of people in the way.

I try and ease myself between the Saturday shoppers who, like him, are waiting for those lights to change. And as I do, I glance into the coffee shop full of Saturday mums and dads and their playful toddlers. An old lady in a big purple hat with her back to me moves a pram away from the door so she can leave.

But what I see stops me in my tracks. A reflection in the coffee shop front window. The glass is slightly angled so the window acts like a mirror and what it reflects isn't so much the church opposite, but its roof and the sky above, bright and open. And right now something is hurtling down through the air, heading straight towards the church. It's big. A rock? No, it's gleaming white with jagged edges. More like a crystal.

Then I realise – ice! A huge boulder of ice. And it's about to hit the church roof.

What's strange, as I think back now, is that it seemed as if my mind's eye were witness to what would happen even before it struck. I could see it all – the crystalline ice would pierce a hole in the slates as if it were a bullet. The wound would be deep, but there'd be no yawning gash, for the hit would be precise and exact. Almost as if the ice had known all along the job it had to do.

Someone I was yet to meet would often tell me that all human life was at the mercy of the next tile that fell. Ah, but you must wait to hear from her. Yet she was right. *Chance is everywhere.*

I now spin around from that reflection in the coffee shop window and see the impact of the ice on the church roof for real. The roof tiles are already falling everywhere and the workmen below are forced to clamber out of their trench. Those yellow hats won't be enough to save them. In the scramble, a workman knocks over a sign that says: DANGER: EXPOSED ELECTRICAL CABLES.

But what happened next, I did not foresee, for from the sky now comes a huge boulder that strikes the tarmac right in front of me, scattering ice like diamonds.

There's screaming all around. From a mother with an already crying child. From a little girl who, without thought, lets go of her balloon. From a man too drunk even to know why he is even screaming. The postman I bumped into earlier now stands beside me. He doesn't scream, just stares ahead, a letter yet to be delivered in his hand.

People don't know where to turn. And nor do I, but through the many cries I hear something only I could. Another strike of ice. Smaller than the first two but with it comes danger... No, more than danger: *Death.*

I can feel it. The Man is about to die and only I can save him.

CHAPTER TWO

The First Attack

THE STRIKE FROM the sky on the church roof had startled everyone and the crash onto the tarmacked road brought panic, but in the commotion no one but me had heard that third hit of ice on the roof of the coffee shop. And that was the moment I knew it would be a falling tile from that roof above us that would kill The Man. For it would land exactly where The Man was standing. Where he is will be where he'll die.

Without thought, just the instinct that makes us who we are, I grab at his tool bag and pull it towards me. The Australian is strong and fit, but that unexpected tug does what it was meant to do. He loses his balance and falls backwards. A split second later the tile flies by, passing before his eyes like the blade of a guillotine. The grey tile then crashes onto the hard Yorkstone paving and shatters into a dozen harmless fragments.

And all my plumber says is, 'Jeez!'

Well, he was an Aussie. So that was that. My job, I thought, was finally done. I could walk away and that would be that. Oh, but how wrong I was. For in truth, a whole new life was about to begin.

You see, in the reflection of the window, I saw another loosened tile on the church roof beginning to pull itself away. Most of the others had landed harmlessly on a pile of rubble nearby, yet, as this last one slid over the ridge of the roof, it was as if it already knew its target, for it shot through the air, pointing like an arrow with its aim in sight. And, as it disappeared into the trench, a cold wave of fear washed over me.

It was then it happened.

That flash. Blinding. Penetrating. Like lightning. Only… not lightning.

Something more powerful. Something somehow released. And with that burst of light, came a menacing noise, like the cracking of a whip.

My eyes adjusted. It was then I realised. That strange and frightening light just now hadn't come from the sky. No, its genesis was that dugout pit beside the church.

Creeping and threatening, out from that hollow ground emerged two lengths of electrical cable, spewing sparks. Each had a severed end like the mouth of a snake and the flares spat out were not white and pure but green and vicious. These cables, muddied orange in colour, now twisted and curled – *as if alive!* Not really cables at all but two venomous vipers in battle.

One rose high in the air and struck its coiled twin down with a blistering bolt, but its foe fought back with its own strike and once more they were evenly matched. The first rose up high again and then hit its rival with such a mighty blast that it fell back, shaken and wounded. The attacker then moved in for the kill, with a vicious bolt cracking through its opponent's head. The victor now raised itself higher, twisting this way and that, as if on the lookout for fresh prey.

The cable snake grew tall and lifted itself high above us all. It was clearly able to strike out at any moment and in any direction, and so much so, that those nearby could do nothing but watch in helpless desperation. Among them, that postman, still gripping his letter, and the little girl who had lost her balloon. Only now she was terrified.

'Whaaaah! Wah!' she cries.

Don't do that, I think, *or the serpent will notice you.*

Too late, it has, for it now moves towards her, spitting venom.

'Ahhssss! Ahhhsss! Ahaaarrssssshhhrrrr!!'

The serpent's mouth widens, as if ravenous and ready to kill.

Is the viper about to strike?

Yes, it is! I turn away in horror. And yet again I see it all in the refection of the coffee shop window. The cable, snake, or whatever it was, strikes and in an instant the little girl becomes no more than charred and blackened cinders.

I feel a deep empty pain within me, the like of which I have never lived before. A dark shadow spreads far and wide that seems to last beyond forever.

But then everything suddenly stopped. And I mean, really stopped. No noise, no movement. Not from anywhere. Not from anyone. It was as if people all around me had become cast in fear like statues.

I then turned away from the coffee shop window, but as I did, the world came alive again – and there was the little girl. Living and breathing!

How to explain the impossible? Had Time somehow moved backwards? Or had what I'd seen in the window reflection been some sort of a vision?

But there was no time to make sense of it, for the cable snake was already on the move. After a bend and a stretch, it began to advance in my direction, with its head pointing straight at me. Only then it began to swivel its neck, as if examining and curious.

All of a sudden, it turned away and fixed its glare instead on the postman who, without thought for himself, now grabbed the little girl and flung her behind him. She screamed and screamed and screamed some more but at least now seemed safe from further harm. The postman then took his sack from his shoulders and threw it to the pavement. He opened his arms wide as if to say to the devouring monster, 'Take me, not the child!'

The cable snake swung its head from side to side, as if, this time, deciding what to do next. 'Will I? Won't I?', it appeared to be thinking. It then stretched itself to full height – and spat out a vile green blast of light.

Again, I spun about in fear, for again, I couldn't watch. Yet once more I saw what was happening in that strange window mirror of the coffee shop. The poor postman – not old, not young, nor thin, nor fat, just, I thought, an ordinary everyday man – was no match for that flashing rod of lightning. It pierced his chest with a strike so powerful I could hear bones break. Scorched and seared, his body then suddenly splattered into a mass of burning red and black.

In that moment it was not pain or grief I felt but a strange absence. A loss of something not yet understood. And then once more, everything froze. There, right in front of me, was the exploding body of the postman, suspended in mid-air. The world again had become a landscape of petrified silence.

What was happening? Had the minutes and seconds somehow – I don't know – stopped? Or was I in some sort of Circle of Time?

So confused, I didn't know what to think. The reflections in the coffee shop window couldn't be true, yet they felt so real. None of this was happening and yet it was. All I knew for sure was that never had I been so afraid.

Perhaps, I thought, *if I close my eyes it'll go away.*

So I do. But now I feel an unearthly bitter cold more frightening than whatever was in front of me. I open them again and turn from the window.

The impossible has happened once more. The postman, back on his feet and alive. The little girl, still there, and still screaming.

The only way I can describe all this is that it was as if *The Now*, the moment we live in, was ever changing. As if Time itself was somehow shifting between *What Is* and *What Could Be*. At least that's what I thought. I wish I could explain it better, but I can't. What I can tell you is it felt like the beginning of madness.

Then I sensed it. The way our kind do. Something truly terrible was about to happen...

Oh no... was it my own life that was about to end?

Would the next strike be my *Now*? Not the little girl's, not the postman's. Mine. If I'm struck down there'll be no coming back for me. Better that way, I think, because it is for the human world that our kind exist. Yes, I might look like a boy, a young lad you might see every day, but I am not what I seem. Besides, my short life has been lived unnoticed and unwanted. There's little to leave behind. The house I left this morning was – and always is – empty. Loveless, too. Few will miss my passing.

And so I shut my eyes again and accept my fate. I then sense the snake coming nearer and nearer.

Oh, it's close, so very close!

Yet nothing happens. I open my eyes. The snake pulls away. I watch as it jerks its head side to side then up and down.

What's it doing? It's almost like it's mocking me. Laughing even.

That head now twists itself towards the mother and her crying child, then back to the postman, as if to say, 'I can take her if I like. Or him.'

But then it stills. It has decided. The cable snake rises high and lurches back upon itself. And strikes! It's scarred and molten mouth flies past my head to attack whoever stands behind me. I turn.

It is The Man! The plumber.

But as look again I see the snake hasn't aimed at his body – more his bag of metal tools. There's a sudden blazing green light as the snake's mouth hits its target. The canvass bag explodes in incandescent flames. The plumber is thrown back by the shock.

I reach out to help, and for all I know I do touch him, but I feel nothing except a tingle as he speeds by. His body lands on the Yorkstone slabs. Is he alive or dead? I cannot tell. Is it pain or loss I feel? Neither. Just defeat. Somehow, I've been tricked.

Just for a moment I have hope. Perhaps, I think, Time will shift once more and the *Now* will change again and I will see the plumber back on his feet as I had with the postman and the little girl.

But that *Now* does not happen. And Time moves on.

The dirty coil has done its worst and it slowly drops to the earth. Its severed end lands where the ice had fallen on the road. Sparks fly, briefly, as it makes contact with the melting water. And then it seems to die. No more a snake, just a grubby, muddy orange cable.

Then – *SMACK!*

A hit. Like one almighty punch. Something heavy landing on my head. A yellow hat comes running towards me. No, two yellow hats. I blink.

There's something in my eye. A thick, blurry crimson. I wipe my face. My hands are red. Blood? I fall. And as I do, I wonder, 'Will anyone even come to my funeral?'

And with that final thought the blurry crimson fades and is replaced by blackness.

CHAPTER THREE

The Get Well Card

'OH, THE SLEEPER doth awake,' speaks a voice with a soft Irish lilt.

I open my eyes. A woman in green stands over me.

'Well good mornin' to you, young sir.'

A uniform with a white band round its edge. A nurse? I look around. Yes, I'm lying in a hospital bed, wearing a patient's gown.

Well, I'm alive. Or at least I think I am. But I suddenly feel a terrible ache. And can't even tell where it's coming from.

'You've made the newspaper!' says the nurse, pointing to *The Chipping Express* spread out on a table beside my bed.

'Just the local. Don't be imaginin' you're big enough news for the nationals!'

News? I don't want to be news.

I have so many questions but there's only one that matters.

'Did the plumber live?' I ask.

She comes closer. The name on her hospital badge reads, Molly, and underneath that, Senior Nursing Sister. I like Nurse Molly. She has a warm tone to her voice. A nice smile. And smells of talc.

'And what plumber was that?' she asks, her head now to one side, the way heads often are when examining you.

'The plumber attacked by the snake!' I answer.

Oh, why did I say that? But I know why, because that's the image that keeps coming in my mind.

I look into her eyes. They've seen it all, haven't they? Perhaps that's why she doesn't seem that surprised by what I've just said.

'A snake, was it? Oh, maybe that bump on your noggin is

worse than the good doctor thought.'

Bump? What bump?

I lift my hands to my head. Bandages.

'Do you remember a postman?' Nurse Molly inquires.

Yes, I say to her, I did. A man struck by an electrical bolt, burnt to a cinder, who then came back to life again. Only I don't tell Molly that bit.

'Well,' she goes on, 'the postman came with you to the hospital. With you and the other fella. But no snake. And no plumber. The postman though, he did leave you this.'

Nurse Molly picks up a sealed envelope lying on the table next to me.

'Shall I do the honours?'

I nod and she opens it. Inside, a Get Well card with a cartoon yellow sun in top hat and white gloves with tiny dancing feet beneath.

'Oh, it's our best seller. But no name, though. See, it's just signed "The Postman". Oh, but very concerned, he was.'

Nurse Molly then stands the card on the table and seats herself on a chair next to my bed.

'So, m'treasure, tell me all about this snake of yours.'

By then, I was becoming more awake. Of course, it wasn't a snake. I knew that. It was just an electrical cable. But the way it spat out those sparks – like molten venom – and how it seemed to think – then pounce…

Nurse Molly sat waiting for my reply. Perhaps she saw how unsettled I had become and so held my hand for a moment.

'Now I'd say you're far too young to be having acid flashbacks. And not yet old enough for the cheese to have fallen off the cracker. So could it be that you dreamt this snake of yours?'

Dreamt? If only she knew. You see, our kind never dream. But I couldn't tell her that either.

'I meant it *looked* like a snake,' I explained. And that was true.

'What looked like a snake?'

'The electrical cable.'

'And what is the very last thing you remember?'

'A man in a yellow hat. No, two hats. Two men.'

'And before that?'

'The electric cable,' I nearly said *attacked* but caught myself in time, 'it struck the plumber. Is he all right?'

'Do you remember being hit on the head?'

'No – I mean yes. There was this big flash. Cables came out of the roadworks. They were moving everywhere... and then... and then... and then there was another flash and the plumber fell. After that I felt this punch on the head. I think. I'm not sure. It all seemed to happen so quickly.'

'Well, this may explain it,' she said, picking up the local newspaper from the side table. 'I was reading the very page when you woke up. Where is it now? Oh yes, here we are. To answer your question, the plumber is fine. Only, he isn't a plumber. See.'

Nurse Molly then pointed to the headline.

'I GOT THE SHOCK OF MY LIFE', SAYS ELECTRICIAN.' Ha! Ha! I bet they came up with that one. But save your eyes, young fella, I'll tell you all about it.'

Molly's face then disappeared behind *The Chipping Express* and she began to read aloud.

'"Aussie electrician, Jayden Mitchell, twenty-eight" – oh, and quite a fit fella he is. I've taken his pulse! – "is recovering in hospital from burns as a result of a severe electrical shock following what has been called "a freak accident". A live electrical cable in the High Street roadworks was severed by falling tiles from the roof of St John's church."'

Nurse Molly then peeked her head over the open pages.

'Oh, I tell you, those old slates are sharper than you'd think. And heavy, too. Easter, I'd say it was, we had a poor fella in here with his arm nearly sliced off from one that fell right outside his own front door.'

She then disappeared again behind her newspaper.

'Where was I? Oh yes – falling tiles from the church roof… "which had been loosened by a bizarre strike of ice, which, it is reported, fell from a plane's undercarriage after it was struck by lightning."'

Again, she gazed at me from above the top of the page.

'Now where else would that block of ice be coming from? Do they think the Man in the Moon has started throwing things? Oh, but these strange electrical storms we've been having, they even have the weathermen flummoxed. But back to the paper. "The electrical cable," said Jayden, "was jumping everywhere at once, with sparks coming out of one end"– oh, I see now why you thought of snakes.

'Well, the Australian pin-up goes on, "with all that electricity about," – here it comes – "you might say it couldn't *resist* me!" Ha! Did he think that terrible joke up himself or again, or did they make him say it? Anyways, The Great Jayden lived. As he explains himself, '"Luckily I was on my way to work and so was wearing my protective insulation boots, otherwise I might have carked it!"' Oh, don't ya just love Australians! "Carked it"! To see the doctor's face if I wrote that on their tag before sending them off to the morgue.'

Nurse Molly closed the newspaper for a second, only to then wink at me, and promptly open it again.

'Now did you think I was going to miss out the best bit: yourself! "An unnamed boy was hit by falling debris and taken to the local hospital but his condition is not thought to be serious." Oh, will there be no end to your fame?'

Nurse Molly now put the newspaper down and went to examine the notes at the end on my bed.

'"William", it says here,' she observed, with a puzzled face, 'but I'm thinking, since you've only just come round, and you had no wallet or anything on you, who was it that told us?'

Of the many questions around the story of this day, that would be one of the last to be answered.

Just then the door opened.

'Oh, good afternoon, doctor,' said Nurse Molly.

But this young doctor was in a hurry. No time for greetings.

'How is the patient?' she asked, promptly.

'Well, we've been chatting away and I'd say his stairs go all the way up to the top floor.'

The doctor didn't reply and the brief smile she gave me went up and down so quickly you'd hardly know it'd been there. She then took from her pocket what I thought was a metal pen, only with the push of a button it lit up at one end.

'Eyes open wide, please,' she instructed.

She and the light came nearer. A pretty face, I thought. Sweet eyes. And no make-up. But then she came so close all I could see was her nose, which twitched slightly, like a rabbit's. Then even that disappeared as the light between her fingers began to blind me.

'A man goes to market and buys an apple, a blackboard and a lipstick. What did I say he bought?'

'An apple, a blackboard and lipstick,' I answered, almost not thinking.

'MSE fine,' said the doctor, turning to Nurse Molly, 'as I thought, just a bad bump on the head. Best keep him under observation for an hour or so but after that he can be discharged. Of course he'll need to be signed for.'

A few lines were written on my notes and then this busy young doctor, whose name I never knew, left the room.

But what she had said worried me. Signed for? Who'd do that? I had no one... or so I believed.

I've always liked to think it was at that moment that the wasps arrived to bring her to me. They'd be there now, swarming round that silly hat of hers. Oh, I'm jumping ahead again. But you've not got that long to wait.

I knew Nurse Molly would want to know who'd be collecting me, so, before she even had time to ask, I said, 'Is he in the hospital? The electrician, I mean.'

'Indeed, he is,' she replied, 'about five doors down.'

'Could I see him?'

This seemed to give Nurse Molly an idea.

'Why not! Oh, but you'll have to fight through that queue o'nurses! Seen his picture in the paper, they have, and now they're all over him like flies on a horse in August!'

She checked her watch.

'Oh, that's good timing. Get dressed now, m'young fella, m'lad, I'll be off to get your discharge letter. You'll find your breeches in the side table.'

And with that, out the door she went. At last I was alone with my thoughts.

All this was wrong. Everything about it.

Our kind are meant to prevent accidents, not be one. Ahead is a Timepath better not taken, so we stop you taking it. I bet it's happened to you. Rushing somewhere, late for something, then someone got in your way – an old lady losing her purse, a kid on a skateboard, a blind man with a stick – under your breath you cursed us, but then a car you didn't see misses you by inches. It's then you think: 'If that boy hadn't run out in front of me, I'd have been under that.' Yet our kind are never meant to *become* the accident. Yet here I was in hospital with a big bandage on my head.

But it wasn't just that which was troubling me. Those visions or images or reflections or whatever they were, they looked so real. And the pain and loss I felt when that little girl died, they seemed real too. But they couldn't have been because the little girl, and the postman, came back to life. Or never died in the first place.

And then there was what that newspaper said. The lightning strike on the plane. The ice that struck. The tiles that fell. The cable that split. One thing following another. As if intended. And as for that snake. Yes, it was only a cable, yet it seemed so alive. As if it knew what it was doing.

As I got dressed that morning, I had no answers, but there'd come a day when I would. Forgive me, I jump ahead again. Better to tell my tale as it happened and not as it came to be understood. And I do this as much for myself as for you. For isn't it sometimes in the very telling of our story that we come to understand it?

Ahhh!

There's a sudden pain across my forehead. It feels like I've been hit again, like I was back on that High Street with that falling tile, only as I look about me, there's no one there.

CHAPTER FOUR

The Australian

THAT PAIN IN my head, how it hurt. Sharp and deep, like a hammer's hit of the nail. Only it felt as if it came from inside me, somehow. What was it? But then it was gone almost as soon as it arrived. Even so, I had to take a deep breath.

'Ahhuuuuuh –'

I turned and there was Nurse Molly standing just inside the door with my letter of discharge, but I don't think she saw my grimace.

'If you want to visit the Australian, m'young fella, come with me.'

I got up from the bed and moved towards the door. I was steady enough on my feet as I walked down the corridor. Perhaps that sudden pain wasn't anything to do with the bump on my head?

Nurse Molly stopped and indicated a door half ajar.

'The dreamboat is in there,' she whispered, 'and it's Nurse Petra who has the good fortune to be looking after him.' She then popped her head round the side and pushed me forward saying, 'This is William, the young miracle who was hit on the noodle and lived. Could he be waiting here? Miracle or no he's only a boy-een and needs to be signed for.'

My discharge letter was then handed to Nurse Petra before she could even say no.

'I'll be seeing you, then. These night shifts will be the death of me, but at least now I'm away to my bed.' And with that cheery goodbye she was gone.

Ah, that's why she was happy to bring me to see the Australian, so she could go home. And who'd sign for me was now not her problem. No fool, that Nurse Molly.

Jayden Mitchell, Australian, aged twenty-eight, was sitting in a hospital bed, bandaged all the way up his right arm and shoulder, with wires from his chest connecting him to some sort of monitoring equipment. Next to him in a chair was a young lady holding his hand.

'Hiya, mate. Come in. I'm Jay. This is Candice. My better half.'

I was a bit confused because both women in the room wore medical uniforms, only Candice's was blue not green like Nurse Molly's. Perhaps Nurse Petra noticed my puzzled face for it was she who spoke first in what I guessed was probably an eastern European accent. What she said was *I am the nurse and Candice is a vet* only with her accent it came out as 'I am ze noose and canned-ice-is-wet'.

Candice began to snigger, but Jayden gave her an embarrassed glance and her giggles soon stopped. An awkward silence followed.

'Do you remember me?' I asked, closing the door nervously.

'Er, were you there too? At the, er, scene of the crime?' Jayden replied smiling, perhaps a little relieved that someone at last had said something.

'Yes. I was hit on the head.'

'Reckon!' he the Australian laughed, pointing his left hand up at me.

How stupid. I had forgotten I too was bandaged. But at least he didn't recognise me.

Jayden then gave me a half thumbs up.

'Won't shake your hand, mate. Cos I can't! Be a few days, they say, before I'm back on the turps! Bodgy tile, that got you, was it? One nearly had me. Don't know how but I fell back and missed it.'

Ah, that's good. He hadn't cottoned on what I'd done either.

'But my luck ran out when that cable chose me.'

That was an odd way of putting it. And his girlfriend Candice thought so too.

'Jay, it didn't *choose* you, it struck in your direction because it was attracted to the metal tools. Electricity, it's like lightning–'

'It's not *like* lightning, Can,' he interrupted. 'Electricity *is* lightning. I should know. But I tell you straight, mate,' looking back at me, 'it was as if that cable was staring right at me.'

Candice shook her head. And Petra smiled again. Another silence followed.

On the table, standing between two vases of flowers, were several Get Well cards, including one I recognised. Jayden must have seen how I was looking at it, and, perhaps relieved at an opportunity to change the subject, said, 'Yeah, got a few cards. That cartoon one with the dancing sun is from the Postie. They say he came with me in the ambulance.'

I'd thoughtlessly left mine behind in my room. Candice passed me the card and I opened it. Again, no words, but simply signed 'The Postman'.

I asked if he had any other injuries, apart from the electrical burns. Jayden said he had a bruise from being thrown by the impact of the strike but otherwise he was fine.

'All this,' added Candice, indicating the wires on Jayden's chest connecting to the monitor, 'is just a precaution. Sometimes, you see, electrical shock can interfere with the heart.'

I glanced at the screen. A silent repeating green peak ran across it. I'd never seen a heart monitor before so, curious, I walked over to take a closer look.

'The reason why people are thrown, as Jayden was,' Candice went on, 'is because of muscular contraction. Electrical shock interferes with nerve control. And the heart is muscle, so that's why the monitor's there. But luckily Jay is quite fit.'

'Not just fit, very, very fit! Ha! Ha! Ha!' added Nurse Petra, laughing away to herself.

Jayden gave a brief half smile but that soon vanished when

he caught sight of his girlfriend's dead-eyed stare. Shuffling awkwardly in his bed, the Australian then turned to me and asked, 'So, er, William is it, would you like to see my tree?'

By now I was standing right beside the heart monitor, my finger in the air following the green pulse that ran across the screen, but on hearing the word 'tree' I instinctively pulled it away.

'Just had my tree photographed by some medical journo,' he went on, 'very rare, they say. I'll show you.'

Jayden tried to loosen his hospital gown with his good arm but struggled with the bow. Nurse Petra went to help but Candice stepped in quick.

'I'll deal with it,' she said sharply, taking hold of the strings.

'Careful, Can, with those wires.'

'I will be,' she replied, undoing the top bow to reveal Jayden's chest, 'I am medically trained.'

And there it was.

The Tree.

Like a tattoo, only somehow more part of his flesh than mere ink. Its colour was a pinkish red, like a ripening strawberry. I could see why Jayden had called it a tree for it covered his whole chest and had stretching branches and offshoot leaves that spread everywhere. Beautiful in its own way, but, for me, alarming. For our kind, you should know, fear trees. In the past, trees have seemed to sense who I am and even without the wind they have swayed menacingly towards me. I didn't fully understand it then but in that moment, as I looked at that tree on human skin, a jittery sense of unease came upon me. Not just nervousness but fear and dread. Here present, somehow, was something stronger and more powerful than I had ever known.

And a shuddering terror ran through my whole body.

CHAPTER FIVE

The Lightning Flowers

'THEY'RE CALLED LIGHTNING flowers,' explained Candice, pointing to the strange markings on Jayden's skin.

'Rare as rockin' horse sh—!'

'Jayden!' interrupted his girlfriend. 'Mind your language!'

'But that's what the quacks said. Deadset! And there's been enough of them in here wanting to take a squiz.'

'That's true,' agreed Candice, a little more friendly, 'and I wrote some of what they said down.'

Candice opened the drawer of the side table, took out a used envelope and began to examine the notes she'd written on the back.

'Let me read it. "The tree shape is caused by a rupture of the capillaries beneath the skin."'

'Ruptured capillaries!' I blurted out.

'Oh, sorry, when you're medically trained, as I am, you sometimes assume everyone else it. Don't look so worried. Capillaries are just very small blood vessels. The smallest in your body. They're there to help move things like oxygen from the blood in your veins to whatever part of your body needs it.'

'Like bridges,' I said, less anxious now.

'Yes,' answered Candice, 'I suppose you could call them that. And breaking a few won't do that much harm.'

Candice looked again at her notes on the Get Well card envelope.

'But the point is if they are ruptured, as when hit by electricity, they leave – let me get this right – "arborescent", that means tree-like, "erythema keraunographic" markings. These markings are usually only found on people who've been struck by lightning. But, in a way, Jay was.'

Candice then handed the envelope over to me, saying, 'Personally speaking, I think it's lovely. Nice leaves and a big, long branch.'

Nurse Petra then laughed quietly to herself.

'Do they hurt?' I asked, still a little nervous.

'A bit sore, that's all,' Jayden answered, perhaps a tad flustered by Petra's giggling. 'They say they'll fade in time, but the doctors did warn they can spread and turn purple. If they do, I'll be zombified!'

Jayden suddenly bolted upright, stretched out his good arm, and started grunting, 'Ahrrrrah!'

Both Candice and Nurse Petra jumped back.

Jayden then laughed, 'Ha! Gotcha both!'

He next swung his arm side to side, zombie-like, making hissing and snarling noises as he did.

'*Hissss! Snarrrr! Grrrarr!*'

Candice was not happy. 'Stop it!' she insisted, but Jayden just laughed and grunted all the more.

'*Ha! Ha! Hissss! Snarrrr! Ha! Ha! Grrrarr!*'

Then it happened.

The heart monitor had been silent. Muted, perhaps. But now it began to bleep. As I was standing near it, I saw straight away how the pulsating green line became more and more rapid. And as it did, those beeps grew shriller and shriller.

Nurse Petra looked worried. Candice's face too was one of alarm and instinctively she grabbed Jayden's hand, but Jayden himself was neither fearful nor alarmed, just confused.

In the moments that followed I caught only snatches of phrases, from Nurse Petra 'ECG – heart rate – move away!' and from Candice 'Do something – get somebody – press the alarm' – for my attention was focused on that monitor and its unearthly screeches.

Unbelievably, the green pulse on the screen was changing shape. No longer a series of peaks but now the outline of what looked like a clenched fist – which then opened and reached towards me – with a grab!

I jumped back. But as I did, the hand on the screen lost its shape and became the mere scratchings of an angry child.

All this time the pitch of the bleeps kept rising. From cry to howl, howl to scream, scream to squeal, until they became one deafening shriek that seemed to pierce my very soul.

Then the monitor went blank and the bleeps stopped.

I looked to Jayden. There he was still sitting up in his bed. Still breathing. Still conscious. And his heart, for all I could tell, still pumping.

Nurse Petra must have realised it was the machine that was at fault, not Jayden, for she began to pull away at the wires. But as she did, the bleeps came alive again. And this time, they were more than just the noise of monitor.

'*Uuooohhhahhhhahhh…*'

Was the machine trying to say something? Whatever it was faded to a breathless sigh but then from nowhere came the word:

'*YOU!*'

What followed was more a breathy sound than a word, yet now it found shape and meaning.

'*HHHAVE!*'

The machine put these words together.

'*YOU HAVE…*'

No training could prepare for this. Petra panicked. She ran to the wall and pulled the unit's electric power cable from its socket. Not that the machine seemed to care, for even with no power, it strove on.

'*Eeeeen! Eeeeeeen… Eeeeeeeeeeen…*'

What was it attempting to say? It appeared frustrated only its belief in itself now grew and it cried:

'*BEEN!!!*'

38

It then ran its words together.

'*YOU HAVE BEEN…*'

The screen cracked like breaking ice. The glass fractured and intricate patterns spread across it. Fern like. Tree like. Jayden like. Perfectly matching the lightning flowers on his chest.

By now Petra had removed any and all electrical connections from the machine. But, far from dead, the unit began to swing about of its own accord, this way and that, as if surveying its surroundings. I saw it. Candice saw it. Petra saw it. We all did. And the fear on each other's faces.

The machine then went for its next and final word: '*Sssorrr… sssoorrorr…*' Only suddenly it stopped. And then from nowhere it seemed not only to know what to say but how to say it.

For it yelled, as if in triumph:

'*YOU HAVE BEEN SOUGHT!*'

CHAPTER SIX

The Wasps

THEY'VE PUT ME back in the room where I woke up. I've been told to wait and not touch anything. With me is Nurse Ramesh, who's tall, slender, very eager and very, very chatty. Is he my guard? Do they think I'm gonna do a runner? I am to be questioned, they said, and they want answers, they said, but right now it's Nurse Ramesh who's doing all the talking.

'Most of my work here at the ozzie is in imaging. There's nuclear imaging, that's where you get injected with this radioactive fluid so we can see right inside your kidneys. Then there's sonic imaging. We use that a lot on pregnant women. I'm the first to know the sex of their baby. Proper made up, I am! And X-Ray, of course. Broken bones and the like. Ohhh! Dull! Dull! Dull!'

As Nurse Ramesh speaks, he flicks his hand in the air as if swatting away a bothersome fly, but it's those dyed blonde eyebrows I can't help staring at. So sharply plucked and pointed they look like shooting stars on imminent collision.

'But the MRI Scanner, that's the biggie. Patients lie in this ginormous pod blasting them with this really powerful magnetic field, while I'm in the next room gawping at their insides. How weird is that? Monster-mega if you spot something that shouldn't be there. I mean, I'm seeing their future.'

Nurse Ramesh continues to rattle on, but my mind is elsewhere. I think about those words 'You have been sought'. And how the smoke that came out of the machine rose up in the air, curled and twisted, and then –

'Hello? Anybody in?'

Nurse Ramesh taps me on the hand.

'Sorry, what?' I say.

'Mind gone blank, has it? Soft lad.'

He's wrong there. The minds of our kind are never at rest.

'Oh, I know, I know, I know,' Nurse Ramesh goes on, with more flicks towards that non-existent fly, 'things pop into your head and then do a Houdini. Where do they go? Who knows? Who cares? There's always more to take their place. *Bedpans!* That's what just came into my head. Oh, I'm so random! Me and my mate Julie, who's a bit of a dizzy prinny if you want the truth, have found some in storage. You know, the traditional, kind, porcelain. Oh, you won't know what I'm talking about. Only see them now in those old comedy films. Never mind, your mum or dad will explain.'

No, they won't. I never knew my real mum or dad. And the ones who took me in are gone now. So, with no one to collect me, I begin to wonder if I'll be kept here forever.

I then hear footsteps. Two people. Big. With heavy shoes. Must be men, I think.

'Someone's coming. Two guys,' I say.

Nurse Ramesh listens hard, his lips pursed, clearly doubting what I'd just said, but then those sharp eyebrows of his rise up and he says, 'Spot on, kid. You must have good hearing.'

Yes. Our kind do. And we need it. Many things about us are different. Not that we want to stand out. The opposite. We're the lady on the bus who nods but never says hello. The boy at the back of the class whose name you can't remember. The man across the road who goes out every morning at nine but nobody asks where to. We are seen but never noticed. Unspoken to, unspoken of. And certainly never ever questioned. But that was exactly what was about to happen to me. I began to tense up, sweat even, because, you see, there's something else you should know about our kind. We can't lie. And I knew that today the truth would never be believed.

Without knocking, two men entered the room. One was in a smart blue suit and appeared angry, while the other, in a white coat, who I assumed to be a doctor, seemed more friendly, but still concerned. The man in the dark blue suit spoke even before he shut the door.

'You should know, from the outset, that I have already spoken to the other eyewitnesses.'

Eyewitnesses? Did this man think I had committed some sort of crime?

This same gentleman then noticed Nurse Ramesh.

'Perhaps it would be best, if we spoke to the boy alone?'

'If I may,' said the man in the white coat, 'Nurse Ramesh is very good at finding things to do. And not of the things always medical. If you do not mind.'

'Righty-oh,' said Nurse Ramesh, more than a little irked, I thought. 'I'll take my leave. T.T.F.N. young fella.'

And with a final flick of his fingers, he, and that invisible fly of his, winged it out of the room.

The man in the white coat put out his arm and said, gently, 'William, I am Dr Lorenzo. And this is Mr McClane from Resource Services.'

The doctor shook my hand and he gave me a polite smile, but the other man offered only a steely frown as he reached into his pocket for his notepad. Dr Lorenzo now took a step back and began to fidget with his thick horn-rimmed glasses. Somehow too big for him, I thought, as if he'd accidentally picked up the wrong pair.

Mr McClane wore no glasses, so there was nothing to lessen that iron stare towards me as he began his onslaught of questions.

Why I was in Jayden Mitchell's room? Who had taken me there? Who else was present? What had I said? What had been said to me? I kept all my answers as simple as I could. I mean, I didn't want to get anyone into trouble. Then came the question he had been building up to, for his voice was now even more stern and severe.

'Why did you touch the ECG unit?'

'I didn't,' I replied.

'Are you sure?'

'No.'

I was nervous and Mr Resource Services leapt on my reply.

'No, you're not sure or no, you did not touch it?'

'No, I did not touch that machine. I never did. Honestly!'

This was true. My finger had got close but when Jayden mentioned his 'tree', I pulled it away.

'If you did not touch the machine, then who was the culprit?'

I hesitated.

'I will ask you again,' said the man in the blue suit, now very insistent, 'who touched that machine?'

I had no choice. We have to tell the truth.

'Nurse Petra,' I answered, not wanting to say more.

'So it was she who interfered with the ECG unit?'

I didn't like Mr McClane. I didn't know what Resource Services were but I didn't like them either. But perhaps there was a way round all these questions if I answered his with one of my own.

'What's an ECG unit?'

I suspected Dr Lorenzo didn't like Mr McClane much either, for as soon as Mr McClane said, 'interfered with', Dr Lorenzo, who had been cleaning his glasses with his hankie, put them on again, as if ready for battle.

'If I may,' said the doctor, stepping forward, and, I thought, intentionally placing his back to Mr McClane, 'as you may know, William, the heart is a pump and when it pumps, little electric impulses are made. ECG –'

'I don't think we need to explain to the boy what the unit does.'

'If I may. If I explain to young William how it works, it may help.'

Resource Services could hardly argue with that. Instead, he rested his pen on his note pad and put on a sulky face. But I liked that face a lot. Because it kept its mouth shut.

'ECG Electrocardiogram,' continued Dr Lorenzo, 'measures the electric impulses of the heart. The squeeze as blood is pumped. But these electric waves are tiny, so the machine, makes them bigger.'

Dr Lorenzo turned round and gave Mr McClane a friendly enough smile, though not, I suspected, the smile of a friend.

Mr McClane took up his pen again as if ready with a question, only Dr Lorenzo got in first.

'Tell me, William, what is it you were seeing on the ECG unit?'

'The green line, you mean?'

'Yes, the green line.'

'Different shapes,' I replied. 'Pointy. Round. Then all scribbly.'

'All scribbly!' exclaimed Mr McClane.

'That's what it looked like to me,' I said, 'like angry scribble, filling the whole screen.'

'If that were the case,' replied the blue suit, 'the patient would be dead.'

'Not only dead,' interrupted Dr Lorenzo. 'Boom! Boom! Dead.'

If Dr Lorenzo meant that as a joke, Mr McClane wasn't laughing.

'Tell me, young William, what sort of noise was the machine making during all this?' Mr McClane asked.

'Loud,' I said, 'like someone screaming.'

'Tell me what it –'

Mr McClane stopped in mid-sentence. Had he been about to say, 'Tell me what it said?' Perhaps. But I'm glad he didn't, for I would have had to tell him the truth. Then they'd think I was completely nuts.

'Tell me, did it make any other sounds?'

I thought for a moment how best to reply, then answered, 'It was a sound like words.'

'What words?' he queried.

I was about to say, 'You have been sought', only suddenly Dr Lorenzo came to my rescue.

'If I may. The ECG unit contains a sound amplifier, no? Remember your physics. Is it not possible for amplifier to be also a receiver?'

'You mean like when you hear radio signals from taxis and police cars on your television?' replied Mr McClane.

'Yes. Exactly. A voice that comes from who knows where?'

I could see by the speed of his pen that the words 'amplifier' and 'radio signals' would feature very heavily in his report.

Mr McClane then asked, 'And what happened after that?'

'There was a burning smell and smoke began to come out of the machine,' I replied. 'It must have set off an alarm because soon after that a load of people rushed in. And I was pulled out.'

That wasn't a lie, yet not the whole truth. What I didn't tell him was how the rising smoke curled itself into one long twisting line, slithered towards me and in front of my eyes scrawled out a name in the empty air. My name.

William

It was as I was remembering this that I heard them. The wasps. A distant buzzing at first, but getting louder and louder. If Mr McClane had another question, he never had chance to ask it, for there was a knock at the door and Nurse Ramesh entered.

'Sorry to interrupt, but there's a lady come to collect the young lad. And she's already signed the form. Well, sort of.'

'Who is this woman? Does she have a name?'

'All she said to me was "Granny".'

Granny? I thought. I don't have a granny.

CHAPTER SEVEN

The Wasps Bring a Friend

'DO YOU KNOW, luv, I put on three layers of underwear this morning, oooh, and I'm still feeling a chill! Sometimes flannel knickers aren't worth the wearing. And they give you the itch!'

'Granny' arrived in the room as if carried on a wave of her own whirlwind of words. And all of them spoken in a broad Yorkshire tongue that told you that she was not a woman to be messed with.

'Yes, I will admit there's been some advances in medical science – transplants, vaccines, plus, thankfully, that bandage offering new hope to the ruptured. But today something went wrong. Very, very wrong. I'll take that, I think,' Granny said, grabbing Mr McClane's notepad with her gloved hands and quickly tearing out the pages. 'Yes, must be serious for the money man to be brought in on the Sabbath – it's the suit that gives it away, luv. I knew a woman once, wouldn't even put her washing out on a Sunday. Chapel, she was. All sin and Alleluia. Like them American Evangenitals.'

A dozen or so wasps suddenly emerged from her tangled hair and began flying round her shoulders.

Bzzzzz... Bzzzzzz...

When she lifted those creamy gloved hands of hers, I thought she was about to swat them away with Mr McClane's notepad, but no, she instead opened the top pocket of her dress and with an encouraging wave all the wasps obligingly flew in.

'They're my friends,' she said smiling, while gently patting the flap. 'And such misunderstood creatures.' As she said this, a long loose curl of unruly hair fell down across her brow. 'Entropy, I curse you,' she declared, immediately sweeping it back into place before returning the now empty notepad to a dumbfounded Mr McClane.

If candy floss could grow in the wild that would be Granny's hair. And no doubt, given the colour, it would taste of spicy ginger. And there was so much of it. And all in a tall heap above her head, with strands jutting out everywhere. Another strand fell, this time across her bewilderingly green eyes.

'Entropy, I curse you once more! And gravity, too!'

I didn't know who this woman was but somehow I felt she was here to help me.

'Now where was I?' She paused for a moment and then ploughed forcefully on. 'Oh yes. My own health, if you're asking, is very good. Except, of course, for those ailments any lady beyond the age of expectation would be prone to when sitting too long on a cold wall. A while ago I did worry I was breathing out more than I was breathing in, but I put that down to spending too much time with men who'd lived all their lives at sea – oh dear, them pillow cases could do with a boil wash!'

Without warning Granny then ran her gloved fingers through McClane's hair. It had been neatly combed back. Until now.

'Oh yes, luv, a fringe suits you so much better.' She pursed her lip as she surveyed his loosened hair, and then nodded to herself as if very pleased with her creation. 'Now, I was saying something. What was it? Oh, yes. If you expect me to take legal proceedings for the distress caused to our William due to that cockeyed machine of yours, you'd be mistaken, because I don't hold with lawyers. As Mother used to say, "Courts are where you go in a pig but come out a sausage." So don't trouble yourselves with worry. And you worry too much,' she added, bringing her nose within sniffing distance of Mr McClane's own. 'Oh dear, you've got a face no woman should witness before breakfast. Try and smile a bit more. When you smell flowers, don't always look for the coffin. Talking of flowers, here's some chrysanthemums.'

From inside the sleeve of her blouse Granny then produced several stems of the flower and immediately planted them in various pockets of Mr McClane's suit. Granny then spun sharply on her heels like a whipping top – 'Weeeeeeee!' – before coming to an abrupt stop in front of the Dr Lorenzo.

'Good for the thigh muscles,' she declared. 'Yes, they built my sort to last. Oh, and you must be the doctor. A rock among pebbles. I was a nurse, myself, once. Well, I'd sit with the dying until it was Goodnight, Vienna. Did you notice if it was raining out? Another storm is brewing. I can feel it in my bones. But that's rheumatism for you. You'll understand that, being medicinal. Joints, I mean, acting as a baromic indicator of low pressure often associated with imminent precipitation.'

Mr McClane and Dr Lorenzo may have understood all those words but even so, they just stood there, dazed.

But I wasn't really looking at them. My eyes were locked on her. It wasn't just the impossible untamed hair and those stunning green eyes, it was everything. The scarf round her neck, red roses one side, yellow daffodils on the other. The bluebell embroidered waistcoat, the summer blouse patterned with golden tulips and that long lace dress of white lilies. And sprouting out from that hair of hers, several real sunflowers. Bright and golden. All in all, she simply bloomed.

'1958. That was the last time I was in hospital. Happy days! Pregnant women were prescribed Guinness. A very good source of iron. Of course, it wasn't me that was pregnant. How could I be? I was – oh, close your ears, William, you're far too young – I was back then almost a virgin.' She said this with both a whisper and a smile. And she kept that smile all through the long silence that followed.

'By the way, did I mention I have a liking for Guinness?' she said at last. 'If you've got a spare pint going, I wouldn't say no.'

At last Dr Lorenzo felt able to make a reply.

'I must tell that we are not doing that anymore.'

'Pity. Not that I'm one of them alcofrolics, but as you know, you can't go wrong with a bit of haemogoblin.'

Now I began to giggle. I think she'd meant to say 'haemoglobin', which I knew were in blood cells because we'd done that at school, but the way she kept getting her words mixed was making me laugh.

Granny now did another spin on her heels only this time when she came to a halt her mood had changed. Not angry or cross, but, as they say, she wasn't taking any prisoners.

'Now I'll say this one time only, because I'm not the sort of woman who boils her cabbage twice. William never touched that silly machine. So don't be incinerating he did. Accidents happen. I accept that. Is not all human life at the mercy of the next tile that falls? So we'll leave it there. And while we're on the subject of leaving – come along, our William, best be on our way. I don't want you becoming a victim of medical malfunction again. And ending up all discombobulated.'

My hand was then grabbed by Granny's own. Well, her creamy white glove which, as I looked down, I could see was sewn with a chain of cotton daisies and fastened with a ladybird button.

As we walked out of the door, Granny whispered to me, 'I'll warn you now, William, if I do have a fault, it's I'm a very loose knitter, which one day may or may not be to your advantage. Oh, isn't it wonderful we've met at last. I've been so looking forward to it!'

CHAPTER EIGHT

Those Amazing Green Eyes

ONCE WE WERE outside the hospital room, Granny picked up a large carpet bag that she must have left by the door and we were on our way.

'Now I can see from your face you'll be wanting explanations,' she said, as I walked hurriedly along the corridor behind her, trying to keep up. 'But, let me tell you, William, from the off, I'm not the sort of woman who holds with explanations. But I am in favour of having lots of names. So, what are yours, other than William?'

Odd question. But I would get used to those.

'Only Arthur.'

'"Only Arthur"'! But Arthur is a name that stands for courage! Goes well with William. A name with the desire to protect! Oh yes, William Arthur! What a bucketful of wonderment you must be!'

'I… don't think so,' I said, still nervous about who this woman was and what exactly was going on.

'Oh, but we can't have you thinking like that. But the young learn quickly. Is it not the little pot that's soonest hot? Talking of learning, would you like me to prove that two equals one? Or save that for another day.'

'Er, another day, I think,' I answered, believing her to be quite beyond even bonkers.

'Oh, well, I suppose it'll keep,' she replied, a little disappointed, 'Mathematical laws do not change their nature overnight. Unlike husbands and bubble gum. But they'll come at a time when I will prove to you that two equals one. And that's a promise.'

Granny then came to a stop in order to deal with yet another strand of ginger hair that had dropped across her face, but it was soon swept up and given a new home thanks to a butterfly clip, taken from one of the many side pockets in her lily lace dress.

'Entropy, I curse you!'

'You keep saying that,' I blurted out. 'Entropy. But I've no idea what it means.'

'You *do* know what it means, only you've never had the word for it. Big difference.' Granny tightened her lips for a moment and then said, 'An ice cube. On a hot day. What happens?'

'It melts,' I replied.

'Into what?' she then asked.

'A pool of water,' I answered.

'So, on a freezing day that pool of water will turn back into an ice cube.'

'No, it won't! Not by itself!'

'You mean someone has to come along and go to the trouble of turning it back into the shape of a cube?'

'Yes!'

'Well, that's entropy for you. How something is put together and arranged. And we all need arranging. Only even when we are, everything still eventually goes to pot. That's the sad rule of the universe.'

Another curl fell across her face, this time landing on her nose. And then I got it.

'Your hair, it can go anywhere. Anywhere at all. But for it to go where you want it, your hair needs organising. But even if you do put it back, it will still fall down again.'

'You see, William Arthur, you *did* know what entropy is. The universe, like my hair, is full of many possibilities, but even when it's put in place nicely, as mine always is, curls will still fall down – because things that can go wrong, will go wrong. So, we have to make the effort to set them right again,' she said, clasping another curl back in place with yet another butterfly clip, 'which is, I suppose, why you and me have been put in the universe in the first place.'

And with that she was off again, her steps now more a skip than a walk. As I raced after her, I began to wonder at her age. She had the face of an old woman, but with a joy of life that somehow cancelled out the many wrinkles. And though her legs were bony, they could skip like a hare. And as for those amazing green eyes, they didn't seem old at all, more child-like and playful. Naughty even. And they had noticed how I was looking at her.

'William Arthur, whatever age one is, always remember you'll never be younger than you are today. And if you believe the most exciting day of your life could be tomorrow – which, with me, it will be – it's impossible ever to grow old.'

'You're not my granny!' I shouted, hoping she'd stop, but she didn't miss a step and just carried on.

'It matters little what you call me. The question is: Does the collar fit the cuff? I think it does. Besides, my friends the wasps have again brought me to you. And they are never wrong. But best not to know too much too soon, for, as Mother used to say: "Sometimes it's the blind pig that finds the truffle!"'

'I never had one. A mother, I mean,' I said sadly.

On hearing that, Granny did stop, came over and gently took my hands and held them in her gloves.

'I know. I know you didn't. And that's been hard for you. But I must ask you now to look on me with the eye of faith. Trust in me, William Arthur, for I am all that you have.'

This was true. I had people who had taken me in, but now even they were gone. And again Granny seemed to sense what I was thinking.

'We are all orphans in the storm. Unwanted and uncared for.'

Those words hit me hard, because that's how I'd always felt.

'Can I ask you something?'

'Is the elephant heavy? The grasshopper thin? The jellyfish wobbly, as you would be if you were lacking a stable molecular structure? Yes, yes and yes. So ask away, my inquisitive young friend, but, if I feel it best not to answer, I'll offer you some advice instead.'

So many questions were bouncing about in my head, but for starters, I just wanted to know how she knew what had happened in that room.

'Oh, that's an easy one. There are many places in life to discover secrets, but the best is always the pub next door. Rumours were flying round that bar like bats at midnight. Poor Nurse Petra was very upset so I offered her a shoulder to cry on. Which is what one woman gives another in exchange for more information. And, as I held her hand tight, it was Nurse Petra who told me what went on.'

'But why would she do that?'

'Because she thought I was Polish.'

'Why did she think you were Polish?'

'Because I spoke to her in Polish! Are you the full shilling or what?'

'Well, how come you can speak Polish? And what's a shilling?'

Granny's wide green eyes now became more of a narrow squint.

'A shilling is coin. Twelve pennies in a shilling, twenty shillings in a pound. But by the look of your puzzled face, I'm guessing they don't exist anymore. As to your first question, well, William Arthur, let me offer you some advice. Never hold a cat and a bag of flour at the same time. And now I have a question for you.'

'I didn't touch that machine,' I protested.

'I know you didn't, why would you? But was there anyone in that room you did touch. Even if only for a second. With your hands? With those hands? Jayden? Candice? Nurse Petra?'

I wasn't surprised that Granny knew all their names, but why say 'with those hands'? What else would I touch with?

'No, I didn't,' I replied. 'Jayden couldn't shake my hand because of the bandages. I did shake the doctor's hand, but that was later.'

As I said this, Granny's face tightened and became thoughtful.

'Hmmm. All a bit of a puzzle.'

Then I remembered the envelope. I must have put it in my pocket without realising.

'Candice did pass me this,' I told her, taking it out, 'but I don't think our hands touched.'

'Are you sure? Not even a finger?'

'Well, I can't be certain, but I don't think so.'

'Try and remember. It's important.'

I closed my eyes and thought hard.

'No. Our fingers didn't touch. She held one end then I took the other.'

I hadn't given the envelope much thought until now. Written on the front in ink was the word 'Electrician' and on the back Candice's notes in pencil.

'You can look at it if you like. It's what Candice wrote about the lightning flowers, the strange markings on Jayden's body because of the electric shock,' I explained, offering it to Granny. 'I never gave it back to her. Do you want to read what it says?'

'Don't be daft!' she said, dismissively. 'Why would I be interested in that load of old nonsense? Put it in the bin.'

But I wasn't convinced this was the whole truth. Granny seemed irritated by the envelope. Something inside told me I should hold on to it. Perhaps there was more to discover about these lightning flowers.

Granny by now had moved off again, only this time at a slower and more thoughtful pace.

'Why is it so important what I touched?'

'It isn't if you didn't.'

'Then why did you ask?'

Granny replied simply, 'Let me offer you some more advice. Never trust a man who can't eat two puddings.'

I could see I wasn't making much progress.

'You're not my grandma,' I told her again, 'and in fact, I don't think you've ever been anyone's grandma.'

I expected her to stop again. But no.

'It matters not *who* am, the only thing that matters is *what* I am. And I, William Arthur, am a Swidger. Just like you.'

'A Swidger?'

'Yes, that's what we are. Swidgers. Put on this earth to change lives for the better with a switch or a dodge, a shove or a nudge.'

Wow. To know *what* you are but never before have a name for it. Only now I did.

Swidger. I am a Swidger.

I wanted to ask Granny more but she had become suddenly frozen and motionless, her eyes staring ahead. I tried to follow what she was looking at, but it was just a Hospital Notice Board, full of posters about flu jabs and measles. Nothing much out of the ordinary. Only then I saw how Granny's eyes were drawn to a flyer with a picture of a young man on a stage holding a skull. Underneath was a warning about the dangers of smoking.

'The Time is out of joint,' she whispered, half to herself, her voice quivering. 'A young prince once said that in an old story, cursing the world that he'd been born to set it right. But Swidgers,' she added, her tone now more assured, 'we don't curse what we do, we relish it!'

The Time is out of joint.

I had no idea what it meant, yet the day would come when I did. And never would I see the universe in the same way again.

'Oh dear,' declared Granny, looking at the board hanging above our heads, 'like the one-legged duck we seem to have gone round in a circle. Twice we've passed that sign of that poor mother holding her baby, but not once have I seen an arrow pointing to the way out.'

Granny sniffed the air and then gave me a big cheeky-faced smile.

'Oh, but is that chrysanthemums, I smell? *Sniff, sniff.* Yes, it is. We can follow the scent. A lady was selling them at the entrance, though of course she gave me mine for nothing. Very kind.'

A buzzing sound suddenly came from one of her pockets.

'Ah, my dear friends, the wasps! Why didn't I think of you before?'

Granny opened the flap to let them out and after flying round her head three or four times they headed left down a corridor we hadn't tried before. Granny immediately chased after them.

'William Arthur,' she cried, calling back to me, 'are you coming with us or not?'

'Of course I am,' I answered, needing only a second to think. 'Is the elephant heavy, the grasshopper thin...'

CHAPTER NINE

In the Park with the Trees

'I'M ONE OF the lucky ones,' Granny declares in a low voice as we sit on a bench in the park near the hospital. 'I knew my mother, though obviously not my father. I did ask her once what sort of hair he had, but she said she didn't know 'cos he never took off his cap.'

'I'm adopted,' I tell her.

'Many Swidgers are,' she says gently. 'Foundlings left on a doorstep.'

'No one ever told me who my real parents were. If they were alive or dead. I was brought here, you see, from Romania when I was a baby. From an orphanage, I think. But I've never known for sure. When I grew up I did once hear voices downstairs that I didn't recognise talking about me not being legal and money in "brown envelopes". My mother – my adopted one, I mean – had been, I think, desperate for a child, but within days of coming back to England, she died. Some sort of illness she'd caught travelling, I'd heard them say.'

'And so your new father didn't want you...'

'No, he didn't. But I never really knew him, either. I was told he'd gone to live in America, but I'm not sure that's true. He blamed me, I think, for her death. If she hadn't gone to Romania... oh, I don't know. I try not to think about it too much. My mother – well, the lady who wanted to adopt me – had a sister who took me in for while, but when she wanted to get married...'

'You don't have to say any more. We're the parcel passed pillar to post.'

'I'm nobody,' I say to her, looking at all those sat alone on the park benches nearby.

'What nonsense! You're William Arthur. And you must have something about you, because, as I've said, the wasps are never wrong. What about hobbies? Origami? Toenail painting? Are you by any chance a collector of earwax or navel fluff?'

I answer with a shrug, then drop my head and stare down at the yellowing grass. A breeze goes by and the leaves of the trees begin to flutter and so I shiver a little, but Granny's hand rests itself on my shoulder and I settle.

'When did you discover what you were?' I ask.

Granny sighs and says, 'When does the fox know it's not a rabbit? We Swidgers feel who are.'

She was right. Like swans that can swim or bees that can fly, we do what we do and we are what we are. Born that way, I suppose. Only now I had a name for what I was.

Swidger. I am a Swidger.

'I know *what* to do,' I tell Granny, 'as a Swidger, I mean, and the way to do it – those bumps and shoves that change the paths of Time – but what I don't understand is the *why*. Why we do what we do?'

'To help the Commonality sing the song they were meant to sing.'

The Commonality?

She must mean everyone who isn't a Swidger. A good name, the Commonality. Yeah, I like that. I like that a lot.

'What do you think of that one, over there,' she whispers, awkwardly nodding her head in the direction of an old gentleman on the next bench.

'I've never seen him before,' I say to her.

'Maybe so, but that doesn't mean you can't tell me all about him.'

'He's lonely.'

'Why say that?'

'Because, he's not just looking at people, he's trying to catch their eye. See, just then. He was about to say something to that women with her two toddlers.'

'Only she was busy with her pram.'

'Yes. And look at all those sandwiches he's brought. Far more than he can eat by himself. I bet he was hoping to find someone to share them with.'

'William Arthur! You see all that and you tell me you're not a bucketful of wonderment? Huh! Who needs hobbies when we have the fascination of the Commonality right there in front of us. That said, between you, me and the donkey's hind leg, I have been known to enjoy a bit of skinny-dipping. And I would again, even if nowadays I do look like the last turkey in the shop.'

Ah, that makes me smile. And Granny smiles back. You know, I don't think anyone's ever smiled at me like that before.

The wind blows, and the leaves on the trees gently flutter in the breeze.

All the time we'd been sitting there was one question I'd been wanting to ask.

'When you were in the pub, Nurse Petra must have told you that the machine spoke to me.'

Granny's smile fades.

'It even wrote my name in smoke before my eyes.'

Granny's face is now as still as stone.

'But what I want to know is why it said what it did. Why have I been sought?'

Granny points to a large mound of earth near some trees.

'See that ant hill? Inside are hundreds of tiny little anties. Each one knows where its blob of mud must go but few will ever see the hill they build. Most Swidgers are like that. All their lives acting only on instinct, never knowing the why.'

The breeze now blows strong and a branch sways above my head with a sudden boldness.

'You said *most*,' I reply, quivering a little.

'*Most*,' says Granny again.

'And that's why you're here, isn't it? Why the wasps brought you to me. Because I'm not *most*, am I?'

'No, William Arthur,' says Granny, 'you are not as other Swidgers are. You are very different. But I have already said too much.'

So I was different, yet did not know how or why. To be a Swidger was one thing, but I was discovering I was something else too. But what? And when would I find out?

A sudden gust of wind, and leaves start to fall. I become distinctly uneasy.

'Why are we Swidgers afraid of trees?' I ask.

'To learn not to be!' she proclaims, leaping up from the bench and grabbing my arm. 'Stand up and let me look properly into those eyes of yours.'

My eyes. Why my eyes?

'Good,' she then says, staring deep into them. 'Nothing fancy. Hazel with a bit of grey. Yes, they'll do just fine for now. But I do think we'd better do something about these bandages on your head, so what I want you to do is go over there, stand in front of that tree, say "Hello, Tree" and then give it a big hug.'

I hesitated and Granny, I think, could see I was scared.

'William Arthur, let fear rule you and you'll be its slave for life.'

'Are you sure I'll be okay?'

'Is the owl awake? The cat asleep? The sloth a case of both and neither?'

There was no point in arguing with her, so I slowly went over and stood by the tree.

'No, you daft a'peth, I said in *front* of the tree. Go round the other side,' she yelled.

I began to move, but then stopped.

'No, it's you that's been daft,' I shouted. 'Trees don't have a front or back.'

'Oh yes, I knew it! Able to think for yourself. And not afraid to answer back. Indeed the wasps were right – you and me, we're going to get on just fine. Now do what I said, give that tree a great big hug. Press the palms of your hands tight against its trunk. So tight it makes its leaves shake. Go on, trust me!'

Trust.

Until today it had only ever been a word people said, but now it really meant something. I was still frightened, so, before saying 'Hello, tree,' I closed my eyes. But then, when I did grip the tree, I felt a real sense of freedom, and shook and shook and shook.

'Oooh! That's enough, don't get carried away,' she shouted, calling me back to the bench. As I returned to where we'd been sitting, my body seemed strangely full of energy.

'And now, I think, we'll be able to get rid of this nonsense,' Granny said, whipping the bandage from my head.

I lifted my hand and felt around. No bump, no blood. Not even the hint of a scab.

'Right as rain, but,' she declared casually, 'best no Swidging for a while. Not now there's been an attack.'

'An attack!' I exclaimed.

CHAPTER TEN

Granny Laughs

'AN ATTACK!' I cried again.

'Oh dear, I shouldn't have said that. But since I have, I better ask: do you know why that electric cable went for the Australian and not you?'

'No, I don't.'

'Well, that makes two of us. Very puzzling. But not to worry, you'll be safe enough when we get to Dungeness.'

Dungeness? I'd heard of Dungeness. It was by the sea and, if I remembered right, had a nuclear power station. *But why there*, I thought. Granny must have seen the question on my face.

'I know what you're gonna say, so don't even ask. Instead, here's some more advice: never give a two-year-old a tomato and always buy a plunger before you need one.' Granny paused, then added, 'But in a way, you could say that Dungeness is your plunger. For you need to be prepared.'

Granny then looked at me with a face of sudden disappointment. 'But, I suppose, you're now too old for a bucket and spade. Oh, and I do like building forts and castles. Not that it matters, because Dungeness ain't that sort of beach anyway. Even so, we'll make a week of it.'

'A week! I can't do that. I've got school.'

'What! You're still at school?' she replied, with surprise.

'Of course I'm still at school,' I answered, equally surprised she should even ask.

'Oh botheration, that's a nut to be cracked.'

'But it's school training day tomorrow,' I told her, beginning to giggle as I remembered what had happened to Mr Flynn.

'What's so funny?'

Trust, I suppose, must work both ways. But will Granny laugh if I tell her? Yes, I think so.

'Our maths teacher, Mr Flynn,' I began to explain, 'had to leave, after the last training day.'

'Why?'

'The Law of Averages.'

Granny looked puzzled.

Ah, I thought, at last something I knew she didn't. Oh yes, I was going to enjoy this.

'Mr Flynn, well, "Finbar" we called him, because we found out that was his first name. Anyway, Finbar wasn't the sort of teacher to tell jokes but apparently on one of these training days he'd been told to add more humour to his lessons.'

I hesitated for a second.

'Go on,' Granny insisted, 'take the bridle from thy tongue!'

Trust. Yes, she'll see the funny side. I know she will.

'Well,' I continued, 'Mr Flynn, Finbar, said to the class that "the human population was, on average, half male, half female, and therefore, statistically speaking, all human beings should have one breast and one testicle."'

I began to giggle.

'Well, yes, but that's not that funny,' she said, still stony faced.

'I know,' I replied, 'but then Tommy Lee climbed onto his desk and proved that the Law of Averages was wrong. By dropping his trousers. And then, er, the rest.'

Trust... so was I right to put mine in her?

'Ha! Hah! Hah! Ha! Hah! Hah! Ha! Ha! Hah! Hah! Ha!'

Yes!

It was a laugh that was longer, louder and more mischievous than any I'd ever heard.

'Oh, I see now why that Mr Finbar of yours had to walk his bike home! Doing that must have started a riot!' Laughing now even louder, 'Hi-ee! Oooh! Ohhh! Oh, William Arthur, I bet you're glad you're not washing my bloomers! Ha! Ha!'

It was an odd laugh at times. Half giggle, half snort. Her 'gruffle', I called it. But then she said something that surprised me.

'Yes, but, as with the man who thought it safe to cross the river because he was told the average depth was only three foot six, putting your faith in a mathematical hypothesis not in step with experienced reality is very foolish, for mathematics is often a begetter of anomalous statistics.'

Anomalous statistics?

The words were hers, yet somehow not. Very strange.

Drops of rain began to land on my nose. So, she was right about a storm coming as well. What did she say at the hospital? 'Imminent precipitation'.

Well, that rain was here now. And coming down fast, too.

'What became of the lad,' she asked, as she reached inside her carpet bag for an umbrella, 'who showed you all his unspeakables?'

'Oh,' I replied. 'Tommy Lee, he was expelled. No one ever saw him again. His brother Jimmy is now in my class. He's a right bully.'

There was a sudden change in Granny's expression, as if a wonderful thought had taken hold.

'Ooh! So tomorrow, you have to go into school and help with this training day thingamabob?'

'No, that's the point. Experts come in and train the teachers, so we get the day off.'

As soon as I'd said this, Granny jumped up from our park bench and began to jump about excitedly.

'My Swidger instinct was right! Good job as well because I'd already got the tickets. For yes, William Arthur, we shall go to Dungeness! Where seagulls are as big as dogs. And stars shine as bright as silver bells.'

But the rain was falling heavy now and clouds were darkening.

'And cracking that nut will have to wait. Come along now,

we better get a move on. I don't want you anywhere near a big storm,' she said, opening up her umbrella, 'I pity that woman who's left her washing out in this. Oh, it's coming down like stair-rods. Where's the nearest railway station?'

'Totteridge and Whetstone tube isn't far,' I told her, 'but if we do go to Dungeness, I'd need to get back for Cider Night.'

'Cider Night!' she cried, waltzing her way towards the park gate and swinging her umbrella as if it were her dancing partner, 'Well, that sounds fun!'

'It isn't really,' I shouted after her, 'that's just what the lads call the Parent Teacher Meeting.'

'Well do you get a chance to knock back a bit of cider or not?'

'Not us,' I said, finally catching up with her. 'You see, at the beginning of term, the science class bring in apples for an experiment in fermentation. And they're told they can try the cider when it's ready. Only the teachers drink the lot at the PT Meeting. And that's why the lads call it Cider Night.'

'Fibbing and theft!' Granny replied, lifting her umbrella over my head to protect me from the downpour. 'And I don't approve of either.'

'Yes, but they're teachers – so what can you do?'

'William Arthur!' she declared with a passion, 'You have much to learn about we Swidgers. And Dungeness is the very place to start. For a stratagem begins to grow in my brain – the nut to be cracked – and two birds with one stone –'

Granny wouldn't say what the 'nut' or the 'birds' were, but the 'stone', as she kept calling it, she'd get from an old friend called Echo who lived in a converted railway carriage on the beach at Dungeness.

I didn't really care where we stayed, I was just glad to be getting away from all that had happened. And school too. That Jimmy Lee had turned into a real bully. Yes, a day away by the sea, I thought, would do me good.

Granny was right about the bucket and spade, for, as I was

to discover, the beach at Dungeness was a mystifying desert of shingle with a strange bleak beauty. And what I was to find there would change how I saw the world – but it's what happened on the train on the way that still sends shivers down my spine.

CHAPTER ELEVEN

The Brownies

OUR JOURNEY BEGAN at Victoria Station. For the trip Granny wore a purple pillbox hat which sat awkwardly on her head, as if someone had accidentally put the wrong lid on a teapot.

'Nothing quite like a railway station for Swidgers!' observed Granny as we came into daylight from the underground. 'For everywhere you look are hopes, wishes and promises.'

We'd missed the worst of the storm, but it was still raining heavily. Granny said she didn't want her lovely hat ruined so we made a dash for the old Victorian canopy above the station's entrance where underneath there was a line of stalls.

'Oh look, doughnuts! One of the great inventions of the Commonality. A combination of starch, sugar and fat unknown in nature. Yummy! And I'll get you one while I'm at it,' she says, rushing off to a stand with red and white stripes.

The stall directly in front of me belonged to a fruit trader. Apples, pears, lemons and those shiny-skinned orange fruits with the fleshy inside. What are they called? What's the word? Sharon fruit, that's right. Odd, for a moment then, I couldn't remember their name.

The fruit-seller catches my eye. With hands like shovels, he now fills a bag with red apples. Is it him? Is it him who's watching me?

Watching me? Where did that thought come from? Not sure, but I have a strong sense of a Watcher.

The fruit-seller takes a ten-pound note from his customer and turns round to sort out her change. His eyes are no longer on me, yet I still feel watched.

It's not him, then, I think.

The next stall along has a sign that reads 'THE DEVON PLOUGHMAN – IRWIN'S CHEESE, CURDS AND CHUTNEY', but it seems unattended. But then a man in white overalls and a matching hat emerges from beneath the display table. He's been fetching some cheese for a customer but now she doesn't want it and so walks away. Towards me. His eyes follow her and then catch mine. I look into them.

No, he's not the Watcher, either. But someone out there is. It's strange because I feel observed, yet not looked at. Does that make sense? It's as if the Watcher is hiding somewhere. Maybe behind one of those ornate pillars holding up the canopy.

'Mine's apricot, yours is raspberry 'cos I can't cope with them pips.'

Granny is back. And that feeling of being watched suddenly disappears.

We walk towards the canopy and there, at the back of one of the pillars, is a man in a dark Mackintosh coat and black hat, but I can't see his face, for the brim of his hat has been pulled down.

How long has he been standing there, I wonder?

A lady in a pink scarf with a white poodle on a lead passes us by. Only the dog stops and begins to bark at the man.

Woof! Woof! Woof!

'Dover!' cries the lady, bending down to quieten the dog. 'Stop it! Stop it now. Silly Dover!'

The poodle dog barks on, yet the man in the black hat remains as rigid as ice.

That Mackintosh coat. Something's not quite right. Out of place somehow, yet I can't think why. As we pass him, I try and sneak a look under that brim, only as I do, the man pulls it down even further.

'We'll have to change at Folkestone,' Granny tells me. 'I had a friend called Eileen who had good cause to remember Folkestone. Met a fella there once. Wouldn't go into details. Except to say he was the sort of man who said he had a double-garage but inside he kept a bike.'

But I'm not really listening, for the man in the Mackintosh coat has suddenly disappeared into the crowds.

When we reached the platform and the waiting train, Granny lingered for a while as if expecting something to happen.

'Are we getting on or not?' I asked.

'Oh, I'm waiting for the station master to shout "All aboard!" I've always liked that bit.'

'They don't do that anymore.'

Granny's face turned to disappointment, then defiance.

'Well, I'm gonna at least wait for the whistle.'

A long troop of young Brownies marched by, all neatly turned out in their smart chestnut uniforms. About a dozen or so, aged around seven or eight. In charge of the group were a couple of Brown Owls, one to the front, one to the rear.

'Oh,' beamed Granny, 'like a line of little chicks out on a stroll with mummy. Oh, and a second mummy behind. How very modern.'

Towards the back of this procession was a young Brownie on crutches. Agile enough, but not quite as speedy as her friends.

'Oh dear,' Granny said, 'have you been int' wars?'

The Brown Owl leading the pack was now by the train door, counting each girl aboard, only on seeing the steps up, the girl on crutches hesitated. Brown Owl encouraged her to take them one at a time, only the engine started and then stalled, taking her by surprise.

'Don't worry, my angel,' said Granny reassuringly, 'it won't set off without you. Do you know what's yellow and white and travels ninety miles an hour? An engine driver's egg sandwich!'

This young Brownie attempted a smile, but the shudder of the train had unsettled her.

Granny nodded for me to back pull the door as far as it would go to give her more space to climb up. As I did this, I was able to look along the whole length of the train and there at the other end was the man in the Mackintosh coat, resting his hand against his door.

'Ooh!' a voice suddenly cried out. I turned to see Brown Owl frantically shaking her fingers.

'Static shock! All I did was put my hand on this handlebar,' she went on, 'and now I've gone all tingly.'

Granny laughed. 'I go all tingly sometimes, but that's one of the hazards of wearing a loose gusset.'

The young Brownie on crutches now appeared even more nervous. The Brown Owl still on the platform, a cumbersome woman whose uniform was stretched to its very limits, couldn't assist much as she was weighed down by holdalls and rucksacks, so Granny nodded to me to help the young Brownie with her first step.

As I did, I glanced again along the platform. The man in the Mackintosh coat still had his palm resting against the train. At that moment, the engine started up and the whole train shook. The poor Brownie lost her footing and fell back, but somehow she caught my hand and I saved us both from falling down by grabbing hold of the metal handlebar.

'Ahh!'

Another static shock? Not sure, but I definitely felt a tingle. Perhaps something about this train was not right.

CHAPTER TWELVE

Stray Currents

BROWN OWL ON the train took the other hand of the young Brownie on crutches and gave her a heave up and at last she was aboard. Brown Owl on the platform now followed, first throwing on the various holdalls and rucksacks before taking hold of the metal bar.

'Oh, my word! What was that!' she exclaimed.

Yet another static shock? Must be.

I looked down the platform and, yes, the man in the Mackintosh coat was still there, pressing his hand against the train.

A whistle blew.

I turned round. It came from a short, sturdy looking woman in a navy uniform. I then looked back along the platform but now the man in the Mackintosh coat had gone.

The Brown Owls called over the lady who had blown the whistle.

'We've both had static shocks from this metal bar.'

'Quite strong, too.'

'Oh yeah, that happens sometimes,' confirmed the railway lady. 'An earth bonding gets disconnected and you get stray currents. It's thieves nicking the copper. Unusual in a station, but it does happen. But nothing to worry about, madam. Doors locking in one minute!'

I climbed aboard half expecting Granny to follow, only she remained on the platform, chatting to the railway lady. I couldn't work out what was going on as Granny had her back to me, except it looked like she was tapping the lady's wrist as if thanking her for something. Granny then turned towards the train and as she did I saw that she was putting her gloves back on.

But why, I wondered, had she even taken them off?

Granny winked at me. And as she did the station lady blew her whistle and cried out, 'All aboard! All aboard the Choo-choo Train!'

What to make of that? I'd not heard anyone say, 'All aboard!' except in films. And no one ever called it 'Choo-choo Train'. Perhaps the lady had done it for the Brownies.

As we walked down the train, Granny was all for choosing a carriage with lots of people – 'I like it when it's noisy. Folk make the mistake of thinking they can't be overheard' – but I wanted one less crowded so we could talk. We finally found a busy carriage that still had free seats with a table. Granny insisted on being near the window, with her back to the engine.

'Did you notice the man in the Mackintosh coat?' I said in a quiet voice as soon as we'd settled.

Granny said she hadn't.

'Do you remember outside the station,' I went on, 'there was that poodle and the lady who tried to calm it?'

'Yes, I do. And with a scarf that shade of pink she was probably as equally yakety-yak.'

So, Granny had noticed her.

'Did you see who the poodle was barking at?'

'No. Poodles bark because they like barking. And no point trying to stop 'em, you might as well nail jelly to a swing door.'

'The poodle was barking at –'

'– the man in the Mackintosh coat,' interrupted Granny.

'So you did see him!'

'No, I just guessed that's what you were gonna say,' she replied, with a mischievous grin.

'But it was like he was expecting it to bark.'

'Well, he would if he had a dog himself. The poodle smelt it on him and so he expected it to bark because it had happened before.'

'But he also had this hat and as we walked by, he pulled down the brim as if not wanting to be seen.'

'Oooh, a private detective on the trail of two young lovers whose parents didn't want them to marry. How very romantic!'

'Yes, but that same man had his palm resting on the train.'

'Perhaps he was tired? Or drunk. Or just checking the sign on the door to make sure it was the right train.'

I could see this was a losing battle.

'But the railway lady said that static in a station was unusual.'

'Unusual things happen every day. We should know. I tell you what was peculiar, them thighs of hers. Like tree trunks! And no wonder she has bunions walking up and down that platform all day. Lucky for her I was able to give her a remedy.'

Granny's face became one big tender smile.

'A clever Scotsman once observed,' she said softly, 'that when something follows something else it doesn't necessarily mean it's *because* of that something else. The man, the static, the barking dog. Not connected at all. What does your Swidger instinct tell you?'

I closed my eyes and thought hard, but something seemed to be holding me back.

'I don't know,' I told her.

'I understand why you're worried, but, my young Sherlock, it might be best if you stopped seeing danger round every corner. Harbour fear and you're landlord to a ghost. Not that I believe in ghosts. On that subject I've always been very septical.'

I smiled. Poor Granny and words – they did sometimes get the better of her.

'You should take up knitting,' she said, opening her carpet bag and bringing out needles and a ball of wool, 'very thermapeutic. Besides, knitting is the best way to listen to other people's conversations without them realising you are.'

Despite Granny's reassurances, something still bothered me about that Mackintosh coat. I couldn't put my finger on it. Was it the material? The colour? And I could hardly ask Granny because she hadn't even seen him. I decided as well not to tell her about my sense of being watched. She'd only put it down to worry.

Besides, by then a rather refined lady in a tweed jacket had taken one of the seats opposite and began to enquire about Granny's knitting. It was a hat, Granny told her, for the man we were visiting in Dungeness. The lady then asked if she would be adding a pompom. 'Certainly not! I don't want people thinking he still lives with his mother.'

The poor woman never spoke again, except for a polite goodbye before getting off at Ashford.

'Odd to think people choose to live here on purpose,' observed Granny, looking out the window. Not sure the lady heard her, but by the pointed look on her face I suspected she had.

By now Granny's ill-fitting pillbox hat had shifted to the other side of her head, as if attempting a sneaky escape. And it soon got its wish for it just then it fell off completely.

'Never mind,' said Granny, not bothering to put it back on, 'I fancy a bit of gongoozling. And it's the wrong hat for that.'

Gongoozling? Was there such a word? Seems so.

'That's why I wanted the window. To gongoozle. Let all thoughts drift way away as you idly watch the world pass by – difficult for us Swidgers to clear our mind – but lovely when it happens, you should try it sometime.'

Granny stared out at the passing fields.

'Buttercups and daisies, heather and violets, gold in the meadow, and jewels on the hills –'

I didn't watch the world go by. I just watched her. How restful she looked. So calm and peaceful.

And soon I began to nod off too.

CHAPTER THIRTEEN

The Clapping Game

A TRAIN ANNOUNCEMENT woke me up. We were now at Folkestone and we had to disembark and take a short bus ride to Hythe.

'I prefer trains to buses,' declared Granny, 'because they stop, even if you don't put your arm out. But there's a far better reason too, as you are about to discover.'

And on arriving at Hythe I did. Grand and majestic. Graceful and stylish. A gleaming metal beauty.

'Welcome, William Arthur, to the Golden Age of Steam!'

Wow!

Never had I seen a train like it for as the steam rose from her funnel it was almost as if she were breathing.

'Oh yes, in my day, they weren't just engine drivers, they were cavalrymen riding iron steeds. Not as fast as she used to be, but then again, who is?'

The name of the train was *The Gift of Pluto* and it truly was a wonder to behold. And I wasn't alone in thinking that, for that same party of Brownies we had met at Victoria were now eagerly climbing aboard.

The carriages were made up of individual compartments and most were already jam packed so Granny asked Brown Owl if we could squeeze in with the Brownies in theirs.

'Room for two little ones?' laughed Granny, sliding open the door. 'Oh, we'll all have to sit hugger-mugger, it'll be like the Skegness Special on Whit Monday.'

'I'm afraid they're rather excitable, they've never been on a steam train before,' said Brown Owl.

'Oh, they can make as much noise as they like. Let exuberance be the watchword of the day.'

There weren't quite enough seats for everyone but the girls were young and thin enough to squash together and share. Granny sat herself next to the little girl with the crutches.

'Oh, isn't this cosy? All as close as the rice pudding to its skin.'

The train engine now let off a piercing whistle and all the Brownies screamed back just as loudly, and then with a chug and splutter we were on our way.

The young Brownie with crutches became fascinated by the carpet bag which Granny held tight in her lap. She began to follow its flowery patterns with her fingers. This entertained her all the way to Dymchurch, our first stop. Here there was a brief train announcement that amused Granny and the two Brown Owls.

'Please remember to take all your personal belongings with you because the truth is my shed's already pretty full.'

By the time we had arrived at Romney Sands the excitement of the Brownies had subsided and they had begun to play a clapping game to amuse themselves. Granny's eyes were half-closed and her head had dozily fallen back to one side. The gentle rocking of the train must have sent her off to sleep.

The little girl's fascination with the carpet bag had moved on to the embroidered cotton daisies on Granny's glove. The young Brownie now undid the ladybird button and slowly put her finger inside. As she did this, the other Brownies continued with their clapping game.

'*A sailor went to sea, sea, sea,*
To see what he could see, see, see.
But all that he could see, see, see
Was the bottom of the deep blue sea, sea, sea.'

The curious Brownie then seemed to get bored with Granny's glove, took her finger out and then joined the others in their clapping song.

It was hardly noticeable at first. The change in the game. But as it went on the clapping was growing louder. Their hands were hitting really hard. More slaps than claps. Yet the Brownies kept up a perfect rhythm. Almost too perfect.

I looked at their palms. They were becoming redder. One of the Brown Owls noticed this too.

'Calm down girls,' she instructed.

But the girls wouldn't calm down. And by now they weren't even looking at each other, they were simply staring ahead, trance like.

Brown Owl had had enough.

'Stop it! Stop it!'

But the little girls just stared ahead as if unable to hear. The second Brown Owl intervened by raising her hand but it was slapped away with brutal force by the young Brownie with the crutches. And as she struck, this innocent little girl didn't even blink.

'Stop this at once!' pleaded Brown Owl. 'Stop it!'

But her entreaty made no difference. The clapping game went on, only its rhythm began to change. For hands were now hitting faces. No, not just hitting but smacking hard. Yet not one of the Brownies even flinched.

'*A sailor went to slap, slap, slap,*
To see what he could slap, slap, slap.
But all that he could slap, slap, slap,
Was the bottom of the deep blue slap, slap, slap.'

Those hits were now coming at the rate of a Gatling Gun. And those young cheeks grew more and more red. Brown Owl again tried to intervene only when she did she was smacked in the eye by a sharp elbow.

'Arrh!' she cries.

Not that the Brownies either see or hear her, for slowly, and together, as if one being, they all now turn their reddened faces to me and sing that clapping song with new words.

'*A foolish boy was SOUGHT, SOUGHT, SOUGHT.*

And now that he's been CAUGHT, CAUGHT, CAUGHT,
He'll find that when he's TAUGHT, TAUGHT, TAUGHT,
He's nothing at all but NOUGHT, NOUGHT, NOUGHT!'
What to do? I couldn't think. But something was telling me
to pull off *Granny's glove. Why, I did not know, but I wrench*
it away.

The clapping game instantly stopped, as if the Brownies had all of a sudden awoken. The pain of the slaps was now being felt for the first time. They saw each other's burning red faces and began to scream. And scream. And scream.

I look at Granny's hands. Strange to say it, but I'd never set eyes on them till that moment. They'd always been hidden beneath those cream-coloured gloves. But perhaps I shouldn't have been surprised by what I do now see: the deep ingrained pattern of lightning flowers.

CHAPTER FOURTEEN

The Rainbow Boy

'YOU HAVE TO tell me, what's going on?' I say to her, as we stand on the platform. 'No more of that stonewalling you call advice.'

By now we had reached Dungeness and disembarked from the train. But the Brownies had stayed on. Their fun day out had come to a premature and alarming end. The palms of their hands had soon lost their redness, yet the terror in their troubled eyes would take longer to fade.

Granny hadn't yet replied to what I'd said. She just picked up her carpet bag and walked the few steps from the stone platform into the tiny Dungeness terminal. More house than railway station. A brass mirror hung on the wall. Granny looked into it and adjusted her hair. Errant strands had tumbled across her eyes, but as she put them back in place that now familiar curse to entropy was left unspoken.

I was angry and wanted answers. The lightning flowers, the clapping game, that message – I'd heard it twice now – through machine and human: 'You have been sought.' What did it mean?

I asked my question again about what was going on and Granny after a moment of thought began her reply.

'It's a fair way to Echo's place. As we walk, I will answer as best I can, but to tell you all I know would put you in more danger. And I will speak only until we reach his door. Agreed?'

I looked around, not that there was much to be seen so perhaps this promise of Granny's was my best chance to understand what was going on so I nodded and we began to walk across the hard, dense shingle.

'Life can grow in funny ways. And in the Commonality's evolution there is what is called "divergent others". Heterogenesis – that's the posh word. Not very poetic so a nice German fella came up with Hopeful Monster. You see, evolution doesn't always just tiptoe along, sometimes it leaps and jumps. A big change all at once. A man covered with hair. A man with no hair. Which is better for survival? That's how evolution works sometimes. And we Swidgers are no different. Only our leaps are way beyond the world of their science.'

Granny stops for a moment in that vast Dungeness landscape and looks up to the pale blue sky and its snowy white clouds.

'There is the story of the Rainbow Boy.'

'The Rainbow Boy?'

'No interrupting,' says Granny, sharply. 'Who can say if he really existed? Not that it matters, he's now part of Swidger legend. Did you know that a true rainbow is a circle, not an arc?'

But that's not a question I'm even given time to answer.

'Well, the Rainbow Boy did. So the story goes, he was walking along the beach with his friend. It had been raining, but the sun was out so there appeared in the sky a big rainbow. The friend wondered whether there really was a pot of gold at its end. But the boy said, "What do you mean, at its end? There is no end. For what I see is a circle." The Rainbow Boy had discovered he could see right through the sand and the pebbles. Even the ocean. No Swidger had had that gift before, nor ever will again.'

'What became of him?'

'Nobody really knows. Some say he became so frightened of what he saw, he closed his eyes and pretended to be blind. Others will tell you he ran away to the top of a mountain to live with people who had always seen the rainbow in its true glory.'

'But what's all this got to do with me?'

'The Rainbow Boy discovered his Swidger gift when he came of age. As you are now becoming of age. That, you see, is when all gifts are given.'

Granny, with a determined stride, now heads towards an old railway carriage that stands alone on the desolate shingle.

Not much time left, then.

'But I don't have a gift,' I say, trying to catch her up.

'Oh, but you do,' she says, 'only you don't know what it is yet. That's good. You're safer that way. But be in no doubt, William Arthur, you are our Swidger Hopeful Monster.'

She's now walking so fast that I can't even see her face. I ask if she can tell me who or what it is that seeks me.

'I dare not say. Not yet.'

A few more steps and she'll be at the door.

'Whoever it is, will you be there to protect me?' I shout.

She turns and smiles at me, yet there is sadness in her eyes.

'Umbrellas are useful in the rain but they're no roof when the big storm comes. That you must build yourself. And to do it you need Time, but Time, my young friend, is what you do not have. As Mother often said, "You can't fatten a pig on market day". But yes, I will stay with you for as long as I am needed.'

'Do you know what my gift is?' I ask, knowing Granny couldn't lie.

'No, I do not,' she says firmly, putting her hand to the handle of the carriage.

'One more question before we go in. If you don't know what my gift is, then how can you be so sure I'll be safe here in Dungeness?'

Granny did not answer. Well, not exactly. She did though glance over her shoulder to the nuclear power station. Perhaps she was trying to tell me more than she was willing to say.

Granny then opened the railway carriage door and as she did three chickens flew out, one catching its claws in her hair.

'Blinking Heck! They're living with him now,' she yelled, untangling the chicken before stepping inside, 'I don't think Echo's home yet. Might be useful to open a few windows before he comes back. He's not the sort of fella you want in a room without ventilation. If you follow my meaning.'

As I waited outside, gazing unseeingly at the nuclear power station, it suddenly came to me. *Electricity!*

The static on the train, the severed cable, the lightning flowers – that's why Granny was keen for me not to be out in the storm. It wasn't the rain she was worried about but a lightning strike.

There must be some connection between all these things. I shut my eyes and thought.

What was my Swidger instinct telling me? I was close, it was saying, but no – not there yet. Something didn't quite fit.

Granny then stuck her head through one of the windows and chucked out another couple of chickens.

'You shouldn't be in here, Gertrude. And you, too Pistol. Disappear now, like your namesake. These chickens, they get everywhere, but that's what comes of liking eggs. *Sniff! Sniff!* Oh dear, this place does need an airing. I'll warn you, Echo is a stranger to scissors and comb. Enough hair to stuff a mattress. Black it is. With a neck to match.'

Granny then popped her head back in again.

Pushed against the windows of the carriage were various herbs and plants.

'I see Echo likes tomatoes as well as eggs,' I said.

'Tomatoes?' queried Granny, her face now peering out of a different window, and struggling with yet another chicken. 'Where?'

'Those green plants with the spiky leaves and the red fruit,' I replied, 'aren't they tomatoes?'

Granny looked at the shrubbery and smiled.

'Ha! No, they're not. Enter his little iron palace and see for yourself. But best leave your shoes on the doorstep, that's if you want to keep 'em clean. Out you go, Bassanio! Do your cluck-cluck-clucking somewhere else.'

Echo's iron home had kept its wheels but only for show, for it stood on a brick base. Even so, it was still recognisable as, well, a railway carriage. I took a quick peep round the side. A wooden chicken coop and next to it a pile of something distinctly smelly. And behind all this, a small generator. Only it didn't look as if it was working.

I came back round to the door at the front, took off my shoes, laid them on the shingle and went in.

If you could fit a lot of everything into a narrow bit of not much, then that would be Echo's railway home. Shelves overflowed with cracked plates, battered pots, twisted forks, lidless kettles and broken knives. A shabby leather chair, two legs missing, stood in a corner on the brink of falling over. Velvet orange drapes formed a partition between one half of the carriage and the other, but sewn into them were so many other fabrics it looked more quilt than curtain. A tiger rug with staring eyes in its head stretched across the floor.

And everywhere there were plants. Plants in chamber pots, plants in Toby jugs, plants climbing up fishing nets, plants running down barrels. Even a plant in an upturned smoky-glass lampshade. Putting all this as simply as I can, it was a cabin of curiosities living inside a greenhouse.

I sniffed the air. Hmm, a distinct smell of damp. Unless it was my own smelly feet.

'My job when I arrive,' announced Granny, squeezing past me to get to the only door, 'is to collect some driftwood from the beach for the night fire. I won't be long. By the way, I wouldn't be eating any of those tomatoes if I were you. Ha! Ha! Ha!'

She slammed the door shut but even so I could still hear that gruffling laughter of hers as she went on her way.

Time for a closer look at those spiky green leaves and ripening fruit. Ah, yes, definitely not tomatoes, but ping pong balls painted red. They'd fooled me. And they were meant to. I was very naive thinking that was a tomato plant.

And what, I wondered, lay hidden behind those orange drapes? I took a step forward.

'Owww!'

Something just bit my toe. That tiger head! It had real teeth! Sharp too. I couldn't help myself. I kicked it. Really hard. I mean, what sort of crazy place was this? A carpet that bites? But as my foot hit the head, the tiger skin slid and revealed a trap door. A damp smell, stronger than before, now filled the air.

Ah, so that bad stench wasn't my bare feet. It was coming from under the floor.

KNOCK, KNOCK!

A tapping at the door. I slip the rug back into place as the door opened.

Whoever it is, I hope they hadn't looked through the window and seen me prying.

CHAPTER FIFTEEN

Echo

'YOU IN THERE! Are you real? Or just a figment of my unconscious mind?'

It was a sad, soulful voice. A man with long black hair all the way down to his knees entered. He stared at me. It was the sort of stare that genuinely seemed to expect an answer. So I gave him one.

'Yes, I'm real. I'm William Arthur.'

'And the shoes outside. Are they real, too?'

'Yes.'

'Could I have them?'

'Well, you could but they're all I've brought with me.'

'Oh, in that case you must keep them. Real shoes are best. If not, your feet begin to notice. It's the shingle, you see. That never stops being real. It's a shame, though, that you are. Today I was half expecting to meet somebody who wasn't. Imaginary people, you know, are far more accepting. Of me, I mean. It's my mind. Reality is to blame. There's simply too much of it. And it gets everywhere. Is that why you're here? To escape from it too? If that's the case, then I'm glad you're real. An unreality running away from a reality that it itself created, well, that would be a paradox beyond even my own mind. But now we've sorted all that out, how about a cup of tea? Nothing more real than a cup of tea.'

So, this was Echo. With hair as long and as black as night just as Granny had described, though she hadn't said it would be braided – not neatly – but twisted and knotted like rope.

I'd say red, gold and green were Echo's colours for he wore a long scarlet military jacket from days gone by, open at the front with brass buttons down each side. Beneath this coat was what looked like an old nightshirt, coarse and yellow with age, and around his neck hung an array of gold moons and stars on a chain. His trousers, baggy, more like those of a clown, were a bright emerald green and on his feet he had sandals tied with string. All in all, he looked like a pixie who'd fallen on hard times.

But none of this was quite as extraordinary as what he said next.

'It wasn't witchcraft. No, it was like the nuns who meowed.'

I didn't reply. What could I say? Yet those engaging green eyes, I believed, somehow expected me to understand what he meant. But my bewildered expression must have told him I hadn't a clue what he was talking about.

'The Brownies. On the train,' he explained softly, 'people are saying it was Mimetic Mass Hysteria. Like the Cat Nuns.'

The Brownies? I thought. How could he possibly know about them? They'd stayed on the train and never even set foot on Dungeness.

Echo all of a sudden clapped his hands and began to dance.

'Once upon a time, in a French nunnery, there lived a nun. And one day at noon, for a reason known only to herself, she began to meow like a cat. Other nuns heard her and joined in. From then on, every day at noon, all the nuns of the convent gathered round to meow like cats.'

Echo dropped his arms to the ground and began to strut about on all fours, meowing. Only he then became angry with himself and stood up again.

'No! No! No! You do not know they *walked* liked cats,' he said to himself, 'you made that bit up. Yes, but that was centuries ago,' he replied, as if responding to his own telling off, 'so the nuns are no longer alive to mind.'

Echo then raised his arms high in the air.

'The story ends,' he went on, looking deep into my eyes, 'when soldiers lined up the nuns and threatened to beat them with rods. Then they had to stop. Never to meow again. Only I like to think,' he whispered in low voice, 'they did it quietly sometimes. When the soldiers weren't listening.'

Echo now lowered his arms.

'I would have heard it, of course. I hear everything. No matter how far away. The Sound Mirror helps. And what people are saying, young William Arthur, is that what happened to the Brownies on the train was the same as the nuns. Mimetic Hysteria. Where one copies the other, only never knowing why.'

Echo then dropped his head, as if he'd suddenly gone to sleep. He then started snoring. He *had* gone to sleep!

I waited a moment or so to see if he'd wake up. But he didn't.

I began to think about what he'd said. *Mimetic Hysteria.* Yes, I suppose that could be said to describe what happened. The Brownies had copied each other and then become hysterical. But nothing could explain how they knew I'd been sought.

Well, if Granny wasn't willing or able to tell me, then perhaps Echo might know. But it would mean waking him up.

'Hello,' I said quietly. Then said it again louder.

No response.

'Echo!' I cried, louder still.

'ECHO!!!' I repeated, now at the top of my voice.

His head lifted and his eyes opened.

'William Arthur,' he said, calmly. 'Are you sure we've not met before? I never forget a voice.'

He now looked me up and down.

'Oh, yes I believe we have, but I think you were older then. And a girl.'

The man's bananas, I thought. Bananas, crackers and nuts! Best get out of here.

I turned intending to make my escape, but someone was already at the door struggling to push it open.

CHAPTER SIXTEEN

The Fire on the Beach

THE DOOR SOUNDED as if it was being battered and ramped, and suddenly it was forced open, but it was only Granny with an armful of driftwood. And now the world seemed normal again. Well, almost.

'Oh, Echo,' she said, putting down the wood. 'Look at your hair! You've gone all Rapunzel. I'll be needing more wool for that new hat of yours. Come here and give me a love.'

Granny hugged him close and there was talk of chickens and plants and trains and knitting and beaches. Only after all that did Echo mention that mad theory about the Brownies, and when he did, Granny listened as if he were telling her about a walk round the park for none of it surprised her at all. After he'd finished, he then repeated that offer of a cup of tea.

'Oh yes please, but none of your nettle and caterpillar nonsense. I want proper builders' tea, not boiled grass. Oh, and I almost forgot. There's a letter for you.'

Granny passed an envelope over to Echo, who then cut it open with one of his broken knives.

What was inside looked more like parchment than paper. There was something written on it, just a few scribbled words, but Echo folded it so quickly I couldn't tell what they were.

'I will make my special tea for William Arthur and me,' he said, putting the letter in his inside jacket pocket. 'It's too warm a day for the stove, so I'll use some of that driftwood of yours to build a fire outside.'

Echo then took a kettle, two teapots, various tins, which I assumed held the tea, and left.

'You'll be wanting answers, not advice, I suppose?' Granny declared. 'Well, on this occasion I'll tell you. You know that all Swidgers can hear more than the Commonality, but Echo has a listening gift that's way beyond what can be measured. For he, like you, is a Hopeful Monster. And there's no Swidger like him.'

Granny beckoned me to look out of the window at the far side of the carriage.

'Eagle those eyes and tell me what you see.'

I surveyed the bleak Dungeness landscape. In the distance was something grey, round and bulky. Difficult to say exactly how big as the ground was flat, so nothing near to compare it with, but, at a guess, I'd say it was about the size of a house. The sun emerged briefly from behind a cloud and now I could see it more clearly. The grey was concrete and it wasn't so much round as hollowed out.

'It looks like an ashtray that's been stood up on its side,' I said. 'Well, an ashtray once owned by a giant.'

'And that's a good a description as any I've ever heard,' Granny replied. 'What that is, William Arthur, is a Sound Mirror. The clue as to what it does is in the name. You'll find quite a few of them along the Kent Coast. The idea was that these giant ashtrays, as you put it, would help detect incoming enemy aircraft during the Second World War. Say what you like about the Germans – Mother always had it they ate their boots for breakfast – but they're damn good engineers. So you could always tell it was them by the engine. Standing in front of a Sound Mirror, well, that would enhance the noise and so you could hear the enemy coming twenty miles off. And what that meant was our artillery would now have just enough time to prepare our defence. Only then someone invented radar so the Sound Mirrors were no longer needed.'

I was beginning to understand why he was called Echo. That must be the reason, I thought, why Granny had brought us here. To listen.

'For the Commonality, Sound Mirrors are just curios from a bygone age. Relics among the shingle. But for a Swidger whose gift is to hear beyond all that can be heard – need I say more? Echo writes down everything he hears on vellum and parchment. Stores it all away. Says he finds it very useful.

'But with every gift comes a curse. To hear everything, and I mean everything, a bit like Moses and the Burning Bush, it was all a bit too much for him. Every sadness, every hate. He's past understanding most of it now.'

Perhaps, that's why he suddenly fell asleep. Listening had somehow worn him out.

'But be thankful today he did, but expect no more on that front. Besides, we didn't come here for that.'

Oh well, seems I was wrong.

'Then what did we come here for?' I asked.

'Tea, I hope!'

Granny had mentioned a plan. 'Two birds with one stone' she had said. But as yet no sign as to what she meant.

It was decided over tea that when night came we would go down to the beach and build a fire. And we would take with us, said Granny, some of Echo's special Moonshine, as she called it.

Moonshine turned out to be a bottle of clear golden liquor that Echo kept hidden beneath the trap door under the tiger rug. Not as brown as brandy and less yellow than whiskey, it smelt and flowed like warm honey. For glasses we used three old jam jars.

The shingle on the beach cut like flint so we took heavy blankets to lie on. Granny brought out her knitting needles and a new ball of green wool that Echo had given her. She took her first swig of Moonshine, gulping it down in one, so now she had an empty jam jar in her hand which she waved about in the cold night air.

'We are by the sea, Echo. And you know what sailors say, "The tide should never be out in a glass."'

I was given only a smidgen of moonshine and even that stuck

to the side of the jar like the jam it once held, so I had to use my finger to get at it.

'Ee-eeh, even that little bit will put ink in your nib,' she laughed.

It was the clearest evening sky I had ever seen. For light, we had the sparking fire, the passing beam of the lighthouse and the distant fluorescent presence of Dungeness Nuclear Power Station. And, of course, the unending stars and a waning moon.

This may seem a strange thing to say but I had never witnessed our Universe before. Not like this. The beach was flat. The sea was calm and unbroken. Nothing to disturb the eye except the tranquil beauty of the timeless night.

We sat in silence for a while. How far away the terrors and worries of the day were now. All felt well. Even Echo no longer seemed quite as mad as I knew him to be.

'What do you feel, young William,' he asked, with a slight hiccup in his voice as he sipped his third jar of that now glistering Moonshine, 'when you sit, uggh, beneath my, uggh, stars? Teeny? Weeny? A mere ant?'

'No,' I answered, staring up into the vastness, 'what I feel is part of them. Equal. Like we're all sharing our Universe together.'

'For that,' beamed Granny, producing a second full bottle of Moonshine from somewhere in her baggy tulip blouse, 'you shall have a second jar. But that's your last. At your age you could get drunk on a barman's dishcloth.'

Granny poured more yellow gold into my jam jar, but she suddenly stopped and looked stern, only to then laugh and fill it to the very brim.

'Give us a story, Echo. To go with the night. Nothing like a good tale to end a dog-weary day.'

'What sort of story?'

Granny lent back, spread herself across her blanket, rested her head on her arm and sighed, 'Tell us *our* story. The Swidger Story.'

Echo cast his eyes to the stars and began.

'One night, long ago, after a dog-weary day, perhaps on an evening such as this, the Universe was fast asleep. Dreaming. And what was that fantasy of its mind? Well, it was dreaming it had become a real Universe. Oh, such happy thoughts. But then the Universe was shaken from its sleep. Something disturbing had frightened it. The Universe slowly began to open its eyes.

'"Oh my," it said, suddenly seeing the deep blackness of the night, "it was only meant to be a dream." The Universe then shuddered for that night sky was now as real as real can be. And cold. And lonely. And lost. Oh, if only it could go back to its dream, thought the Universe, it had been such a happy dream where all was good and pure and in its place. So that's what the Universe tried to do. Remember its dream. But somehow it was always just out of reach. But, William Arthur, our Universe never gave up. It's still hoping, one day, to dream its dream again. If Time will allow. And when it does, all will be well once more.'

As Echo said those words, he looked me straight in the eye and for a few brief seconds he became the sanest man I had ever known.

'You see, that is what we are, young Swidger,' he whispered, the night fire flickering on his face, 'the hope of a dream in a world, a sad world, that awoke too soon.'

A long silence followed, until all thoughts were at rest.

'But why is it, though, that we Swidgers don't dream?' I said, at last. 'I never have. I've heard people talk about dreams. They sound weird. Like living inside a madhouse. I'm not sure I'd even want to dream, even if I could.'

Granny sat up and exchanged glances with Echo. Perhaps, I thought, they were deciding which one of them should tell me. In the end, it was Granny who spoke first.

'Dreams, the Commonality believe, are omens or portents.'

'Like shadowing clouds before a storm,' added Echo.

'Yet such fancies can't always to be trusted. Dream of a wedding, but along comes a hearse.'

'And in bad times,' Echo warned, 'dreams can dance with

your fears. And give you nightmares! And yet, and yet, and yet,' he went on, in a more hushed tone, 'there is much to learn from the dark places of the fairground. For, always remember, my dear friend, the Universe is far stranger than you can ever know.'

Granny now stretched her arms high and looked to the sky.

'Well, at least there's no shadowing clouds tonight,' she said. 'Not that I'm against all storms. If it hadn't been for that big one once in the English Channel all those years ago, we'd now be speaking Spanish. Echo, do you have a roll up? Nothing like a nice ciggie to go with the stars. You're too young to smoke, William Arthur, but I'm allowed, if only to have something to give up if my health fails.'

Echo lit two cigarettes, one for himself, one for Granny. He then turned his head to the breaking waters of the sea.

'The English Channel is looking a bit empty, so I think I'll go and add a little something to it,' he said, getting to his feet and then beginning an unsteady meander across the beach.

'I've never taken drugs,' whispered Granny, as he walked away, 'and neither should you. Not that there were any in my day. Except senna pods, which you took as a laxative. And snuff tobacco, which you shoved up your nose. Wise not to take the two together. If you did, the snuff would make you want to sneeze and the senna pods would dare you to!'

Granny then gave one of her little gruffle laughs which slowly softened into long sighs.

'Oh, the Commonality – I sometimes wonder. No matter where they are in life, they always want to be somewhere else. Yes, we Swidgers make a difference. We stop the ruin of promise. But sometimes the real harm comes from what the Commonality say to each other. Mother to daughter. Father to son. Lover to lover. Even Swidgers can't stop that. And the universe is shaken once more and we start again.'

Granny stretched her arms wide and let out a worn and weary aimless sigh. 'Ahhhh...'

I then heard splintering footsteps approach.

'I think I need another glass of Moonshine, Echo. To cheer me up. And don't be skinny with it. They stopped rationing in 1952.'

As Echo came nearer, even with the flickering fire, his face seemly strangely lost against the blackness of the sky.

Odd drink, I thought, *this Moonshine.* Makes you happy and content one minute, sad and melancholic the next.

'You go back to the railway carriage,' Granny suggested to me. 'Echo and I need to sort a few things.'

'The generator runs on methane, but isn't working at the moment, so I've left a lantern for you by the door,' said Echo. 'I think you'll be safe enough.'

Well, the methane generator explained the poo-ey smell round the back. The chickens gave Echo not just eggs but electricity too. Ironic with a nuclear power station right on his doorstep.

'You sleep in my bed tonight. Behind the orange curtain. I want to be here, beneath my stars. For sometimes, when we look up at the stars, what we are really seeing is what's inside ourselves.'

'Oh, that's true. And our reward will be the sight of the dawn of a new day. And by the time that comes, I hope I'll have finished your lovely new hat, Echo.'

Granny picked up her needles and that large ball of wool that Echo had given her and began to knit.

I was happy enough to go back to the railway carriage by myself. There was something I wanted to do, something I wanted to find. And it would have to be done in secret.

CHAPTER SEVENTEEN

Beneath the Tiger

I THOUGHT ABOUT what Granny had said. And the way she said it. Before this evening everything had been so upbeat and cheery, but her words tonight about the Commonality made what we do sound completely useless. I've already told you a little bit about myself and I feel I can now trust you enough to say that I'd had these doubts and feelings too.

Yes, even if I didn't have a name for it, I'd always known what I was, what I had to do and how to do it. But the *why* had worried me long before today.

I mean – being a Swidger – what was the point of it all? Yes, we somehow helped people, changed their Timepath, but why, when we never know the result? When we never see the outcome? Is that fair? I mean, what about us? Our lives – the distance we keep from those around us – the loneliness – it all makes me feel so empty sometimes. All lives need a purpose. Where was mine?

I thought again about the plumber or electrician, or whatever he was. Yes I had saved him from that falling tile, but hadn't he then nearly died from that electric shock? It was his shoes that saved him then. Not me. Somewhere in this gigantic jigsaw I sensed there was a piece missing. And I was determined to find it.

As I walked back to the railway carriage, I could hear Granny and Echo talking behind me. They were discussing the merits of talking to plants.

'I'm no gardener, Echo, if I gabbed to plants it'd be tantamount to giving them the Last Rites. They'd be dead before the Amen.'

My Swidger hearing was good but nowhere near that of

Echo's and as I walked further away all I could catch were snippets of their conversation.

'I could try some flower juice…'

'What about Daphne berries…?'

'I'd say Mandragora is always very useful…'

'A bit of transgressing might help…'

'Wolfberries, definitely Wolfberries…'

'He needs to be brave…'

'The Latin name be *Carduus Benedictus*…'

'… honeysuckle leaves…'

'… you want three bottles…'

As I ambled back, I suddenly felt the sharp night air on my cheeks and my head began to spin. And as it did, more questions went round and round in my mind – this time about the story Echo had told.

What had shaken the Universe awake? How would all be well once more? And why was whatever it was so out of reach?

No, no, that was just a silly fairy tale, but then those words of Granny came back into my mind – '*The Time is out of joint*' – and Swidgers, she said 'were born to set it right'. There was what Echo said as well: 'We are the hope of a dream', but how can that be when Swidgers aren't even able to dream?

I suddenly had to stop and breathe slowly for a while. That Moonshine had made me befuddled. And was now doing my thinking for me.

Oh, take no notice of it. It was only a stupid bedtime story. That's all. Besides, there were far more important things to think about such as what else, apart from bottles of Moonshine, lay hidden under that trap door? Granny said Echo writes down all he hears. Was that where he kept his notes? Under that tiger rug? I needed to know. Perhaps there I'd find the answers to some of my own questions.

It took a while to reach the railway carriage. My legs had begun to stray a bit.

That Moonshine must be really strong stuff, I thought, but, after the third or fourth attempt, I managed to open the door. It was dark inside the carriage but after some fumbling, I eventually found the lantern and switched it on. At last, light.

Oh, hello Mr Lion… Sorry… Mister Tiger… whatever you are, once King of the Jungle… now flat at my feet… there to be walked all over… you're not going to eat me, are you?

Oh, no, that's the Moonshine talking for me again. I shake myself and breath long and hard. At least now I'm steady on my feet. And sober enough to slide that tiger rug away. I put the lantern to the side and lift the trapdoor.

Echo may live with the fairies but he's not stupid – yes – he's left a torch on the ledge. And what am I hoping to find?

Swidger secrets.

On the way to the beach earlier this evening, I'd overheard Granny and Echo talking. I don't think I was meant to catch what they said, but from what I could make out, Echo liked to listen to how Swidgers had changed people's lives.

Would it be so wrong to read what he'd written?

I thought again about Granny. What had she done since I met her? As a Swidger, I mean? And Echo? In all his years here in Dungeness what could he have achieved? What lives had he changed?

I flicked on the torch. What did I see? Papers! Reams upon reams running the whole underbelly of the railway carriage.

At first I was elated. Here were the stories of lives we had changed. But torches in unsteady hands tell only half a truth, for as I looked again, now with a firmer grip, I saw the true reason these papers had been left here in the dark and damp.

To grow mushrooms.

They weren't really piles of papers at all but one sodden mass of mulch. And from it, the fungi grew. So that was what Granny had meant when she had said Echo found his writings useful. As bedding.

I put my finger into a wet pile. It went straight through. Mush. Just mush. And all the ink had run. Not one word could be read. These papers held their secrets still.

But then I see them. Some loose notes, damp yes, but not yet lost to the soggy mound. In a red ink made from berries, probably, knowing Echo. Handwritten on parchment. I pick one up. And there is my own name, 'William Arthur'. I sit and look through what I can. It is enough.

I switched off the torch.

I will not tell you what I read. It would not be right. These were the lives of others. Private lives that truly belonged only to themselves. Not me. Not you.

But there is one word I can reveal…

If.

That word kept repeating. *If.*

'If it hadn't been for that boy…'

If.

'If he were not there…'

If.

'If it wasn't for him…'

If.

'If that young lad had not jumped out.'

Me. I had changed lives. And for the better. I think perhaps I smiled, not at what I had discovered but in realising that Echo had made a difference to at least one life. My own.

That night I slept well in Echo's bed. So very, very well.

And now I feel the dawn light of day on my face. My eyes open. And there is Granny wearing that green woolly hat she'd knitted. It goes down all the way to the floor. Oh, she does look silly! And now in comes Echo wearing Granny's purple pillbox hat that I thought had escaped. He looks even sillier! I hear a kettle boil outside. Its steam produces a loud whistle. But it's not the whistle of the kettle anymore but a train. The carriage door opens and people come in. Mr Flynn, my maths teacher! What's he doing here? And why's he got a tiger on a lead? And that little girl who lost her balloon. Well, she has twenty – no forty – no a hundred now. And she's laughing and pointing at them. And there's Nurse Molly taking the postman's pulse. Suddenly Echo's railway carriage shakes. The engine has started up and we're setting off! We've already passed the lighthouse and the Sound Mirrors. There are people waving. They smile. I smile back. I recognise their faces. They are all the people I have helped in my life. Hundreds of them. And then I wake. Happy.

I have just dreamt for the first time.

CHAPTER EIGHTEEN

Piccadilly Circus

'DID YOU EVER wipe your sticky chocolate fingers on lace curtains?'

'No.'

'Tie a dustbin lid to a door, knock hard and then run off?'

'No.'

'And I don't suppose then you've ever spent a night in a Peruvian jail? Or tasted the forbidden fruits of a Moroccan house of ill-repute?'

'No. And definitely not.'

I told her I just wasn't that sort of boy. I don't do banter or dares or mischief.

Granny seemed disappointed.

'Well, William Arthur, I think it's time you went out into the world and got yourself a past! In other words, put a bit of bold in your life.'

'In the meantime,' Granny went on, 'do you want another slice of toast with your eggs?'

Breakfast at Dungeness came courtesy of the chickens. And by the smell of it, the bread was home-made too.

'I've tried hard all my life not to be noticed,' I said, dripping the runny yellow yolk all down my chin. 'That's our way, isn't it?'

Granny ignored me. Or at least my question.

'All women should have a past, it's why men find us so beguiling. But I don't see why you shouldn't have one as well. There's more to life than geography revision.'

In Dungeness it was almost as if school didn't exist. That wasn't a bad thing. Jimmy Lee, the bully of our class, was becoming a bit of a menace to me and others.

'How can I put dare into my life or get a past when we Swidgers even can't fight back?'

That was true. You see, our bodies won't let us fight. Jimmy Lee once belted me really hard. I just about managed to make a fist to thump him back but, try as I might, and I really wanted to, my hand simply wouldn't move. I must have looked stupid. Jimmy Lee called me a coward and laughed. And then hammered me again.

'I think it's better,' said Granny, 'that we can't fight or be violent. I mean, look at the mess the Commonality get themselves into always hitting each other. Or worse. We can't use force, so we find another way. That's just how we are.'

Maybe so but it wasn't easy. I then told Granny all about Jimmy Lee.

'Well,' she said, 'in that case, maybe we should just stay here for another week.'

I then had to tell her that if I missed school even for one day, she'd have to write me a note.

'I'll do no such thing,' she exclaimed, 'not with the rheumatism in my fingers. No, I'll have a chat with your teachers when I meet them tonight.'

'Tonight? You mean tomorrow, don't you?' I asked.

'No, tonight. You slept right through Monday. That's what happens when Swidgers dream for the first time.'

So Granny had planned the whole thing.

'Was it the Moonshine that made me dream?'

'Certainly not! Moonshine enhances contemplation of the cosmos – and then makes you fall over. No, it was the tea. That's why I had builders. For you and Echo, Lady's Mantle and Sneezewort. Poisonous to the Commonality but it helps a Swidger to dream. But only, my little stargazer, if you need to.'

'Why did you want me to dream?'

'Because, in my opinion, you are suffering from fantasy

malnutrition. You need to become a "Third-Eyer".'

'A what?'

'"One-Eyers", they see the world as only atoms and molecules. Things you can touch. "Two-Eyers" believe in hope and wishes. Things that aren't there but could be. But the "Third-Eyers" are the true poets, because they see way beyond the possible. And for the battle ahead, my little stick of rhubarb, you must become a poet, develop a corkscrew mind, learn to think round corners, and, most importantly, imagine.'

Imagine. That was something I never did.

I cast my eyes down to the floor.

'And how do I do that? By eating funny mushrooms?'

'Oh, you found those, did you? Not the sort you put on toast.'

'Yes, I had worked that out.'

'Poor Echo,' sighs Granny, 'with all he's heard in life, is it any wonder he needs an alternative reality? But imagination is different,' she went on, walking over to the iron oil stove for more eggs, 'for with imagination you can turn the world into whatever you want it to be.'

As Granny stepped across the tiger, she tripped over its tail sending strands of hair flying across her face. 'Damn you, entropy! And damn, you tiger!' she huffed, annoyed as much at herself as that poor dead beast on the floor. 'Come on, one more egg and we'll set off back to London and you can go to that silly school of yours.'

'But I have no uniform.'

'Then today you will be the boy without one.'

'But everyone has to wear a uniform.'

'Don't your teachers know it's only dead fish that swim with the tide?'

'If I'm not in uniform, I'll be sent home.'

'Then we'll go home first.'

'But if we do that, by the time I get to school it'll be time to come home.'

'Let me get this straight. Go to school and you'll be sent home. Go home and you'll be too late for school.'

'Yes.'

'Well, that's settled then. We'll bunk off. Is that the right word?'

Our kind are rarely ill. Physically we're very robust. If we are injured, our bodies recover very quickly. Our kind, therefore, do not miss school. And we certainly don't bunk off. But none of this seemed to matter to Granny. If anything, she was growing ever more excited by the whole idea of going AWOL, as she now called it.

'Piccadilly! That's where we'll go,' she announced, picking up her beloved carpet bag and now singing very loudly and out of tune a silly song about Piccadilly where the traffic only went one way.

'*La-da-dee!* Oh, I wonder if they've still got that big neon Bovril sign opposite Eros? Yes, there's a place on Piccadilly that will help you to become the Swidger you need to be. Trust me William Arthur, for everything I do has a purpose!'

Echo had left the carriage early for his morning stroll which meant, according to Granny, he could be gone for weeks. But we did manage a goodbye to the chickens.

'See you soon, Gertrude and Pistol. Don't you just love how the two of them walk. Wattling, I call it. Not a strut, not a waddle but somewhere in between.'

On our way back to the Dungeness Railway Station we passed some small houses that had a plaque in front saying 'Pluto Bungalows'. Not sure why they were called that. Not then. Maybe, I thought at the time, because the landscape of Dungeness was more like a deserted planet than a beach. The truth was, I was so angry that day we arrived that I didn't take much interest in anything that was around me. Except that I did notice even then that the Dungeness terminal seemed to have been built from what looked like reclaimed timbers, perhaps a boat or ship. And that inside the station there were framed photographs on the wall of World War Two soldiers all smiling and eating ice cream. Oh, but the importance of all that comes later. For what was really on my mind that particular morning was what I now saw through the window: the Dungeness nuclear power station that dominated the horizon.

Almost like a fortress.

Granny must have seen how intensely I was looking at it.

'That's right, here the electricity is always fresh. And always so much of it.'

Strange to say it but all the while we'd been in Dungeness, I'd felt no sense of danger. Well, what I mean is that feeling of being watched had gone away.

But would it, I wondered, come back when we returned to London?

CHAPTER NINETEEN

The Third Eye

THE TRAIN JOURNEY back to the capital was uneventful. No Brownies, no barking dogs, no men in Mackintosh coats and, most importantly, no sense of being watched.

As it was a sunny day, Granny thought it would be a good idea to walk from Victoria Station to Piccadilly by way of Green Park and Buckingham Palace.

'Oh, see up there, the flag's flying. We're at home.'

She was in a joyous mood, skipping along at a breakneck speed, but on the more uphill incline through the park her stride became more of a jaunty jog. Besides, Granny loved looking at people. And making comments as they passed by.

'Oh, isn't that nice? Seeing old folk holding hands. Saying to the world, "I may be old and ugly, but look at me, I'm loved."' Oh, will you listen to them Hare Krishnas? Still singing the same song. You'd have thought they'd have come up with a B-Side by now. Did I hear that young couple right? They're going to Hawaii for their honeymoon? Why Hawaii? It's only Blackpool with coconuts.'

I think she'd have been happy to wander around the park all day earwigging and gawping at people but eventually we arrived on Piccadilly.

'Very posh area now but it wasn't that long ago it was fifteen shillings a night and find your own railings.'

'So where exactly are we going?' I asked.

'Nowhere. Because we're already here. The Royal Academy of Arts. And the beginning of your journey into the impossible.'

The Royal Academy of Arts was an imposing building with a wide courtyard. In the centre, on cobbled stone, stood a large metal sculpture. As we walked in, Granny asked, 'What do you think that is?'

'Bronze?' I suggested.

'No, Mister One-Eye, not what's it made of, what is it meant to be?'

It looked like a brown egg. Split down the middle.

'A big brown egg,' I replied, 'split down the middle.'

'Yes, yes, but what's it doing?'

I tried again. The egg was divided into two halves and had bits of metal sticking out, representing, I guessed, bits of shell.

'Hatching,' I suggested.

'Anything else?'

This wasn't going to be easy. I mean, it was only a big brown egg about to hatch.

'Look beyond what you think it is and see what it could be.'

I didn't really understand art, but, I thought, I'll give it another go. And suddenly I did see it. It wasn't just a breaking egg. You see, the surface of the shell wasn't smooth, it had engravings with shapes – like feathers. And now I saw the breaking egg could be two chickens, one on top of the other. And those cracked bits of shell at the edges, they could be, if I wanted to see them that way, ruffled feathers. I told Granny this and she did a quick spin on her heels.

'Oh, very good, very good, very good. And what is it these chickens are doing?'

Hmmm. The chickens – well, now I saw them as chickens – were doing exactly was what I'd seen Gertrude and Pistol doing at Echo's. Only this was the Royal Academy of Art so, I thought, I'd better use the word that we'd been taught to say at school.

'They're, er, copulating,' I mumbled.

'Copulating!' shouted Granny, attracting the attention of a group of bemused Chinese tourists and two elderly English ladies.

'They're not copulating, *they're at it! At it!*'

Yes, they certainly were.

'The curve of the lady chicken's beak. That's a smile that's never turned away a stranger! Oh, but look at the fella on top. See where his eyes are, wandering off, already on the lookout for his next conquest. Not ones for loyalty, aren't cockerels. As Mother used to say, "All sail and no anchor." So then, my budding Leonardo, what it you see now? Egg or chickens?'

'Both,' I replied. 'And something else.'

The elderly ladies began to move closer.

'Go on,' said Granny, encouragingly.

'Well, it's what people say: "Which came first, the chicken or the egg?" But here what the chickens are doing will lead to the egg. So perhaps it doesn't matter which came first because chicken and egg are ultimately one and the same thing?'

'Hells, bells and buckets of frogs! And you've worked that out for yourself? Well done, my brush of many colours! That is what art does: makes you see this as that, and that as this. Similtanasity. Yes, I agree, it sounds more like a cure for haemorrhoids, but it's given you a new idea. And ideas are what will make you into a poet. The Third-Eyer thinker you will need to be.'

One of the elderly ladies now tapped Granny on the shoulder.

'Excuse me,' she enquired, 'are you here every day? You're so much better than the audio guide.'

Our visit round the Royal Academy of Arts took several hours. Granny said that art shouldn't just be about filling up empty walls

'That said,' she went on, 'I sometimes wonder if, when Michelangelo had finished painting that ceiling on the Cistern Chapel, the Pope didn't point and say, "Oh look, you've missed a bit!" Perhaps that became the Pope's nickname for Michelangelo.'

'What?'

'"Mister Bit!" Oh, me and my silly jokes. Mind you, it has always been a bit of a puzzle why Michelangelo painted Adam with a bellybutton.'

Granny, though, wasn't keen on everything she saw in galleries. 'I'm no connisewer, but if you are going to do a portrait of royalty, it seems only polite to include ears and a nose. I don't think we'll see that interpretation of majesty on a biscuit tin anytime soon.'

According to Granny though, I was still 'a frame without a picture', and so it would be better, she said, if I went round the galleries by myself. One painting made me smile: 'Telemachus and Athena'. A young man being told what to do by a woman in armour.

Oh yes, I know how you feel, I thought.

As I looked, that sudden pain came again across my forehead. Ahhhhhaaah!

It stopped me in my tracks. Less sharp than at the hospital, more a throb. I tried blinking and eventually it faded.

Something within me was changing. If it was anything to do with this gift of mine, well, I couldn't yet sense what that was. How art or imagining was going to help, I didn't know either. But Granny was right: my mind was too literal. No one ever read me stories or fairytales when I was little. For me, gingerbread was for eating, not building houses. A grandma was a grandma, not a wolf. And cables were cables, not snakes.

Snakes.

That day on the High Street. Perhaps those snakes had been omens like in dreams? Yet Granny warned that such things shouldn't always be trusted. And so, on our journey back to Chipping Barnet on the underground, I began to argue with her that imagining, like dreams, could be dangerous.

'Well,' she agreed, 'you're right in a way because the mind can become its own prison. Live in that world too long and you'll end up chasing windmills, like that doolally Spaniard.'

Granny then pulled her hat over her eyes and began to nap. It had been a long day and we still had that Parent Teacher Meeting to come.

Granny had said there was purpose in everything she did

and so, to show her that our visit to the art galleries hadn't been wasted, I began to see if I could think up something artistic of my own. I mean, if art could be a chicken or an egg, then why not anything and everything around us?

And with that thought, I looked out the underground carriage window. And then it came into my mind – I saw it there in front of me.

Most of the underground system has tunnels with bricks on both sides, but there are places on the Northern Line where there's no divide, no wall, where trains run alongside each other and you can see right into compartments on the adjacent track. Doesn't happen often, and the timing has to be just right, but as I was thinking about art that's what I saw. And that gave me the idea for my picture.

I quickly poked Granny and lifted up her hat so she could see.

'Look,' I blurted out, 'that's what I'd paint!'

'What?' she asked, her eyes struggling to wake.

'Two trains in parallel. That's what was there just then. You know how that can sometimes happen on the Northern Line,' I told her.

After rubbing her brow for a moment, she looked to where I'd seen the other carriage but by then it was gone and we were back to the solid brick wall of the tunnel.

'You missed the other train,' I said.

'Yes,' she sighed, 'seems I have.'

But my artistic idea excited me so much I wanted to tell her all about it.

'I'd paint two trains, you see, but really they'd be the *same* train, with the *same* people. Only in different place. The second train, you see, would represent an altered Timeline for everyone. As if I had Swidgered them when they got on. I suppose for the idea to work I'd have to paint the compartments from above, that way you could really see that they had changed places. There'd be no ceiling, but that's all right, isn't it? Art doesn't need to be real, does it?'

Granny seemed lost in thought and said simply, 'Oh William. You are full of surprises. Your picture sounds very artistic, but can you actually paint?'

'No. Can you?'

'Not really. I doubt that Michelangelo would've trusted me with a brush. The only thing he'd have let me paint would have been the back door of his dog's kennel.'

'Dog kennels don't have a backdoor.'

'Exactly! Ha! Ha!'

As Granny began to gruffle at her own terrible joke, she again closed her eyes for 'a quick twenty winks', yet I could tell something was troubling her.

Perhaps it was the thought of that Parent Teacher Meeting.

CHAPTER TWENTY

The Glass Bottle

'SAD BUT TRUE,' declared Granny, as we left the tube station and began the walk to my school, 'but the world of the Commonality is run by clever idiots, who believe that only *they* know what's right, so when folk think for themselves, they're called ignorant and stupid. Clever idiots have many names such as Bishop, Politician and, tonight, Teacher.'

As we went along, Granny asked if there were any iron railings on route as she always enjoyed, from her own days on her way to Sunday school, running a stick along the bars. There were some near the abandoned railway line, so that was the path we took.

'Walking has the advantage over cars and bicycles,' she said, making a rat-ta-ta-tat across the bars with a broken branch she'd found in the grass verge, 'in that legs do not require what people call "parking".'

She was enjoying her game with her stick, but I wasn't because coming from the other direction was Jimmy Lee and some of his mates. What a sight we must have looked. Jimmy pointed and laughed. He then lifted his fist, directed it at me and mouthed, 'Tomorrow!'

I wasn't surprised Jimmy Lee was off in the opposite direction to the school. His family weren't the sort to attend a Parent Teacher Meeting.

Granny's rat-tat-tatting came to an abrupt end when she saw the imposing school building ahead. The savage grey steel and lifeless glass dominated the entire length of the road.

'Oh, do you know, William, I'm as nervous as a kitten in a

Doncaster butchers. So you'd better show me where the bins are.'

'The bins?' I asked.

'Well, at the hospital I told you the easiest way to discover secrets was the pub next door, but the next best is the bins. Because that's where all the grief ends up.'

The school refuse was kept near a side gate but that was out of bounds, though Granny couldn't see that this mattered as we weren't in school hours.

'Besides,' she added, 'it's not my school, so not my rules. And even if it were, rules, like piecrusts, are made to be broken.'

The bins, large with flat orange lids, were stored in an open shed under a corrugated roof.

'I'll lift the lid with my stick here, then you can climb inside.'

'I'm not climbing in a bin,' I protested.

'Well,' she replied, pointing to a pile of old milk crates, 'stand on one of them and bend over the edge and I'll hang on to you as best I can. Oh, I've not done anything like this since I went apple bobbing on Mischievous Night.'

As ever, her eager expression told me there was no getting round this, so I took a milk crate and stepped unsteadily onto it.

'Grab whatever's there,' she croaked, now struggling to hold my legs.

'The school isn't stupid, you know. This is the recycling bin and most of what's in here has already gone through the shredder.'

'Anything solid?'

My hands found what felt like a small cardboard box.

'There's this,' I said, passing it over.

She took it from me and let go of my ankles, leaving me hanging over the side like forgotten washing.

'Ah! It's a medication packet, I think. I can make out a lot of 'Z's so it must be very serious. Always good to know the enemy has a weakness. Thank you, bin, for that, but if you've nothing else to offer we'd better try the one in the staff room so we can discover, close-up, the problems and pressures your poor teachers face in life. Oh look, William, up the side of that wall: a fire escape, all the way to the top. I bet that will take us anywhere we need to go.'

Have you ever thought about something you've done only to wonder how and why you ever did it? Well, I do when I think back on that Parent Teacher Meeting. You see, I foolishly told Granny those iron steps would take us straight to the staff room – and as soon as I had she was on her way like a ferret up a drainpipe.

The climbing was the easy part but when we reached the top, we discovered the obvious: the fire escape only opened from the inside. Granny, though, was nothing if not resourceful.

'They say love laughs at locked doors – well, so do old ladies with a hairpin.'

You couldn't help but be impressed. But another feeling ran through me too. *Excitement*. I mean, we could be spotted any minute. But it was worth it. That said, when she finally unpicked the locked and we were in, I felt something a bit more familiar. *Relief*.

Next though came disappointment, for the bins in the staff room had already been emptied, but Granny cheered up when she saw a large metal barrel standing in the corner.

'Is that the cider you talked about?'

'Must be,' I answered, 'bet they've moved it here to drink it later.'

Granny then started to undo her blouse. Just two or three buttons, yet I couldn't help but notice the beginnings of lace.

'Look away, William Arthur, you're too young for such sights. But being a woman blessed with a very large upper circumference has its advantages. For bosoms can hide a multitude of sins.'

When Granny said I could look now I saw she had several small glass bottles in her hand, the sort that probably once contained perfume. She checked these various coloured vials against the light, and then passed me the purple one before putting the others back down her blouse.

'Echo gave me these,' she confided, 'and if you add a few drops of this one to the cider, justice will prevail.'

'What will it do?'

'Some more advice, I think, William Arthur. Life is like Penicillin: sometimes it needs a little bit of wrong to make it right. Let's just say any teacher who drinks cider tonight will be in for a morning surprise. Well, are you going to take the stopper off or just stand there with a face like a wet Wednesday?'

You may have broken a few school rules in your life. But not me. Not till today. Perhaps I never would spend a night in a jail in Peru or taste the pleasures of that house in Morocco but right now I felt like a true rebel. And I do the deed.

I take off the elegant glass stopper, remove the lid of the metal keg, and carefully pour that strange violet liquid into the barrel.

But when I turn round, Granny is gone. Worse, the door opens and in walks the headmaster, Mr Benjamin. A towering six foot six. No wonder all the lads call him 'Big Ben'.

'You, boy! What are you doing in here?'

I look behind him half expecting Granny to pop out with some brilliant explanation. Only she doesn't.

'What's your name, boy?'

Don't panic now, William Arthur, stand up straight, put your arms behind your back and tell the headmaster your name.

'Er, it's er, William, sir. William Arthur.'

'You have no right to be in here, William. Are your parents with you tonight?'

Good. He hasn't noticed what I'm trying to do with the keg top behind me – it's still in my hand, if only I can screw it back on to the keg.

'No, sir,' I reply.

'Then who is with you? And why are you in the staff room?

It's not easy twisting the top round and round when it's behind your back but I don't think Big Ben can tell that's what I'm doing.

'My guardian is with me, sir. It was her idea for me to come into the staff room. She said –'

That's two full turns now. I'll try for a third...

'Yes?' Mr Benjamin demands. 'Tell me exactly what she said.'

Yes, the top is tightening now...

'She said, er, that, er –'

'Her exact words now!'

'She said that coming in here I would discover, close-up, "the problems and pressures your poor teachers face in life".'

Just one final twist...

'Did she now? Well, I'd like to meet this guardian of yours and inform her that our staff room is strictly out of bounds for pupils, parents and guardians alike. Is that understood? Now take your arms from behind your back, boy, this isn't a passing out parade.'

I obediently brought my arms to my side and then left the staff room red faced with heart pounding.

Oh, why had I gone along with her crazy plan? And where was Granny now?

I ran down the main staircase, eyes darting everywhere. Then out from the girls' toilet came a large hat covered in daffodils. With Granny somewhere underneath.

'Who are you looking round for, the rent man? Do you like my new hat? You're in trouble, aren't you? But don't worry, it's all part of my ingenious plan. No time to explain, but I do need that glass bottle back.'

I'd put the purple vial in my pocket but now I couldn't find the stopper. I told Granny that perhaps I'd left it behind on the metal barrel or maybe just dropped it as I ran down the stairs? I really wasn't sure.

'Not to worry, Echo gave me a spare,' she said, taking a yellow stopper from a pocket and putting it on the bottle. 'Just a tiny drop left, but it's a truth of life that the Mother of Mischief need only be as big as a midge's wing. Now, let's go and meet these so-called teachers of yours.'

As we walked together along the corridor, people were already staring. I felt hot and flushed so I put my hand to my cheek. How red was I getting? And how much more embarrassed would I get?

CHAPTER TWENTY-ONE

Questions to Teacher

THE PT MEETING was taking place in the gym as the school hall was being refurbished. Various signs pointed the way, along with notices saying that this evening the school band would be playing *Tales from the Vienna Woods*. Not that Granny bothered to look at them. Instead she tried a door I'd never noticed previously and without a second's thought we were already halfway across the science lab.

'Oh dear, I've never been that good with technology,' she declared, stopping at a desk and spinning round a pipestem triangle. 'I can hardly dare trust myself with an egg whisk.'

Granny then went over to a cupboard with a glass window through which we could see dozens of bottles and jars all full up with every kind of compound and ingredient.

'Oh, wouldn't it be fun to mix up all these lovely colours and see what happens! But I don't suppose we have the time. Still, it's good to experiment, you know. I did know a fella once who invented a clock that could do an hour in fifty minutes. But it never caught on. Shame, really.'

Granny then moved along to what I thought was a large cupboard in the wall but when she opened it what was there was the hallway with the entrance to the school gym right in front of us.

'This, I think, is what we want,' she said, cheerfully.

Protective mats had been laid on the wooden floor to stop it being damaged by outdoor shoes and high heels. Spread across the room were tables, teachers sitting one side, parents and offspring the other.

'Oooh! They're all here tonight,' noted Granny, as we walked in, 'the world, her lover, the cat and his goldfish. Now, let me guess who's who. Your English teacher. I'm thinking young and trendy, but with receding hair. Wearing an old green jacket but no tie. Am I right?'

'Yes,' I replied, 'but how did you know?'

'His wife told me. We had a chat in the girls' toilet. Another place where secrets are revealed. Including short cuts through chemistry labs.'

'His name is Mr Roper but the lads all call him "Stringy".'

'Well, teaching English, he'll appreciate that nickname for its lexical synonymity. Yes, I see him now. And Mrs Stringy wasn't wrong about that jacket. I've seen better dressed tripe. And that hair of his is living on borrowed time. He'll be bald as a coot before he's thirty.'

Granny went straight over, sat herself down and, without even introducing herself, was off.

'They tell me you're in charge of words. Now if truth be known, very few people in our village could read or write. Except Ada Barraclough. Or so she claimed. Of an evening, for a penny an hour, she'd read to us from the newspapers what was going on in the warring world. But then one day, one of village lads came home. Or most of him did. Turned out France wasn't overrun by giant toads. And in Italy, hairy bats hadn't hatched from coconuts and eaten all the spaghetti. As for that Mediterranean fella who made love to a cloud that then gave birth to a horse, well, that *did* turn out to be true, but that's Greek mythology for you.

'But the point was, Ada Barraclough's two brothers were serving in France and Italy, and she couldn't face what was truly going on, so to cope she made up her own tales. Now don't get me wrong, I'm not against words. I like them. My favourite is "custard". But, it's *why* words are put together that counts. Ada's tales weren't real, like bricks and mortar and mushy peas, but in a way they had their own truth. And it's those stories we should be telling. Well, I'm glad I've cleared that up. Nice to have met you, Mr Stringy.'

And with that, Granny tapped him gently on the hand and walked off, leaving the teacher of words lost for any of his own.

When I caught up with Granny, I tried to explain that the main idea of the PT evening was for teachers to tell parents how their child was getting on, but she thought it should be the other way round.

'I want to make sure they're learning you right. Do you do Shakespeare?'

'Yes. We had a lesson last week on the nature of gender in *As You Like It*.'

'Well, there you are, it's a good job I came. I think we'll do physics next. I'm picturing a face with all the joys of cold porridge.'

She wasn't wrong.

'Mr Draper. He's over there,' I said, pointing, 'only we call him "Droopy Draper".'

'Yes, and I can see why. Oh, I'd hate to look like that and not be ill. Come along, William Arthur, and you'll discover that education isn't about knowing the correct answers, but rather asking the right questions.'

Before plonking herself down at Droopy Draper's table, Granny whispered, 'By the way, William Arthur, do you have a nickname?'

I shook my head.

'Hmm,' she murmured, 'well, I'm giving you notice that by tomorrow you will.'

Of course, I didn't know what she meant. Not then.

Droopy Draper must have been expecting many questions that evening but not, I suspect, Granny's.

'Why doesn't the moon fall down? It's been up there an awfully long time. Not that I want it to. I might get hit on the head and end up daft.'

Droopy face now became Droopy jaw, as his chin dropped well below his tie.

'Well, Mr Droopy,' she went on, moving her chair round to sit right next to him, 'you're a man of science but you seem unable to answer that simple question, so I will enlighten you.'

Granny now grabbed his arms and started to use them to demonstrate her theory.

'The moon, you see, is caught betwixt the gravitational pull of the Earth, this hand of yours here doing the pulling – oh my words, these nails do need cutting – and its own projectile force, that hand there wanting to go in the other direction. You find yourself caught in an equilibrium of opposites. It's like when you're drunk, say, with cider.'

Granny now started swaying his arms back and forth as illustration.

'The alcohol makes you want to fall over, only your pride keeps you upright. So you sort of stay where you are. Except with the occasionally wobble. Just like our own dear Luna orb.'

Granny now left Mr Draper's arms hanging in mid-air.

'Had Sir Isaac expressed it thus in his *Principia Mathematica* perhaps it might well have sold a few more copies.'

Granny then lifted her herself from her chair.

'And now, Mr Droopy-Draws, in my own petulant denial of gravity, I will rise and leave you. Do you know, I'm up and down tonight like a rubber yo-yo.'

And with that she was away again.

'I'm none too impressed with your teachers,' she said loudly, so everyone could hear, 'I wouldn't trust most of 'em to feed rabbits.'

People were beginning to notice Granny, but she was at a loss as to understand why.

'I do wish people wouldn't keep staring at me. I mean, I didn't come here with a duck under me arm. It's not my daffodil hat, is it? I'll have you know it cost me nineteen shillings and sixpence, reduced from two guineas. Who's next? Oh, I think we'll give

Geography a miss. How mountains are formed is their business. As for History, well, I've lived too much of that already.'

Granny then spotted a nervous looking figure standing next to a makeshift platform at the far end of the gym. 'Who is the gentleman over there? Poor chap, looks like he's carrying all the troubles of the world.'

'That's Mr Mansukhani. Our new music teacher.'

'And if he's new, he's an innocent who's never drunk the cider. Oh, but look at them shoulders of his. He's worried about something.'

'Well, I'm not surprised. He's conducting the school band later on. It said so on the notices. They're playing Strauss's *Tales from the Vienna Woods*.'

'Strauss. Nice tunes, no depth. And a bit old-fashioned, but we can fix that. Yes, I understand people can get nervous before a performance, but with him it's much more than that. He looks very troubled.'

'Well, that's because the band are terrible. A school joke. He's probably worried for them.'

'Oh, an incorrigible empathiser. A man after my own heart. Time, methinks, to shimmy over and show a bit of leg.'

And Granny did just that. She lifted her skirt, tucked it in to whatever unmentionables were beneath and cheekily walked over to Mr Mansukhani, removing her gloves as she went.

What on earth was she going to do now?

CHAPTER TWENTY-TWO

And the Band Played On

AS GRANNY TOOK our new music teacher Mr Mansukhani by the hand, I heard her say, 'Goodness me, what a big beard you have. And it's not even the full moon!'

My heart sank. But instead of being in any way offended Mr Mansukhani's face beamed and smiled.

'Ha! Ha! Why thank you! And may I say, how beautiful is your hat. Daffodils. My favourite. And so becoming.'

'Oh, you are too kind. May I call you Abhijeet?'

'Of course.'

'A name that means "Victory", does it not?'

'You are right, it does.'

Granny then held his palm gently and spoke in a language I did not understand. Mr Mansukhani looked taken aback by this but then replied, 'You speak Punjabi?'

Granny nodded and now they went on chatting as if old friends.

Speaking Polish was one thing, but Punjabi as well. And somehow she knew his name by just holding his hand.

They continued in Punjabi until Mr Mansukhani said, 'You are a very wise lady.'

'Not really,' replied Granny, 'I've just lived a long life. Older than dirt, I am. Remember: Victory over fear. I did notice some water jugs in the corridor. Why don't I make myself useful and pour some glasses for your lovely orchestra?'

And with that she walked cheerfully away and Mr Mansukhani moved off to prepare for the concert.

I was now by myself but parents and pupils alike were still staring. A new experience for me. I mean, I was always just the quiet lad at the back of the class but now I was centre of attention. They didn't realise it, but with my Swidger hearing I could tell everything they were saying.

'That boy who was with that peculiar woman in the ridiculous hat, is he in your class?'

'No, Mummy, I don't know who his is.'

'Well, keep away from him, just in case. I don't want you catching anything.'

Yesterday I might have cared what they said, but not tonight. No, I was proud.

All eyes though soon turned to the makeshift platform where the band had gathered. Some lads at the back of the gym were already sniggering at the prospect of yet another embarrassing performance.

The musicians started to play. A few random notes here and there. It sounded more like they were tuning up, but Mr Mansukhani was already waving his baton. Was this how Strauss's *Tales from the Vienna Woods* was meant to begin? I hoped so. For his sake.

The room hushed.

The band was made up of six violins, four trumpets, three cellos, two flutes and one trombone. After that uncertain start the trumpets suddenly came in with a fanfare: *Da-da-da-Da-da-ad-da-da-da-da-dah!*

Now that was good. Very good. Not only loud and brassy, but also, for once, in tune.

Next the violins. Subtle and sweet. One played a gentle solo, the flutes responded and then all the violins came back in. The tune of the waltz rose up, held for a moment, then gracefully floated on.

It was... beautiful, really beautiful. Was it just me that thought so? No, even lads at the back had stopped their sniggers.

Something about the band was very different. I moved closer. All the musicians were looking at each other as if to say, 'What's going on? We've never played like this before.'

The trumpets now came in strong and with purpose. And the violins followed, full of energy and vigour. Captivating, playful, teasing.

Then it happened. One of the trumpeters broke away, taking the melody of the waltz with him. Yet somehow he turned that tune around, as if those notes had suddenly discovered a life of their own. More alive. Vibrant. Bluesy. A real jazz sound.

Then the flutes caught the same fever and the strings too. One player threw her bow to the floor, stood up and started plucking her cello as if it were a double bass. Another joined her, spinning her cello, and making the music dance. Soon the whole band begun to jive. We were swinging with Strauss. And it was brilliant! Totally brilliant!

I heard a door behind me open and saw Granny slip quietly into the gym. She rested herself against the wooden frame of the climbing wall and took out from her ample bosom a perfume bottle with a nozzle spray top. The liquid in the vial was a sunny yellow colour and perfectly matched the abundant display of daffodils in her hat. Granny then squirted some of it in the air and wafted it around.

I looked back to the band. They were having the ride of their life, even if they weren't sure where they were heading. I don't think that audience had heard anything like it. Feet began to tap but as the gym floor was covered with mats so the sound was muffled.

But then someone stood up on one of the tables, others followed, and soon the tapping of feet could be heard. Those who chose to stay on the ground simply clapped along in rhythm. Eventually the whole room became the percussion section, throbbing with joy. Even the sniggering lads had clamber up the climbing wall and now beating their fists against the bars.

Granny winked at me. This was her doing. And I loved her for it.

The reception that greeted the band as they hit that last pulsating note was beyond words and the walls and ceiling echoed the tumultuous applause as if they too wanted to join in.

But by far the happiest man in the room was Mr Mansukhani. I couldn't say for sure as there were so many clapping hands raised high in the air, but I would have sworn he was crying.

Granny tapped me on the shoulder. 'There you see a human being fully alive. And that, my little semi-quaver, is why we Swidgers have been put on this earth. As I've said, we are here to help them sing the song they are meant to sing. Stand back and enjoy it too. Be happy for him.'

And I was. At Dungeness I'd only read about how being a Swidger had altered lives. Now I was seeing it for real. Yes, it was Granny who had done this, not me, but it was a joy to behold all the same.

The applause eventually subsided. A tall figure approached. It was the Headmaster, Mr Benjamin. But Big Ben didn't speak to me but to Granny.

'Are you this boy's mother?'

'Oh, you flatter me, Headmaster, I'm old enough to be yours!'

I'm not sure the headmaster knew how to take this, but he went on undaunted.

'Earlier tonight I found William in the staff room. He told me that you suggested he go in there. If this is true, I would like an explanation.'

'Oh, that's going to be difficult because, as our William will confirm, I don't hold with explanations.'

The headmaster certainly didn't expect that. But he hadn't finished yet.

'I've also been informed that William was not at school today. That's truancy. And I've had reports of someone seeing a boy and a woman breaking into the school via the fire escape. Are you aware of this incident?'

'Maybe I am, maybe I'm not. That's for me to know and you to find out.'

The headmaster wasn't going to stand for that.

'That is not the reply I would expect from a responsible guardian.'

'Oh, I agree, but that's because as I've got older, I've immatured with age. My motto is: *Never set a good example to children because that would take all the fun out of life.* But, I tell you what, Ben, luv, in the morning I'll come in and we can have a little chat over a cup of tea. I could bring one of my currant buns, if you'd like? Toasted. I like mine lemon curd one side, marmalade the other. What about you?'

Mr Benjamin didn't know how to take this either and so simply said, 'My wife provides me with an adequate breakfast of fresh fruit and fibre.'

Granny looked him up and down and said, 'I'll have my currant bun before I set off, then. By the way, Headmaster, can I just say to you that I've never met a man who wears a grey suit better. I'll be here first thing – I wouldn't miss our little chat for all the rats in the barley barn. Come along, our William, it's getting late. And time does not stand still, except in close proximity to matter of infinite density and immeasurable gravitational pull. My friend Albert taught me that. Eeeh, we had some laughs.'

And with that we turned and left.

CHAPTER TWENTY-THREE

Two Equals One

I'VE BEEN A latch-key kid for a while now. The woman I stay with now, a distant cousin of the lady who adopted me but then died, is away a lot. That's why the house was empty that Saturday morning. The place is beautifully decorated, but as Granny said when I told her about it, 'That's often the case with unhappy houses that have never been a home.' The woman does have a son, much older than me, who's sometimes around, but we never talk.

No matter. For we Swidgers learn to paddle our own canoe. Become our own navigators.

I did offer to put Granny up but she said she preferred the night air and, if needs must, she knew a place where she could get a bed.

We agreed to meet near the iron railings of the abandoned railway line. I brought with me two sticks so we could both skip along to a rat-ta-ta-tat. But I was already having difficulty keeping up with her. Even with that ever-present carpet bag in hand, Granny had a real bounce in her boots.

The previous night Granny had insisted that human happiness was too rare a spell to be ruined by silly explanations. Fair enough, but that was then and this is now.

'So how did you do it?' I ask. 'Get the school band to play like that?'

'Well, Abhijeet had said that although his musicians could hit all the right notes and in the right order, they rarely did it at the same time. Talent they had, but not the confidence. And it's wise in life to know the difference. Anyway, I slipped what we used to call a Mickey Finn into the water jugs to kill their doubt. Something Echo gave me.'

'You drugged the band!'

'Not really drugs. Medicinal herbs. Prepared by Echo's own Swidger hands.'

'But how did you know?'

'Know what?'

'That you would need Echo's… whatever for the band.'

'I didn't. Echo gave it to me for you, but you'd already proved to be wonderfully daring without it. "Waste not, want not", as Mother used to say. I must admit I was worried about giving the Commonality a Swidger concoction but it seemed to work all right. Even better than I thought. A bit of boogie-woogie thanks to Circe's Cup.'

I hadn't slept much the previous night. My mind kept reliving all the good parts of that evening. Especially the breath-taking joy on people's faces. It was Granny's doing and I was pleased for her and it was good to see, but I couldn't help wondering if I would ever witness for myself something I had brought about. Perhaps then my doubts about my life would go.

By now we had reached the railings overlooking the steep embankment down to the old disused railway line. Granny stopped and became more thoughtful.

'But there is no herb, William Arthur, that can make you ready for what is to come. And your Time is coming. It cannot be held back. Not here.'

Granny threw her stick over the weeds of the bank and it was immediately lost among the discarded mattresses and trolleys that cluttered the edges of track.

'Is there anything we can do?' I asked.

Granny pondered for a moment then picked up a large stone and aimed it towards the railway tunnel. Her throw was surprisingly powerful, and landed, I think, just inside its shadowy entrance but difficult to tell for sure as it made no noise.

She then turned to me and said, 'Remember the Rainbow Boy? We could do the same as him, run away and hide.'

'Hide?' I asked.

'There is a place we could go where you'd be safe. But there'd be a price to pay.'

'I don't have any money.'

'It's not that sort of cost.'

'Then what sort of cost is it?'

Granny gave me one of her looks.

'Let me give you some advice, William Arthur: the grass is always greener on the other side – until you start digging.'

And with that she walked slowly towards the school. But I felt, in her own odd way, she had been trying to answer my question.

When we arrived at the gate there weren't many teachers around. We must have got here early. Perhaps it was all that skipping.

'What's your first class?' enquired Granny.

'Double Maths. With Mr Cooper.'

'Would he have drunk the cider?'

'Definitely.'

'Yes, well, we all have our lesson to learn in life.'

I did wonder what she meant but right now I was more concerned about her meeting with Mr Benjamin.

'What you gonna say when you see the headmaster?'

'Ask me no questions and I'll tell thee no lies,' she replied, picking up her carpet bag and jauntily skipping off. As she swung from side to side, I noticed it was perhaps a bit bulkier than I'd seen it before. But she was gone before I could ask why.

Except for science and PE, most lessons took place in our allocated form rooms. As I walked in ours, I noticed my classmates were more jittery and jumpier than was usual for Double Maths. Something was up.

The bell went. Time for lessons to begin. But there was no Mr Cooper. And Mr Cooper was never late. I've never worn a watch, but, as they say, if you need to set the time then the always punctual Mr Cooper would be your man. Yet the clock on the wall was now seven minutes past nine, and still there was no sign of him. And now I heard the distinct sound of skipping coming down the corridor. It was a rhythm I was familiar with.

Oh, please no, let me be wrong. But I wasn't, for into the classroom walked a woman wearing a long academic gown and a teacher's mortar board, the sort you only ever see now in comic books. It was very odd, but even odder was that Granny was wearing it.

'Now boys and girls, Mr Cooper has been taken peculiar. So this morning, it has been decided, unanimously, by me, to provide a lesson on the eternal truths of Mathematical Law. And the fibs they tell. Today,' she announced, now looking in my directions, 'for a promise is a promise, I am going to prove that two equals one.'

The class were silent, staring. Were they mesmerised or dumbstruck? Or both? Either way, they just gawped at her. Everyone except Jimmy Lee. He turned and smirked in my direction. And his fingers began to twist themselves into a fist.

Granny now picked up some chalk and wrote at the top of the blackboard: $X = Y$.

'Let's agree that X equals Y. If X equals Y, then X times Y will equal Y times X.'

Next, she scribbled $X \times Y = Y \times X$.

'Now it's as true as turnips that X times X, or X squared, will equal X times Y.'

Underneath she put $X^2 = X \times Y$.

'And it is equally the case that X squared minus Y squared will equal X times Y minus Y squared. Why? Because it does.'

Next, she wrote $X^2 - Y^2 = XY - Y^2$ and looked at it for a moment.

'And now time to see how good is my allergybra. I fear I may lose some of you but trust me, it's all perfectly correct. Here we go. X squared minus Y squared can be expressed as, bracket, X plus Y, close bracket, open bracket, X minus Y, close bracket.'

Granny wrote $(X + Y)(X - Y)$ on the board as she spoke.

'But of course,' she went on, 'X times Y minus Y squared can be expressed as Y, bracket, X minus Y.'

The next line now read $(X + Y)(X - Y) = Y(X - Y)$.

'We now come to the clever bit,' she said, brightly, writing the same line again, 'where we start cancelling things out.'

Granny then took some red chalk and crossed out $(X - Y)$ on both sides of the equation leaving just $(X + Y) = Y$.

'We find ourselves left with X plus Y equals Y. But did we not agree at the off that X equals Y. So, we can change now that X to a Y.'

Granny then wrote $Y + Y = Y$.

'So, according to mathematically logic, Y plus Y equals Y. In other words, I have proved that two equals one.'

Granny stood back and admired her work on the blackboard.

$X = Y$

$X \times Y = Y \times X$

$X^2 = X \times Y$

$X^2 - Y^2 = XY - Y^2$

$(X + Y)(X - Y) = Y(X - Y)$

$(X + Y)\cancel{(X - Y)} = Y\cancel{(X - Y)}$

$(X + Y) = Y$

$Y + Y = Y$

$2 = 1$

'Such is the indubitable truth of Mathematical Law.'

Granny next spun herself round on her heels with a great flourish.

No one said a word. Except Jimmy Lee. And the two words he uttered he'd often said before. They were the reason he'd been placed at the front of the class. Not that Granny was aware of that.

'I knew a lad once, used to sit at the front because he had

ambition to be an engine driver. Is that your calling?'

This made the rest of the class laugh.

'Nothing wrong with being an engine driver. An occupation with much responsibility,' added Granny, firmly. She was saying all this, I think, as a way of winning Jimmy Lee over, only Jimmy Lee didn't take it like that and so uttered those two words again.

'Tell me,' inquired Granny, with a smile, 'do you have a particular fondness for Anglo-Saxon or is your only knowledge of language that which you find written on the lavatory wall?'

Jimmy Lee just grunted.

'Grrugh!'

'Oh, don't worry, I understand the meaning of those sort of grunts because I spent a summer once working on a pig farm.'

The class roared with laughter.

Jimmy Lee may have been the school bully, but he had met his match today.

'You watch yourself, m'lad, because I'll warn you, if someone spits in my face, I don't pretend it's raining.'

Then Jimmy Lee said the most unsayable of all words.

How would Granny react?

'Say that again,' she said, her vibrant green eyes now scowling deep into his, 'and I'll take a brush to that tongue o'yours and post the mucky scrapings to y'mother.'

Jimmy Lee tried to out stare Granny but that was a battle he was not going to win. His head fell in defeat and never really came back up again.

The classroom door suddenly flew open. The headmaster.

'Good morning, Big Ben,' chirped Granny cheerfully, as if his arrival was an everyday occurrence. But Mr Benjamin was so shocked he simply stood there, mouth wide open.

'Oh, Headmaster, please say something soon or I'll be tempted to throw you a fish.'

This brought a giggle from one or two in the class, but Mr Benjamin was much feared and any laughter was swiftly stifled with a sharp stare. And then he did speak.

'Madam, what on earth do you think you doing?'

Granny was undeterred by his admonishing tone.

'I've been learning them, Headmaster, the mathematical formula that proves two equals one. Of course what my lesson was really doing was showing that all theory is bunkum if it doesn't work in real life. Make X and Y proper numbers and you'll find you've been multiplying by zero. And do that with any number, no matter how big, and you'll always end up with nothing.'

'My office. Immediately. Both of you. William will join us.'

I stood up and sheepishly walked to the door as the whole class watched in awe. Everyone except Jimmy Lee. For he now had a smirking grin on his face and his hand was once again turning into a fist.

'Out! Now! Both of you!' the headmaster barked.

I think the last thing the classroom heard as we left was Granny asking Mr Benjamin, 'So then, Headmaster, what would you say were the two best things about your job? Apart from July and August?'

CHAPTER TWENTY-FOUR

The Chimes of Big Ben

AS WE WALKED along the corridor, Granny was still jabbering away, but I don't think Mr Benjamin was listening.

'Education in my view,' Granny was saying, 'gives too much credence to reason and not enough to flights of fancy. Curiosity and wonder are the keys to learning. And never be afraid of foolishness, for knowing you're a fool is the first step to wisdom. That's my opinion, and as my heart thinks, my tongue speaks.'

The headmaster himself spoke not a word until we reached his office. I'd never been in it before, even so, my eyes focused on just one thing: that purple glass bottle stopper I'd lost. There it stood, centre stage on the headmaster's desk.

Mr Benjamin got straight to the point.

'William is expelled,' he frowned, picking up the bottle stopper and presenting it to Granny, 'unless you, madam, or he, can account as to how this came to be found next to the cider barrel? I assume it does belong to you.'

Granny nonchalantly took the stopper from Mr Benjamin.

'In addition to the contamination of the cider,' the headmaster went on, 'there is the crime of breaking and entering. Do not deny it. We now have witnesses who have confirmed they saw you both on the fire escape.'

Granny by now had taken from her pocket the purple vial I'd given to her last night. I assumed she was simply going to swap the stoppers over, the yellow for the purple, but oh no, she now shoved that open bottle right under Mr Benjamin's nose.

'Smell this. It's very unusual. Undiluted it's very pungent. And instant acting.'

The headmaster flinched, and his head pulled back, but it was too late for his poor nostrils had already succumbed to the potion.

'And there is the issue,' he continued, at last pushing the bottle away, 'of your behaviour in the recycle refuse collection area. Unless you or he –'

The headmaster was then interrupted by a noise. And he seemed very surprised that this noise had come from him. Not from his mouth, obviously. But another orifice. Lower down. On his other side. His backside.

THHUHRRRHUUHHTHUTHUHR!!!!

It was one of the largest farts I had ever heard.

Granny simply replied, 'Oh dear! Someone's let the New Year in early.'

Then there was another fart.

THHUHRRRHUUHHTHUTHHH!

And another.

THHUHRRRHUUUHHTHUTHTH!

Then two together.

THHUHRRRHUUH... THTHUTHTH!

If this was the 'morning surprise', I thought, then no wonder teachers had stayed at home.

'I did warn you it was potent. Well, if you've got nothing else to say, Headmaster, then William Arthur and I will be off. If that's all right with you?'

The headmaster didn't answer. Except with another fart.

'I'll take that as a "yes", then. Oh, and it's a smelly one!'

Granny put the purple stopper back where it belonged, took me by the hand and led me towards the door.

'Last night you mentioned truancy. Well, I've an idea that might help. Tell the school you're going to have a day where all lessons will be cancelled. And replaced by sex education. They won't want to miss that. But the clever bit, you see, is you don't tell them which day.'

The headmaster let out a final fart, his biggest yet.

THHUHRRRHUUHUUHHTHUTHTHTHUTH
HHHUHRRRHU UHHTHUTHTHTHU
THHHUHRRRHUUHHTHUTHTH!!!!!!!!!!!!!!!!!

'And Big Ben chimes once more!'

And with that we were away.

'Oh, I'm glad we're out of there. That headmaster has one of those faces you can't look at for long. But what a successful morning!'

'What are you on about?'

'You said that boy who got expelled was never seen of again. That was my ingenious plan for you. And now it's worked! Plus those teachers might think twice in future about telling fibs and stealing what isn't truly theirs.'

'Two birds with one stone,' she had said, settling the score for Cider Night, and in the process getting me expelled – she had planned it all.

'But if you wanted me to run away from school there were easier ways of doing it,' I told her.

'True, but none would be as much fun! There's nothing in life better sometimes than just being silly! It's a shame the Commonality don't do it more often.'

Granny then winked at me, stuck her tongue out and blew a big raspberry.

I couldn't help myself, I began to laugh as if there was no tomorrow.

'That's right William Arthur, I mean what's the point of living if we're not laughing!'

'Ha! Ha! Ha! Yes, but I still want to know, what was in the bottle?'

'A bit of Swidger science. What the Commonality don't know, and Echo does, is that with the right herbal concoction the process of making cider can be reversed –'

'Which means fermentation –'

'– the production of hydrogen gas –'

'– which, when emitted from the human body –'

'– comes out as –'

Only Granny let me finish the sentence for her.

'Farts!' I grinned. 'Lots and lots of farts. Especially after an adequate breakfast of fruit and fibre!'

'Not exactly life threatening but a flatulent backside is not what you'd call conducive to the study of simultaneous equations.'

The corridors by now were filling up with pupils all wandering about asking each other what they knew.

'My foray into teaching was fun,' Granny remarked, 'but I wouldn't want to do it for real. I'd rather have me toes cut off and buttered. You see, in life, if you've got the intelligence, you don't need the education, but if you haven't the brains, well, education is what makes up for them.'

We were walking along the main central corridor and there was Jimmy Lee. He had that poor lad he also liked to bully pinned up between two student lockers. No one ever dare challenge him. Not only was he bigger than the rest of us, as he'd been made to do the whole year again, he also had older brothers and cousins who were even tougher and meaner. I did feel sorry though for the lad pinned up, but I didn't want to get involved.

At the end of the walkway the corridor took a sharp left and now coming round it was Miss Schneider who taught German and who the boys all called 'Frau Cow'. It was no surprise she was in today, she had strong views on body fitness and always prided herself on never touching alcohol. She was a formidable and very heavily built woman, who, aside from teaching German, was also the hockey coach.

As Miss Schneider passed by, Granny couldn't resist murmuring under her breath, 'It's been a long time since she's had anything taken in.'

We now turned the corner and Granny began talking more loudly again.

'You see, in life, if you've got the intelligence, you don't need the education, but if you haven't the brains, well, education is what makes up for them.'

Wait a minute, hadn't Granny just said that? Why's she saying it again?

I get distracted because there's Jimmy Lee with another boy pushed against the lockers.

No wait… it's the same boy! And the same Jimmy Lee! What's going on?

I look to the far end of the corridor and there's Miss Schneider, coming round the corner. But she's just passed us, yet here Miss Schneider is again. And Granny whispers as she goes by, 'It's been a long time since she's had anything taken in.'

We take a sharp left. Of course we should be in the next corridor, but once more, we're back where we started. Granny is talking about intelligence and education – and yes, there's Jimmy Lee still bullying that same boy.

No, no, this can't be real. I must have finally gone mad.

CHAPTER TWENTY-FIVE

Seeing a Rainbow

IT WAS THEN that I remembered what happened on the High Street. How even after the cable snake struck, the little girl, the postman, came back to life. Yet, this is different for what I was happening now was some sort of Time Loop.

But how? Another vision? Or maybe it's just the crazy effects of Echo's dream potion?

We turn the corner once more. Again, it's the corridor we've just left. And no one seems to be aware of it but me. Not Granny. Not Jimmy Lee. Or that poor boy pinned against the lockers. We walk on.

Then it comes to me. And I know what it is I must do to break the circle. Swidgers may not be able to use violence but that doesn't mean we can't sometimes bring it about in the Commonality if we need to.

I go back a few steps. To Jimmy Lee. I tap him on the shoulder and say, 'Hello, Jimmy!'

Jimmy takes his hands from the bullied boy and moves threateningly towards me. We both stand in the middle of the corridor. In full view.

'Hit me!' I shout. 'Go on! Hit me hard!'

Jimmy wants to but he senses a trap. And he'd be right. But I must make sure he hits me. And right now.

I have it!

I point to Granny.

'What you told her, I bet that's what you do to yourself, every night. Shove it where the sun doesn't shine, which is a big improvement on your face!'

Not the brightest match in the box, so it took Jimmy Lee a moment or so to work out what I meant. But once he had, his fist did the thinking for him.

WHAMPTH!

Wow! That was one hell of a punch. I was floored. Dazed. And covered in blood. But had I got my timing right? Yes. Frau Cow came round the corner at exactly the right moment. Jimmy Lee was a big lad, but no equal to Miss Schneider – no man was – and he was marched off to the headmaster's office.

It might have been because my head was still spinning from Jimmy's punch, but for a moment, in the reflection of the window, I saw that same lad who Jimmy had bullied walking down that same corridor now smiling and happy. Another vision? I didn't know or care what it was. It made me smile and I was happy because at last I was witnessing what a Swidger's meddling – if that's what you want to call it – can do. These were not words on a page hidden under a tiger or someone else's delight in making wonderful music. No, these images or visions or whatever they were belonged only to me. And it felt magical.

I don't know if I'm explaining myself very well, but it was like a world where you've only ever known grey and suddenly you see a rainbow in all its full magnificent glory and colour.

Yes, that day at school would be long remembered by pupils and teachers alike for the two boys who were expelled. The bully, Jimmy Lee. And the lad they would call 'Cider William'. I had my nickname at last, but something far more important than that. I had a reason to be. A purpose. A life worth living.

Swidger. I am a Swidger. And happy to be one!

As we left through those school gates for the very last time, Granny took off her black academic gown and mortarboard.

'Won't be needing those anymore. Well, William Arthur, I am impressed. Oh yes! How brave and daring you have become.'

'You said no Swidging, but I felt I had to.'

'Once you give a bully your pocket money, he always comes back for more. So, there's no doubt the life of that poor lad will be a lot happier now. And he's you to thank for it.'

'I didn't really have a choice.'

Granny stopped.

Had I said too much?

'William Arthur, is there something I should know?'

What to tell her? I wasn't even sure what had happened myself.

'What about?' I replied. A question can't be a lie, so I was safe enough asking that.

Granny gave me a curious squint, but I don't think she'd twigged. Not about the Time Loop, anyway. And since she didn't know about it perhaps she wasn't meant to.

'Lucky Miss Schneider came along when she did,' I simply added.

'Yes, it was,' acknowledged Granny. 'I suspect –'

But I didn't let her finish.

'You suspect it's been a long time since she had anything taken in.'

Granny gave me another puzzled look.

'How did you know I was going to say that?'

But I was ready with my reply, 'Could it be I'm getting to know you and it's the sort of thing you would say?' That was another question, so again I wasn't lying. Besides, ever since Granny had come into my life, I'd felt I was part of her plan but now, for the first time, I was making my own choices. Even if it had left me with a bloody nose still sore from that punch.

Then suddenly I experienced a terrible ache in my head. But it wasn't like the smarting pain from the punch, for that weird nagging throb was coming once again from deep inside me.

'Ahhh!' I cried out.

And now it wasn't just my head, but everywhere. And it was pain I couldn't hide.

CHAPTER TWENTY-SIX

The Tunnel

'AHHH!' I CRIED again, raising my hands to my head.

'Oh, William Arthur, change is coming,' I heard Granny say. 'I know what you're going through. Swidger growing pains. You're no longer a child but not yet a man. But even with all your daring you're simply not ready for what is to come. Oh, what are we to do with you? It's all happening much too fast. And with it comes danger.'

'What sort of danger?' I ask, still holding my head. 'And why me? Why me?'

'That we never know.'

'You said there was a place we could go?'

'Yes, there is. You'd be as safe as a penny in a Scotsman's purse,' she said, attempting a joke, but I was in no mood for that.

'Safe? But safe from what?'

Granny's eyes saddened.

'You're right. You should be told. You see, William, in some ways we're very like the Commonality. We too are made up of a mixture of carbon compounds and water, making us, like them, bio-depravable. But what makes Swidgers different is that we are born with a special Life Energy that flows through our bodies. It's a good energy, that is there to do good. But out there, in our big Universe, there's another kind of energy too. The Malevolent Energy that hates Life and would do the Commonality harm. And it seeks those Swidgers who are different. Whose gift it desires.'

'Then teach me how to stop it.'

'But that's the problem, this powerful energy cannot be

stopped. Cannot be defeated. And cannot die. And it will come for you as soon as you know what your gift is. But I fear when it does, you will not be ready. And all I can do is take you to a place where it cannot reach you.'

'How long will I have to stay there?'

For the first time since I had known her, Granny appeared lost for words.

'Well, that's a difficult question to answer in so many ways,' she sighed, 'but I should tell you now that what you must face cannot be put off forever. The future is always waiting. And it will bring with it danger.'

Granny put her gloved hand to my cheeks.

'In the battle between the hammer and the nail, the nail can never win. But,' she added, 'with a bit of cunning, sometimes the one who holds the hammer can be made to miss.'

'If we are going to this place, wherever it is, hadn't I better go home and get a change of clothes?'

'You have no home anymore, William Arthur,' she replied, wistfully, now twisting her little finger round a long curl in my hair. 'Nor will you ever again. You were never a boy born to wear grey trousers. I know this because, as I said, you are not "most". And neither was I.'

Granny then took her hand away and picked up her carpet bag.

'Besides,' she went on, taking out a bulky pillowcase and handing it over, 'I already have all that you will need.'

'Where is this place we're going?' I asked.

'I hardly know how to answer that question. But I know what will help take us there. The tunnel.'

There was only one tunnel I knew. What was it with Swidgers and railways? Railway stations. Railway carriages. And now tunnels. I remember wondering as we walked towards that old disused railway tunnel where it would lead. Somewhere north of London probably.

Seems so strange that I still thought like that back then.

Granny's legs were great for skipping but not so expert on the steep slope of the railway embankment and as a result she slipped and tumbled.

'Whoops!' she cried out, landing at the bottom with her legs akimbo, 'you nearly got an eyeful of next week's washing!'

The track itself was filthy, covered in rubbish and you could tell from the smell this was where dogs had done their business. There were flies everywhere. For a moment I thought I even heard wasps again, but looking round I couldn't see any. There was an old man with a white beard staring down at me over the railings. And he was probably wondering what on earth I was doing here among all the old mattresses and junk.

'You go in first,' said Granny, who'd by now got to her feet.

I looked nervously into the tunnel. It had an unusual darkness all of its own. I could just make out the contours of the old Victorian brickwork under a century of soot. Deep, black soot. I suddenly felt scared and my body shivered.

'Why am I so frightened?

'When the Commonality are dying, they sometimes see a bright light. Or a river. But for Swidgers it's a railway tunnel.'

'A railway tunnel? We see that when we're about to die?'

'Yes.'

'Well thanks for telling me that now!'

'You'll come to a special place,' Granny instructed, 'with no light ahead and none behind. Eyes will be useless to you. Remove your old clothes, just let them drop, you'll never see them again. Then, put those on.'

I opened the pillowcase. Shirt, trousers and some sort of jacket. More like a tunic. The shirt, thick coarse cotton, and the trousers, wool, and some braces.

'Do not speak, do not look back. Always face ahead. And when you are ready, walk on. Most of the metal track is gone. All that remains are the wooden sleepers, so keep your feet on these if you can.'

'Where will you be?'

'Don't worry about me, I've made this journey before.'

I've never been afraid of the dark but this tunnel was one of ever-growing blackness. Beyond my experience. What was it that Echo had said? *'The Universe is far stranger than you can ever know.'*

As I walked, I didn't just notice light disappear, I somehow felt it go out inside me. Fading away in my very being. I wanted to turn round to see Granny. But I did as she had told me and looked only ahead.

I had to trust the dark. One step, then another until I felt a sudden death-like chill. The day had been warm and sunny but now my world was oh so very cold.

I took off all my school clothes and put on the others. They were smelly, scratchy and made me itch. Granny said to leave my old things where I stood, but I checked my pockets first. Nothing much, an old hankie and some keys. Well, I wouldn't be needing those anymore. There was also that envelope Candice had given me with her scribbled notes. That, I decided, I would keep.

I let out a sigh. I expected an echo but heard only a deep, empty silence. No sound. No warmth. No light.

I needn't have closed my eyes but I did. And then I strode on. I cannot say for how long I walked but at last I felt a glimmer of shadowy sunshine and I opened my eyes. Ahead of me was a figure. Granny. Already waiting at the tunnel's exit.

'Oh good, glad you made it. We're here.'

CHAPTER TWENTY-SEVEN

Gravestones

THAT DARKNESS IN the railway tunnel. It was like it was touching me, and so now the sudden the dazzling sunlight took a bit of getting used to.

I rubbed my eyes for a few seconds and then began to look around. No abandoned trolleys or mattresses on this side. I breathed the air in deep.

Hmmmm. So fresh. No smell of staleness or decay. No fumes. No stench of dogs, either. And something else was different too, for when I went to scratch my nose, the dried blood from the punch I'd received from Jimmy Lee had gone. And so had the pain and soreness.

I remembered that first day I'd met Granny at the hospital and how she'd made me hug the tree in the park and how when I did the bump on my head somehow disappeared. Yet here there was no tree. Well, not one that I could see.

The embankment this side of the tunnel, I noticed, was much steeper here, more a cliff than a hill.

'Steep climb, stout heart,' announced Granny. 'You go first, I'll follow.'

As she said this, I spotted some receding stone slabs laid into the side of the embankment. Steps of sorts. I moved closer and an engraving on one of them caught my eye. Turning my head to the side, I could now make out the lettering.

'BELOVED.'

It was then I realised: these weren't just slabs, they had once been gravestones. Dug out of the ground at some time or other to be used, one on top of the other, as a quick way to the top, I guess.

Even so, I took my first step up. As I said, it was a sharp incline and I had to concentrate on not slipping, yet I couldn't help thinking about that word 'Beloved'. Where else would you see that word nowadays, except on gravestones?

As a game, I decided to allow myself a step up only if I could think of more words that are only ever used when you're dead. It was childish really, but I needed some sort of distraction.

What about 'Rest in Peace'? 'Never Forgotten'? 'In Loving Memory'? No, my rule must be single words only.

Well, if not 'In Loving Memory', how about 'Remembrance'. Yes, that counts. So I take a step up.

And how about 'Doth'? Surely there's a gravestone somewhere in the world that reads: BENEATH THIS STONE DOTH LIE.

Yes, I've earned myself another step. 'Doth' leads me to 'Sleepeth' and 'Cometh' as I picture in my mind a stone slab that reads, HE SLEEPETH UNTIL THE DAY OF JUDGMENT COMETH. And so, I taketh my 'Sleepeth' and 'Cometh' steps.

What's that word they always put in brackets before a woman's maiden name? Née. Not quite sure what it means. Formerly, I suppose. Is it ever seen nowadays except in a graveyard? I decide not. And as it's such a good word I award myself three steps.

But then I hit a dead-end. I try and reach in my brain for words but none come. Perhaps there's more to be had from how they spelt things in the old days. Yes, there is.

'Stayeth'.

'Goeth'.

'Leaveth'.

'Breatheth'.

No time to work out how they'd be used on a gravestone, but figure they could somehow, and so I take four more steps. Just one more to go now.

I then think back to that first word 'Beloved' – of course, 'Loveth'! But isn't 'Loveth' also used at weddings? Too late. My foot goes up.

I've reached the ridge of the embankment and the ground has begun to level out.

What an odd sort of game to play. Strange how the mind works.

Yet all the time I was climbing those graveyard steps I never thought to ask, 'Where were all the bodies?'

CHAPTER TWENTY-EIGHT

The Seagull

GREETING ME AT the top of the embankment was the puzzled face of a seagull, jerking its beak back and forth as if to ask, 'Where-on-earth-have-you-come-from?' Not that I had time to answer for it now squawked and flew off.

I turned round to see how Granny was getting on. A carpet bag was suddenly flung onto the ridge and Granny's face slowly bobbed up behind it. Not quite trusting herself to take those last few steps in one go, she crawled over the edge on her hands and knees, looking for all the world like a weary crab making its final strides home. With pincer fingers she then raised herself up to full height, tottered slightly, and declared, 'Well, them steps weren't that difficult, were they?'

'They weren't steps,' I replied, 'but gravestones. Look, they're engraved. Wilfred, 1885, the year he must have died.'

'Perhaps a Wilfred did use to live here once, in the Old Coach Inn, for that,' she said, pointing, 'is your new home.'

As I had been looking round to see how Granny was faring I hadn't noticed what was just across the way.

'It's a big house, so there'll be plenty for us to do.'

My first thought on seeing the Old Coach Inn was, was it even a building at all? The outline of one for sure, tall chimney in the middle and what looked like two smaller chimneys at either end. And definitely a roof, in fact several roofs at different levels and angles. But it was all so overgrown with ivy that it looked more like a giant bush in the shape of an inn than an actual inn.

'It's called the Old Coach Inn because in years gone by this is where travellers would stay and change horses. Come along.'

This inn, or whatever it was, stood on the peak of an incline so it was difficult to tell what lay beyond. An upper storey jutted out, making it look as if the house had leaned forward once and then decided to stay there.

But there was something not quite right about this place and I became very uneasy.

'Are you sure we'll be safe here? My Swidger instinct isn't convinced.'

I could tell Granny wanted to respond, for her cheeks filled up like a big balloon, but all that came out was a discouraging sigh. But then she thought again and now said something very odd.

'You must give your consent to their greeting. When we reach the threshold, what you must do, *must,* is accept their welcome. And don't wait to be asked twice,' she said, already pacing towards the house. 'They won't like that.'

'Consent to their greeting?' What on earth did she mean?
Wait! Were they vampires?

No, can't be. I mean, vampires weren't real. Besides, 'consent to their greeting' didn't fit the legend. It's the *vampire* who needs to ask, 'May I come in?', and if the hosts say, 'Yes', they become defenceless. Even with a house filled with garlic and crosses. Yet she'd also said, 'Don't wait to be asked twice'. That's right, part of the vampire myth was the undead must never repeat themselves. Images of black capes, sharp teeth and blood running down my neck began flowing through my mind...

'Come along, don't just stand there doing nothing like cheese at nine pence. I don't know what you're expecting, but if it's tea with a unicorn, you're going to be very disappointed.' Then she added, in a half whisper, 'That said, best only speak when spoken to. You're very much a child in their eyes, always remember that.'

Granny now raised her hand to the knocker.

Would the door slowly creak ajar and a tall, shadowy figure appear, unwilling to show itself in daylight?

No. Because before she even knocked, the door was flung open and there stood a bunch of very short, very lively and very hairy gentlemen. About half a dozen or so. Some were thin, others fat and burly, but all remarkably small in height – and even shorter now for they took off their large velvet hats and barked welcomes from every direction.

'Greetings, dear lady!'

'How now, how now!'

'You will want for nothing that our house affords.'

'We have burnt sweetwood and lavender sticks to make your lodging mellifluous and gladsome.'

'Well met!'

'Well met, indeed!'

'We have hope of ginger. Do not ladies love sugared ginger?'

'And we have hope too of spiced apple!'

And each greeting was accompanied by the intense anticipation of darting eyes.

As I stood at the threshold, I felt a peculiar sort of stillness, broken only by a breeze on the rustling ivy. It can't have lasted more than a few seconds, yet somehow it seemed longer.

The next thing I remember was Granny saying, 'Good welcome and felicitations upon your gracious house.'

A grey robed gentleman then answered soberly, 'Thanks indeed, honoured lady, will you now enter our abode?'

'I will,' replied Granny.

The assemblage parted down the middle, three men one side, three to the other, and now Granny stepped from the stone threshold onto the wooden floor of the inner vestibule. Once she had walked past the group, they again closed together as one. And all those darting eyes now rested on me.

The grey robed man then said, 'Greetings to the Boy.'

Did he just call me, 'the Boy'?

'My name is William,' I wanted to say, but I remembered Granny's warning. Besides, I was still so bemused by their appearance that I was pretty much rendered speechless.

Their hair was so unkempt and matted, you might have mistaken them for wigs. Their faces were old and lined, yet somehow youthful as well. What they wore – how can I explain it? – was part gown, like the one Granny had on at the school, and part smock, like artists wear when they paint. Their big velvet hats, which they still held in their hands, looked like cushions that needed plumping. Each hat had its own design, some were braided, others had embroidered insignias. But what really took my eye was that they were all gripping some sort of needle or pin. And one man had his pointing his right at me.

But then I was distracted by the waving arms of Granny who, from behind the group, was now animatedly signalling me to do something.

That's right! I must accept their greeting.

Those darting eyes were becoming ever more doubtful, hostile even. I panicked and out came:

'God rest ye merry gentlemen, let nothing you dismay.'

Why on earth did I say that?

Immediately I shut my eyes, half expecting a slap. But none came. Instead, I heard a solemn voice announce, 'So said, so done, 'tis well.'

I opened my eyes. The gentleman in long grey robes, looking more at the door than me, then asked, 'Will the Boy enter?'

I heard myself say, 'I will.' And I crossed the threshold.

Lavender scented the air but a sharp acrid smell too that I couldn't quite place. And cats. Definitely a whiff of cats.

I turned back for a second. That man in the grey robes was already closing the entrance door. Through the gap I saw that the day was now fading fast.

Strange, I thought, seems only a few hours ago it was morning, yet here twilight had already come.

I was then ushered into a long, narrow hallway. Here all the windows were shuttered and what little light there was came only through distant doors at either end. My world had suddenly become one of shadows.

Very dark and deepening shadows.

CHAPTER TWENTY-NINE

Gibble and Rutley

I SUPPOSE WHAT I should have noticed even then was the wood. The bare staircase to the upper floor, the exposed panels of the walls and the uncarpeted floorboards at my feet. And most prominent of all, that long bulky jetty beam above my head.

All this I saw and should have noted. But I didn't. You see, I still had vampires on my mind, so all I did was peer round looking for mirrors, but there was nothing hanging on any of the walls. No mirrors, no paintings, no clocks, no flying ducks. There wasn't even a hook for coats.

But my curiosity was interrupted when I heard my name. Well, not exactly my name. It was that man in the grey robes, with a dull grey voice to match, asking Granny, 'Will the Boy be in need of nourishment?'

'Perhaps a little light supper, Marsden.'

'Was your journey fair?' this Marsden now enquired.

'The train tunnel was kind to us,' she answered.

On hearing that word 'train', the smallest of the group immediately started running round, chanting it out as if he were a kid playing a game.

'Train! Train! Train! Train! Train! Train! Train! Train!!!'

Were it not for his long brown beard, I would even have described him as a child. Marsden now raised his grey gloved hand and with an admonishing finger said, 'Rutley, that is enough!'

Poor Rutley was silenced and he then lowered his head to the ground like a dog who'd been told off by its owner.

By now all velvet hats had been put back on. Except one which had dropped to the floor. This I could tell belonged to a gnomish looking man with fuzzy ginger hair who, instead of picking it up, was staring into some sort of round, shiny metal casing in his hand.

What was it, exactly? It was difficult to tell as his sleeves were long and pulled down over his hands. But Marsden, that sombre man in grey, now unwittingly provided the answer.

'Gibble, put away your looking-glass, retrieve your hat and then withdraw.'

The gnome-like Gibble, with a great big bulbous nose that looked like a giant sprout that might explode any minute, caught my eye and gave me a big toothless grin that was all gums. Then out came his tongue and he wiggled like a worm.

Ugh.

The look on my face must have given me away for Gibble quickly put his tongue back in his mouth and his smile vanished. He bent down to pick up his bottle-green hat and as he did, he pocketed his small looking-glass in his tunic.

Well, so much for that theory. If Gibble is a vampire, he'd be the first to carry his own mirror.

Gibble then sheepishly walked backwards down the corridor, his legs tight together like a wound-up toy. The playful Rutley tagged along, all the time chuntering, 'Train! Train! Train! Train!' under his breath.

A delicate looking man, who I had not noticed before, gave me a slight bow of his head. He had long, white hair like a wizard, which fell all the way down his back. He now followed the bow with a gentle wave of his hands. And what it revealed were, I thought, the thinnest fingers I had ever seen. Skeletal. Like twigs on a snowman. What would they call him? I wondered. Wizley? Littley? Scrawnley? Scrinley?

The name of the hairiest man among them was no mystery, as Granny now addressed him in a loud, cheerful voice, 'Brewster Blaxton! What you been feeding that beard of yours, bull marrow and rum punch?'

Was Brewster smiling at this? Hard to tell, as his beard was so thick and bushy it was difficult to see a face underneath, never mind lips or a mouth.

Granny then teasingly tugged at his wild and shaggy beard, and added, 'If truth be known, this wouldn't be out of place in Botany Bay!'

Brewster's mouth now opened wide and out came a thunderous laugh.

And in that moment, two rows of gleaming teeth flashed brightly.

Well, that's a smile you don't see every day, for it was entirely made up of pure golden gnashers! And probably worth a fortune.

Brewster then said something. No idea what, as his accent was too strong. Scottish? Irish? Welsh? I really couldn't tell.

There was one face, though, neither laughed nor spoke. Only stared. The man who had that sharp metal pin pointing at me at the threshold. And it pointed still. I looked closer. It was a hat pin with a decorative handle, enamelled, in the shape of an acorn. And he now raised it and stabbed the spike into his velvet cap. He pulled his shoulders back and pushed his chest out as if standing to attention at an army parade. Whoever it was then turned abruptly and marched off down the corridor. A moment later a door slammed.

No one it seemed wanted to talk to me, so I sought help from Granny.

'The man who walked away,' I said. 'I didn't catch his name.'

The delicate wiry-thin man with twiggy fingers now answered for her.

'Salton. Salton Manning. The would-be soldier who prefers, shall we say, his own company. I am Meeler. Missel Meeler.'

Missel Meeler. Hmm. As good a name as any for a man even thinner than string. And this Missel Meeler might have said more, only Marsden, whose dull voice matched the greyness of his garb, declared, 'The shutters in the upper storey. Is that not your duty, tonight, Meeler?'

His words had a reprimanding effect, for Meeler bowed, waved his thin hands obediently, then turned and left.

As he did, I noticed something I had missed before: all of Meeler's bony fingers were slightly bruised purple and red.

'A chamber shall be prepared for the Boy,' announced Marsden, grimly.

If this was meant to be another instruction, poor Marsden wasn't in luck for there was no one left to hear it. Salton had gone off in a huff, Gibble shuffling backwards, Rutley shunting after him like a train and now poor Meeler had been ordered away. And Brewster and his big beard had trundled off somewhere too.

'The Boy's presence will not go unobserved,' Marsden muttered, almost as if he didn't want anyone else to hear him, but there was only Granny and me left. He then turned and disappeared down the hallway, his grey robes fading into the darkness.

I rounded on Granny. 'What sort of place is this? Who are all these people? There's some poor fellow who thinks he's a train. Your bearded mate looks like he's eaten a pirate sandwich. Then there's the one with no teeth at all, what's his name? Gibble, Gummy Gibble! Who on earth calls anyone Gibble? Worst was that military bloke with the staring eyes – what does he think he is, a Gorgon? And as for the man in grey, he won't even speak to me. Keeps calling me 'the Boy?!'

'Meeler spoke to you.'

'Oh yes, the Celery Stick Man! And as soon as he did, he was sent packing.'

'I thought you did very well at the threshold.'

With all the other weirdness, I'd completely forgotten about that.

'*God rest ye Merry Gentlemen*? I don't even know what it means. Nobody does.'

'Well, it worked a treat. "Merry" doesn't mean being three-sheets-to-the-wind on a Friday night, it's Old English for "strong". "Rest ye" is another way of saying "make you". And "dismay" is the same as "upset".'

'So, what I actually said was, "May you be strong and not worry too much?"'

'Give that man a coconut!' Granny proclaimed, picking up her carpet bag. 'Well, good night, see you in the morning.'

'You can't leave me here all by myself!' I protested. 'You said I'd be safe from outside harm, but what about the inside sort?'

But it was no use, she too disappeared into the shadows before I could even finish the sentence.

So there I was, alone.

All of a sudden, the door at the end of the corridor, by then my only source of light, began to close of its own accord. The murky gloom soon became complete blackness.

SCRATCH! SCRATCH! SCRATCH!

I froze.

A clawing, scraping sound that would make even those with nerves of steel shudder like frightened prey.

I tried to look about me, but the darkness was overpowering. I could see nothing.

More scratching. And it seemed to be coming from everywhere.

Was it behind me?

I turned.

Or down the hallway?

I turned again.

Perhaps the stairs.

I spun once more. I tried to reach out but I'd twisted myself round so many times I'd lost all bearings.

SCRATCH! SCRATCH! SCRATCH!

No, no, no! It is now at my feet. Instinctively I draw my arms about me and bring my legs close together.

Then, I see a blurry redness moving slowly nearer. And with it, a yellow flickering light. A face? Maybe, yet it seems to float upon the air. Closer now. So close now I shut my eyes...

A shadowy voice now begins to speak.

CHAPTER THIRTY

The Red-Faced Man

'WE HAVE VISITORS,' says the voice, with a deathlike sigh.

I open my eyes and I see scarred, red skin. And a nose that's long and curled, and below it a sharp pointed chin.

A strange face, yet familiar too – I know it from somewhere – it reminded me of something or someone. *But who?*

I can't make out the figure's eyes, even when it comes nearer, as it does now, only then to swing away, avoiding too close an acquaintance.

A rasping whisper, more sigh than speech, says again, 'We have visitors.'

The yellow light gradually grows stronger. I see now it is an oil lamp, for the figure shines it towards the staircase, illuminating the 'visitors' he wishes me to see.

'Mice,' says the Red-Faced Man.

The voice is slow and somewhat ill-matched with the creatures I now see scurrying quickly up the stairs.

'Follow where they lead,' orders the Red-Faced Man.

The steps I see before me are my second of the day. There are no chiselled names of the dead, yet I fear these more.

The Red-Faced Man brings his lamp closer. I see why that face appeared to float in mid-air for he is dressed in a long black cloak that goes all the way to the floor, his head covered not by a velvet hat but a monk-like hood.

'Proceed.'

His voice, like his skin, is burnt and scarred.

'It's very dark,' I mumble. 'I can't see very well.'

His reply comes in Latin, I think, making that voice seem all the more scorched and blistered.

'*Non est tanti.* The stairs await.'

The steep wooden steps, bumpy, and of differing heights and widths, are navigable only with care. But with the oil lamp at my back, it's my own darting shadow that puts me most in confusion. I lose my footing and stumble badly where the staircase turns, hitting my jaw hard upon the treads.

The Red-Faced Man stops but does not acknowledge my fall. His oil lamp, now close by his head, lights up a line of sharp, half broken teeth.

Suddenly I know where I've seen that face before: a Punch and Judy show. *Punchinello!* The hooked nose. The pointed chin. A fixed expression that, like a doll, never changes. Even when it commands, as it does now, 'Walk on.'

Only six more steps and I will have reached the landing. Then, from nowhere, the oil lamp gives out. Darkness engulfs us and the caustic smoke from its wick permeates the air. I start to cough uncontrollably.

'Cough, cough, cough!'

I shudder as I feel his hand rest on my shoulder.

'*Non est tanti.* It is of no matter. I know this house without need of light.'

It was then I heard a door open. Footsteps came close. Two pairs of footsteps, I think, for one stopped ahead of me and the other behind.

A gentle voice then called out, 'Did you bring a taper?', then that exact same voice answered from the opposite direction.

'Indeed. I'm lighting it now.'

Something was struck, a match I guessed, for a flickering flame on a long thin stick of wax suddenly appeared and then an oil lamp was lit to reveal a meek but pleasant face. The taper was then passed to the side of me. I followed it round to see it light a second lamp and from the darkness emerged – the exact same face! I spun my head back, yet that first face was still there.

'You –'

'– must be –'

'William.'

Two faces, one voice. Two voices, one face. Twins!

'I am Edwin.'

'I am Elwin.'

And together they said, 'We are brothers.'

Of all that was said to me that day, this last remark, I must say, was the least necessary.

'We are the Meads,' they stated in unison.

'We heard someone fall –'

'– and coughing…'

'… so we came to help.'

'Is young William hurt?'

'We pray not.'

But the Red-Faced Man never allowed me a reply, for he said swiftly, 'I take the child to his chamber.'

The twins, it seemed to me, took this as their opportunity to help.

'Zavier –'

'– let us guide William Arthur –'

'– to his room.'

'Both our lamps are full.'

'And yours is now dead.'

But Zavier was ready with his answer.

'You have surfeit with two. Pass the one you do not require to me. The child's need, not mine.'

Although scarred and wounded, it was not a voice to be quarrelled with. Edwin passed over his lamp and it was exchanged for the empty one held by Zavier.

But the twins were not quite done. Their eyebrows suddenly rose together as if they had at that moment exactly the same thought.

'Aloysius –'

'– is in distemper.'

'He is not a day of season.'

'Sunshine –'

'– and hail –'

'– come as one.'

'And more hail than sunshine.'

'And you are acquainted with where that may lead.'

The silence that followed made me think that the twins had said more than was wise. What I saw next, I would see many times in the Old Coach Inn. Their sign of anger for Zavier now raised his fist and lunged his thumb forward.

'Go. Be gone!'

The twins weren't going to argue with that. They went. Quickly.

Who, I thought, *was this Aloysius? And where may 'what' lead?*

But there was no time to dwell on that, for Zavier grabbed my arm and ordered me on.

The full oil lamp gave off a much brighter light and so now I could see into his eyes. Black and lifeless. As empty as death. It was then I knew: Zavier was blind.

As we made our way through arches and across the landings, Zavier never faltered. One corridor seemed to come to a dead-end, only Zavier, unseeing, now pointed to what looked like a wrought iron handle concealed in the wooden panelling and said, 'Lift.'

When I did the handle moved with surprising ease. The hidden door glided slowly open with a low clunking noise, revealing a simple room, with a single bed, a chair and a table. The window was shuttered and secured with some sort of fastening device.

Without speaking, Zavier passes me the lamp. Without seeing, his hand indicates an inner closet door and, without feeling, adds, 'The necessary.' And then, without another word, he is gone.

As his footsteps disappear, new ones take their place. It is Marsden, the man in grey, carrying a covered plate which he now hands to me.

Food at last, I think, as I lift the lid. Underneath are three large squelchy balls of something in a gooey white pool.

'Boiled onions,' he says. 'In milk. To aid sleep.'

And with that Marsden turns and leaves. Then I hear that low clunking noise again and the door closes, but as it does, I now see there is no handle on my side.

I've been locked in.

I'm way too tired to think about that now. I sit in the chair and fix my eyes on those three soggy onions in a puddle of – slime. Well, let's hope it is just onions.

I pick one up. It's slippery to the touch. I pop it in my mouth. Surprisingly chewy. Doesn't really taste of much, bland more than unpleasant. I manage one, two onions left.

My mind wanders...

Twins and a celery stick man... is that what they ate in Merry England? No trains in those days, and no teeth either. Who did you say died in 1885? Was it Wilfred or Aloysius – or even me?

And with that question in my mind, I slowly drift off to sleep.

CHAPTER THIRTY-ONE

The Loud Knock

I DO NOT dream that night. Nor any other in my stay at that house.

I awake to the smell of bacon. I open my eyes and there is Granny, standing over me.

'You slept well,' she says.

I am no longer in the chair but tucked up in bed. Someone must have moved me. I'm still, though, in the same itchy clothes.

'They say if you want to get young people out of bed the best thing you can do is start frying bacon.'

I try to look around but the morning light from the open window is so overpowering I have to scrunch up my eyes.

'There's eggs, as well,' Granny adds with a grin, as she exits towards the door. 'Just follow your nose downstairs.'

People say, don't they, that whatever happens in life all will be well in the morning. Well, even with Granny's reassuring smile, that wasn't true today. Nevertheless, I take her advice and follow my nose downstairs.

Those eerie landings are now well lit by daylight streaming in through open windows. And those dark staircases no longer threaten injury. Yet in the plain light of day there's something I hadn't noticed before. Everywhere the wooden beams of the house are rough, coarse and veined. It must have been the bumpy tree knots in the timber that made me trip. Perhaps I should have thought about those knots of wood more then, but that smell of bacon was calling me down, and I was very hungry.

Granny's singing was now my guide. A hymn, by the sound of it. Granny always sang, to use her own expression, 'in the key of much too loud'. That was certainly true this morning and the tune was coming through a door half ajar, so I pushed at it and went through.

A large, airy kitchen.

No surprise there, except, unlike the rest of the house, it was built of dark grey stone. No wood at all, apart from a table and chairs. Along one wall stood two big copper washing drums and next to them a hefty, enamelled table. Opposite was a porcelain sink and draining board, with a bulky oil stove next to it. The only other door in the kitchen led to a brick walk-in pantry.

Granny was standing at the stove dropping eggs into a pan, still caterwauling away.

'Nearer, my God, to thee,
'Nearer to thee.

'How do you want your eggs? A dippy-yolk, runny or hard?'

'A dippy-yolk, please,' I said.

'E'en though it be a cross
'That raiseth me.
'Still all my song shall be.'

'What are you doing?'

'Quiet. *Nearer, my God, to thee,*
'Nearer, my God, to thee,
'Nearer to thee!
'Though like the wanderer,
'The sun gone down,
'Darkness be over me,
'My rest a stone,
'Yet in my dreams I'd be.
'Nearer, my God, to thee,
'Nearer, my God, to thee,
'Nearer to thee.'

Granny took the frying pan from the stove.

'That's a lesson for you. Best way to cook eggs: count the verses: one for runny, two for dippy-yolk and three for hard. This house has many amoeboties but an egg-timer isn't one of them.'

I couldn't help but smile at her odd way with words, as I sat myself at the kitchen table.

'You can't go wrong with bacon and eggs. I feel sorry for the French. Forced to eat them croissants that look like what a dog left behind on the pavement. French cooking! Huh! I don't know how they keep it down.'

A large plate of bacon then landed in front of me, immediately followed by three, yes three, dippy-eggs.

'Strength goes in at mouth. You'll need it today, for we have work to do.'

'Work?' I asked.

Granny walked across to the pantry and pointed to various containers and tins.

'Yes, we have to earn our keep,' she said, taking a bottle from the shelf. 'And since today is cleaning and washing day, we'll be needing this. What do you think it is?'

Through the glass I could see a white powder.

'Flour?' I suggested, dipping my bacon into the yolk.

Granny laughed.

'No, hydrogen peroxide. Old-fashioned bleach. Turns yellowing ivory into the gleaming white of Heaven. Now, what else do we have here? Oh yes, borax. The kitchen's friend. Disinfects and dissolves.'

'It looks like sugar,' I said.

Granny laughed again. 'Put that in your tea and you wouldn't be long for this world. Paraffin, we keep in that blue tin. But don't ever use it on a parrot's cage.'

'Why not?'

'They wouldn't like it. Would you? No, to keep a parrot's cage clean, hang a bag of sulphur from the bars. That'll keep away them nasty parasites. Not sure why I'm telling you this as we don't even have a parrot. Oh, but you'll always find something useful in what I say. Them dippy-eggs are all right, aren't they?

Even without an egg-timer?'

I told her they were perfect and she winked at me and then went back to humming her hymn.

What was that all about? Paraffin? Sulphur? Parrots? Was she trying to tell me something?

My chair suddenly moved backwards. One of the legs had splintered.

CRACK!!!

'Oh dear,' she sighed, 'we'll be needing that paraffin after all. And the saucers they use to feed the cat.'

'We're going to feed the cat paraffin?' I asked.

'No, you daft jughead! The chairs have woodworm so we'll stand the legs in the saucers and then the wood can soak it up. But eat your breakfast first.'

Once I'd finished my three dippy-eggs I went into the pantry and took down the paraffin tin from the shelf. There was a handle on top and a spout on one side which I opened and sniffed. Then it came to me: that was the acrid smell I had noticed when I first walked into the house.

'I think sometimes, if it wasn't for the woodworm holding hands, this whole place would fall down. They brush paraffin into the timbers to keep them hungry larviees at bay. Oh, boo and bother! If we do the chairs, we won't have anywhere to sit. Never mind, I'm getting to that age where I'm better standing. Anyway, best get to it.'

So we did. We lined up the chair legs in saucers filled with paraffin. I couldn't help thinking they looked like a row of knobbly-kneed old men bathing their feet.

'What else to do?' Granny then asked herself. 'I know, replace the lime in the pantry. Nothing absorbs damp better than lime. Best kept away from the heat, gives off a strong glow when it burns.'

'Is that why people say, "in the limelight"?'

'My, you know how many beans make five. Yes, in the olden

days they used burning lime to illuminate the stage. But before we do anything else, we need put the kettle on.'

'To clean something?'

'No, for a nice cup of char.'

I filled the large copper kettle and placed it on the stove.

Granny went over to the pantry and took down from the shelf a small container labelled 'Dry Mustard' and scattered some of it under the gap of the kitchen door. This, she claimed, would keep away the cat.

'If that horrible Tom comes sniffing, he'll sneeze himself silly till the cows fly home.'

I thought Granny would be the sort of woman who liked cats. But no.

'Curiosity may be the making of that species, but his nosey-parkering stops at my kitchen door. Females at least are good mousers but that Tom, like most men, is a lazy louch. And ugly. Long hair and horrible pink nose. And a face that looks like a baboon's backside.'

Well, that explained the presence of both the mice and the cat.

'And now, my little sprucer-upper, since it's washing day, you'd better get the mangle out. It's under the lid of that white enamelled table, which, when you raise it up, becomes a sink to catch the water squeezed out by the rollers.'

It was heavy to lift but I managed. As I put my hand on the wheel to test it out, there was a knock at the door. Yet when Granny opened it, all that was there was a basket of velvet hats.

'Well,' murmurs Granny, bringing in the basket and shutting the door, 'we won't have sight nor sound of them for the rest of the day.'

Why not? I wondered.

Could it be the gentlemen who lived here didn't like to be seen without their hats? Old-fashioned courtesy meant they had to take them off last night but they were quick to put them back on for what was underneath was all matted and messed up.

'Why don't they ever cut their hair?' I asked, almost without thinking.

Granny looked at me both impressed and annoyed, that is if such a thing is possible.

'The hair of Swidgers always grows more than the Commonality. Look at mine, at Echo's. And at your lovely black curls.'

Yes, my hair has always been thick and curly. And I'd always wondered why it grew so quickly. Yet that still didn't answer my question. I tried again.

'But they could cut it, couldn't they?'

Granny remained silent.

'Unless there's only one man here who's allowed the scissors.'

Now I'd meant that really as a joke. But as I said this, Granny suddenly seemed anxious. She came close and whispered, 'It is not wise to ask too many questions in this house.'

Had I accidently hit on something? Yes, I think I had. And I wasn't going to be put off.

'And is his name, Aloysius, isn't it?'

Granny's expression went in the instant from worry to dread. And then from dread to fear.

A banging at the door. Granny jumped in alarm. The hammering became more intense, violent even. Louder and louder.

And Granny's face was now full of terror.

CHAPTER THIRTY-TWO

Aloysius

'BETTER IF YOU open it,' Granny instructed, visibly shaking now.

I did as she said, but there was nothing there except a heap of long straggly black hair. Only then it moved and opened its mouth.

Meeoow!

From behind the door, a cane violently struck the timber.

THWWWAACKKKKWWAKK!

A hand emerged as if from nowhere and swept up the black cat.

Meeoow! Meeoow!

Next came a piercing screech.

WHHEEEEEEEEEEEEEEEEESZZ!

I spun round. It was the kettle on the boil, the steam forcing its cry.

A voice now spoke, its pitch almost as high as the kettle's squeal.

'Lady will be needing these.'

I turned back to the doorway and there, cat held in one hand and a long cane in the other, was a short round figure of a man in a scarlet cloak.

Aloysius! It must be him.

He had the pinkest face I had ever seen. And pink head too, for he was completely bald. Not one hair did he have, not even on his chin. And his eyes were green, yet bloodshot. His scarlet cloak was plain enough, except for embroidered oak leaves round the neckline, but unlike the tunics of the other men it went down to the floor and trailed out behind him.

Blind Zavier then appeared from behind the door holding, strange as it may seem, several umbrella frames that had been stripped of their canvas. They looked like legs that had been pulled off from some sort of a giant spider.

'Take, Child,' he instructed, in that same wounded whisper that had guided me to my room. In daylight, he was even more like Punchinello for I now saw that above his dead eyes were painted brows in the shape of crescent moons. And the light too revealed how his hands were horribly red and blistered.

When I took the bare umbrellas, the bending joints of the frames seemed almost to move about by themselves and as I cradled them in my arms the kettle screamed away.

Well, perhaps it knew more than I did.

'Lady, make whistle stop,' said the pink-faced man.

Granny obediently went over to the stove and removed the copper from the heat. The whistle gradually tapered off to a chug, but that fat pink face waited for all noise to die before it spoke again.

'I am Aloysius,' he announced at last, stroking the cat now nuzzling into his neck. 'I am so, so, so, so very sorry not to have greeted Child on the night of his arrival.'

The pink nose of the cat and the pink flesh of Aloysius were so much the same the two seemed to meld together as one.

For some reason I'd imagined Aloysius to be tall and strong. But no. Whatever the source of his control in this house, it certainly wasn't physical strength. The others were child-like in stature but Aloysius was more like an oversized baby. But such thoughts were brief for when Aloysius began to speak, every word had a growing sense of menace.

'What does Aloysius see? Chairs sitting in puddles. Naughty, naughty, naughty Lady. For she has used Beauty's special din-din plates!'

Beauty? Never had a cat been so ill-named.

From Aloysius's pink lips came an equally pink tongue that now slathered itself all over the face of that ugly fur-ball. And if that wasn't disgusting enough, that feline creature got its tongue out and slathered back.

'Uh! Uh! Uh! Don't worry, Daddy will find new din-din plates for Beauty, but first he must decide what must be done with Lady and Child.'

Aloysius then smashed each saucer with his cane, until a river of paraffin ran across the stone floor. Next he sauntered over to the white enamelled table that had opened up to become a mangle.

'Child must be careful,' he warned, turning the wheel with a grim smile, 'not to trap his little fingers in these rollers. Even thin ones cannot avoid the pain and hurt of this tight and unforgiving vice.'

He didn't mean the bruises I'd seen on Meeler's fingers, did he? Yes, I believe he did.

Aloysius now strode across to the copper washing drums.

'And Child must be careful too,' he mused, with a malicious glance towards Zavier, 'of boiling water. It can scald so very, very, very badly.'

This time I didn't have to think who he meant for there was a definite flinching wince in Zavier's painted brow.

Next Aloysius came over to me and brought his face so close to mine we were breath to breath.

'Child will hang umbrellas over boiling coppers with velvet hats carefully placed upon their spikes. Steam will rise and will clean them. Child will do this as I watch. And Lady will not interfere.'

Aloysius struck his cane hard upon the wooden table.

THWWWAACKKKKWWAKK!

A moving mountain of bed sheets now entered the kitchen. Somewhere amongst them was a head. It had no hair or hat and I could see that the scalp had been shaved, and poorly too, for left behind on it were crusts of dried blood. The sheets were dropped in front of the copper cauldrons and a very scruffy, dishevelled stumpy figure was revealed.

'Allard, I wish to sit!'

This Allard now scurried away, eyes to the floor, only moments later to return carrying a throne-like chair on which Aloysius imperiously placed himself.

Well, to be fair, there was one thing this Aloysius was right about, those velvet hats were much cleaner once the steam had got to them. If there was still a mark, he called for oil of eucalyptus and instructed Granny to 'rub the way of the pile'. But boiling those bed sheets was trickier. I was allowed wooden tongs to remove them from the coppers but I had to pass the still steaming linen through the mangle by hand. My skin blistered with the heat and not trapping my fingers wasn't easy, either.

When, after many hours I was done, Aloysius rose and left, but not before lifting his fist and angrily thrusting out his thumb. There was an undercurrent of malice in everything Aloysius said or did, but his command over those who lived here seemed to go way, way beyond that. For a strange sort of tyranny prevailed.

As I went to bed that evening, I knew my door would be locked from the outside with no escape. Yet then and there I was more frightened about someone getting in. So that night, and every night that followed, I propped the table and chair against the door. Nobody in the night would enter without warning.

CHAPTER THIRTY-THREE

A Pile of Dirt

BUT EVEN WITH a barricade against my door, I didn't sleep much that night. So many questions dancing around in my head.

What was the secret of Aloysius's power? Why was everyone afraid of him? Was it perhaps something to do with their hands? And why was I even brought here in the first place?

I restlessly ran my hands along the frame of the bed. The timber was rough here, too – no, more than rough, it was almost bark-like.

Maybe that's it. Maybe the secret of this house was in the wood itself?

Every day from then on as I walked down to breakfast, I sneakily examined every banister and beam. I even put my head on the bumpy knots on the stairs to listen to the wood hoping maybe to hear something. Pretty stupid, I know, but wasn't foolishness the first step to learning? But there was no sound at all except for the odd creak.

I didn't dare listen at the doors. I was too frightened that one might open and they'd think I was snooping. Which, of course, would have been the truth.

Not that I ever saw anyone except for Granny. Even my food was now left in my room when I went to bed and though my door continued to be locked from the outside, I never knew who did it. But at least there were no more visits to the kitchen from Aloysius. And for that I was thankful.

Most days I would spend in cleaning duties. I did wonder if we'd eventually run out of things to scrub, but Granny always came up with something. And her own particular method of doing it.

'Soap on chrome,' she would say, 'but not mother-of-pearl. For that, use olive oil. And for enamel, sodium bicarbonate is best.' I once asked her who'd be doing all this work if we weren't around. 'Allard,' she'd said, 'not that he's as thorough as he should be. There's nooks and crannies in this house never had sight nor sound of a brush or duster.'

One particular morning, just after breakfast, Granny asked me to take all the cutlery from the kitchen drawers and put it in the sink to soak.

'Go get some ammonia,' she instructed. 'It needs to be kept at a low temperature so we store it in the pantry. Add a few drops to the warm water and them spoons will come up as bright as a new sixpence.'

'*We* store it in the pantry,' she had said, not 'they'. Were *we* part of *them* now? I felt despondent. I wanted to ask her so much but every time I opened my mouth Granny simply put a finger to her lips and shook her head.

Over those next hours we cleaned every knife, fork and spoon, neither of us saying a word. When we'd finished, Granny took from a wicker basket a knitted woollen blanket which she then flung on the kitchen table.

'I found this,' she said, breaking the silence. 'A bit moth eaten but there's enough good yarn to make you a nice warm jumper for the winter. But you'll need to unpick it first.'

So distracted with the blanket, Granny didn't hear the creak of the door, nor see Beauty sneak his way in, leaving behind him a wide gap between the frame and door. Beyond it I could now see Gibble and Rutley scampering past carrying some sort of wooden crate or trunk. Gibble saw me, gave a gormless grin, the sort you make when you're caught doing something you shouldn't be, and the trunk slipped and hit the floor. It wasn't a great a drop, given how short they were, and the trunk was quickly picked up and once again they were on their way.

'To uncurl wool,' Granny was saying, still looking at the blanket, 'first put two chairs back to back, then wind the yarn round the tops in a loop. Then put a large tray on the floor between the chairs. Next, boil the kettle – don't forget, spout in – then pour boiling water into a tray and the steam will rise and straighten out the wool. Oh, aren't I clever! After that, I'll give the yarn an alum rinse. Help protects against fire.'

But my mind was elsewhere because when Gibble and Rutley dropped the wooden crate, something had fallen out.

'I've also found these old socks,' she said, returning to the wicker basket. 'We'll fill them with bran and put them in the Wellington boots to absorb the damp. Saves many a cold.'

Wellingtons? They didn't seem the outdoor type. But the mention of a cold gave me an idea. So I sneezed.

'Are you alright?'

'Perhaps I've already caught one. A cold, I mean. I've not been feeling well, at all.'

Well, that was true, if for different reasons, so I wasn't lying.

'Oh dear, it's rare for us Swidgers to get ill, but terrible when we do. Straight to bed. A good night's sleep will help fight it off.'

But I'd no intention of going to bed, for, when I checked where the trunk had slipped outside the kitchen, I saw a pile of soil. At least now I knew what I was looking for.

So far, I'd seen very little of the Old Coach Inn, except the route between my bedroom and the kitchen, but even that suggested this house wasn't just one building but several somehow joined together by branching corridors. Yet most of them, as I was now finding out, led to either barred up doors or blocked off stairwells. I was about to give up when I saw it.

There. On the floor. Another pile of dirt.

I go down on my hands and knees to examine it, even going as far as putting my cheek to the bare boards so I could see it from the side. Then I smelt it. Moist, autumnal. This soil was damp.

Suddenly I hear a cough. Then another.

I stay fixed in place but slowly cast my eyes round and I see the bottom halves of two identical burgundy tunics. And two identical pairs of hands clasped in front of them.

Must be the Mead twins, I think. But I don't say anything and I keep my cheek to the floor, deciding it would appear less suspicious if I didn't suddenly try to hide what I was doing. Not that I really knew what that was.

The question the twins asked was brief enough, yet even that they somehow managed to share the words.

'What is –'

'– William –'

'– Arthur –'

'– doing?'

What was I going to say? A Swidger cannot lie.

CHAPTER THIRTY-FOUR

The Oak Tree

I HAD TO tell Edwin and Elwin the truth.

'Well, er, I've been listening to the wood.'

That was true. I had tried to listen to the timbers. Foolish, I know. And I was sure the twins would think the same. Laugh probably. But they didn't.

'Is this true?'

'Has William –'

'– Arthur –'

'– been allowed to –'

'– meet the Tree?'

I had no idea what they were talking about. 'Meet the Tree'? Was this some joke? How can you meet a tree? But I had to say something in reply.

'No, I haven't met the tree. Not yet. But I'm sure it's a very nice tree. And I'm very much looking forward to our meeting.'

I was winging it, but my nonsense seemed to somehow make sense to the twins, if not to me.

'It's a very special day –'

'– when you meet –'

'– the Oak.'

Then I remembered my experience in the park outside the hospital.

'Yes,' I replied, my confidence growing. 'I hope to hold the tree close with my hands and shake its leaves.'

This seemed to take Edwin and Elwin aback.

'Hold it close?' repeated Edwin.

'With your hands?' echoed his twin.

'And shake its leaves?' added the first.

Perhaps this had been the wrong thing to say.

'I mean, touch its leaves. Touch its leaves.'

The twins looked at each other, with a shared face of wonder.

'Edwin!'

'Elwin!'

'You were right, Edwin. The Boy will change everything.'

And together repeated that last word as if it were almost the end of their world: '*Everything.*'

And they might have said more, only footsteps now approached. I got to my feet to see Marsden, Zavier and Meeler stood in a row like chess pieces awaiting their next move.

It was Marsden who stepped forward and as he did so the bottom of his long grey robes brushed the pile of soil across the floorboards and the dirt disappeared between the joints.

'It has been decided that the Boy will join us for supper,' he announced.

Supper?

Until now all I'd been given at night were boiled onions and sometimes a dry oatmeal biscuit, yet even this seemed preferable to dining with them. However, I didn't wish to appear impolite, so I thanked Marsden and told them I would join them.

As I said this, I began to wonder how they had known where I was. Three of them together. One you could put down to coincidence, but three, that was something else.

Then it dawned. I'd been thinking about the wood the wrong way round. No, it wasn't about listening to timbers but rather timbers that listened.

At the hospital, Granny told me to say, 'Hello, Tree'. I thought she was being silly. But maybe not. And if trees can hear what you're saying, why not their timbers? And maybe that's why Granny keeps putting her finger to her lips. And why Marsden,

Zavier and Meeler knew where I was.

This house could hear everything!

Marsden interrupted these thoughts for he now raised his grey-gloved hand and informed Edwin and Elwin that they were 'required' downstairs. He didn't say why but they seemed to understand for after a short bow the twins turned and left. And as they did, I noticed something hanging down Edwin's back. What looked like a long thread of cobwebs.

I didn't want the others to see what I'd spotted so I said smartly, 'What time is supper?'

A perfectly reasonable question, you may think, yet Marsden and Meeler looked at me in total disbelief and even Zavier's painted eyebrows jumped a little. Marsden composed himself and said simply, 'The Boy will know the call to supper by the strike that he shall hear.'

Then, as one, they dropped their heads slightly, and bowed. Meeler, as he had done on his first meeting, added a wave of his hand which I saw still had signs of bruising.

Their hands! That's where I should be looking.

Zavier's were blistered, I knew that, but what damage, I wondered, lay concealed under those grey gloves of Marsden? Could Aloysius's tyranny be something to do with what he did to their hands?

Yet Edwin's and Elwin's had seemed perfectly normal when they found me just now. Except they were clasped together. And on the first night they had been holding those oil lamps. If there was something wrong with their hands, it would have been easy to miss.

As I walked back to my room, I thought too about those words of Granny's: '*You'll always find something useful in what I say.*' Problem is she says so much. About borax. Parrots. Eggs. Lime. Mustard. Yet nothing seemed to chime. Oh, I was such a fool. Yes, Granny had already told me the secret of this house. I just couldn't see it.

When I arrived at the door to my room I remembered how

on that first night I thought it was a dead-end, mistaking it for wood panelling. Then I thought about the Mead Twins. How they found me just now, it was if they'd appeared from nowhere, and the same happened that first evening as well.

I decided to go back and check the corridor where I'd been spotted, but when I did the soil had gone. I thought at first that footsteps may have spread it across the floor but looking closer, on my my hands and knees, I could see that there wasn't a speck of dirt anywhere. It couldn't have just disappeared. Someone had swept it away.

But it was that wood panelling I had really come to examine. Yes, there, hidden in the timbers, was a small wrought iron handle. I stepped back and it was then that I could make out in the panelling the outline of a door. This must be where Edwin and Elwin had come from when they found me with my ear to the ground.

CHAPTER THIRTY-FIVE

The Door with No Key

I PULLED ON the iron ring, only it wouldn't budge.

Turned it left, then right. Still nothing.

I looked for a place a key might fit, but saw no hole, so I put my shoulder to the panelling and pushed. Solid. Wouldn't move.

So, what unlocks a door with no key... the handle itself.

This time, instead of pulling it towards me, I very gently pushed it up. Something inside the lock mechanism wood clicked and the door opened.

What greeted me were cobwebs, torn and hanging. *Cobwebs*. That's what I'd seen hanging down Edwin's back. Beyond this mesh of web was a dark inner corridor with beams criss-crossing it every few feet. I took a couple of steps forward and my foot hit something. I looked to see what it was. A wooden crate. Perhaps the same one I'd seen Gibble and Rutley carrying.

I did try to lift the lid but it was nailed down. Then I thought if this was the same trunk, then perhaps I might find more soil underneath if, perhaps, it had fallen through from a crack in its base. I gripped the handle tight to lift it and as I did something scuttled over my hand.

A spider!

I let go of the handle and shake my fingers and it scurries away. I've never liked creepy-crawlies, but, I suspected, it was probably more frightened of me.

I try again. Whatever is inside the trunk is heavy. Running my fingers along the base I feel a breach in the wood. When I pick at it the splinters begin to come away. But the box is a weight and a half, and my knee starts to give way and the chest suddenly shudders. And as it shakes, some of the crate's contents fall onto the floor. I lower the crate and slide the box to the side to reveal… more soil. Even bits of decomposing twigs and leaves.

From a distance I then heard what I thought was a cymbal crashing. Was that the call to supper?

I used my foot to spread the dirt I'd disturbed, most of it falling between the gaps in the floorboards, but as I did so I noticed something small and white lying in the dirt. A shell? A broken cup? I picked it up and brushed off the muck. It was a bone. Definitely a bone.

For a second, my thoughts went back to vampires. Aren't they kept in coffins with their native soil? But this crate was too small for a body. At least an adult's.

Vampire children?

Crazy, I know, but the fancy of the mind sometimes leaps in strange directions. Even so, I put that bone safely in my pocket and then placed the box back where I had found it and made my way downstairs.

I'd not been told where supper would be. I assumed near the kitchen. And when I saw a door ajar that had always previously been shut, I walked in.

Marsden was closing the window panels, shutting off the strong glare of tonight's full moon, but what grabbed my attention was a small suit of armour.

So much in this house was sullied and tarnished, yet here was metal that was polished and bright. Putting my flat palm between the top of the helmet and my own head, I could see we were about the same height. I then tapped the metal suit and said to Marsden, 'Good to know I'd have something to wear, if I needed a change of clothes.'

But Marsden wasn't the talkative type. And his reply was blunt and uncompromising.

'This house is not a costumery for fools. And one does not

wear armour. One operates it.'

Again, I tried a light-hearted approach.

'Not sure I'd be that much use to a damsel in distress. More clanking dustbin than knight in shining armour.'

This did not go down well.

'Armour of this workmanship does not clank. It slides gracefully into place.'

One more try.

'Does it come in blue?'

Big mistake. Jokes were not Marsden's thing. And he had had enough.

'Let him that girdeth on armour,' he growled, 'not brag as one who taketh it off. The boy prince, whose suit this was, had been trained, from the age of four, to kill and slaughter.'

I changed track. 'And did he? Kill, I mean?'

'History relates the boy's horse startled and keeled over. The prince fell and became trapped beneath the burden of his stallion. His armour, a cage. Like the snail, whose shell, when upturned, becomes his prison.'

'What happened to the prince?'

'They say, as he lay helpless, his adversary removed his helmet and, at his leisure, made use of it to smash in the boy's skull.'

Marsden then produced from behind his robes a long stick with what looked like a large cricket ball at one end. A mallet of sorts. He then struck the armour and it echoed all about.

Ah, that call to dinner, not a cymbal but the cry of a young man's death suit.

'William Arthur will join us at our banquet?'

Yes, I thought, I had better. Undoubtedly Aloysius will be there too. Head of the table, probably. And him being there means I have no choice, but, as the saying goes, is it ever wise to sup with the Devil?

CHAPTER THIRTY-SIX

Hands

THE DINING CHAMBER was the largest room I had seen so far. The walls were hung with tapestries and candles on tall brass stands provided the only illumination as all the shutters had already been closed. In the centre of the room was a circular oak table made of what looked like old beams and joists. It was almost medieval in its crudeness. The crockery was a complete mismatch, for no cup or plate was the same. Dark blue. Deep green. Shady red. Dirty yellow. With pattern. Without pattern. Each a last survivor, perhaps, of what was once full crockery sets.

I looked around to see who was already here.

Granny was seated, an empty glass in each hand, on a low bench that ran the length of the wall. Brewster Blaxton, his black beard even more overgrown than I remembered, stood over her with a bottle ready to pour.

'When it comes to gin,' she said, laughing, 'I must have *two* glasses, because the first gin always turns me into a different woman – so I think it's only fair *she* should have one as well!'

But it wasn't the gin that I was interested in, but the hands that poured it. Like the man himself, they were thickset and strong, but now I could see his fingernails were black. Not dirt, but the sort of blood-black when fingers get caught in a door. Or hit with a hammer. Yes, and one finger was bent and rigid, as if it had once been badly broken.

I continued to spy round looking at hands. Sprout-nosed Gibble was scratching his backside, so I made a slight bow and waved. He fell for it and dropped his gown, brought his hands round to his front and waved back.

Gibble's palms, usually hidden by long sleeves, were covered in bumpy, lumpy, knotty warts. I only had the candlelight to go by but some looked green and even scabby, as if he'd picked at them and made them worse.

Who next? Salton Manning. The man with the Gorgon eyes was standing alone in the corner, that acorn pin in his hand. Only tonight he was using it to clean underneath his nails. But what were those metal rings across his fingers? Salton raised his hand to a candle, helping him see better. And now so could I. Those weren't rings at all, but some sort of welded band. More manacle than jewellery.

A pattern was emerging. Everyone's hands were fettered, diseased or bruised.

Wait a minute. Granny's first question to me was about hands, whether I'd touched Jayden with them – then she had told me to hug that tree in the park with the palms of my hands, and she always took off her gloves when meeting someone...

I didn't yet know everything about Swidgers but I was pretty certain now that our hands were, somehow, different to the Commonality. And if hands were that important, perhaps when damaged – even slightly – they became useless to us. Like when a cut finger isn't a problem, unless you're a violinist.

Suddenly there was a noise from under the table. That stupid cat, I thought, but no, it was Rutley emerging on all fours playing at being a train. His hands, not blemished or injured but oh, so painfully small. No bigger than those of a boy of six or seven.

The Mead Twins now entered the dining chamber, again, hands clasped together, like vicars at prayer.

I moved closer towards them. My plan was to pretend to examine one of the tapestries hanging on the wall behind them, and as I passed by, catch a closer look at those gripping fingers. Only then a high voice suddenly said, 'Be seated!'

Aloysius had entered, holding his unbeautiful Beauty. 'Be

seated!' he repeated. If the pitch of that voice went any higher, I thought, it'd only ever be heard by that stupid cat.

Aloysius, by now sitting in his throne-like chair, reached for a large, round drinking vessel.

'Fill my pottle!' he commanded.

Such long fingernails, sharp and pointed, but his hand, like his face and head, was pure pink. And without blemish. But not so poor Allard's hands, for I could see as he poured his ruler the drink, how sore and chapped they were. From all that cleaning, maybe?

Aloysius spoke again.

'We welcome our new companion, Master William Arthur.'

Oh, I was 'Master', now, was I?

'Raise your glasses, gentlemen. A toast to this house. May he share in its glory!'

Goblets and wineglasses were taken from the table and lifted in the air.

'To this house!' the gentlemen responded in unison.

Now was my chance. The Mead Twins had picked up wineglasses. Yes, those clasping hands had hidden something, for neither twin had a tip on their little fingers. There was no joint where the fingernail should be. Just a cut-off end.

So, it seemed weakened hands were what connected them all. Gibble's and Rutley's were diseased or small, so perhaps Aloysius needn't worry about them. And both seemed harmless enough, anyway. But the others had hands that had been burnt, hit, chained or even partially dismembered.

Yet if Aloysius did all this to them, why didn't they stop him? Maybe one on his own couldn't have done it, but there were so many of them. And Brewster and Salton were certainly physically stronger than he was.

And there was another thing too. If these men were all Swidgers, and I think they must have been, at least at some stage, how was it possible for a Swidger to harm anyone? I've told you,

I once tried to lift my fist to fight back against that bully Jimmy Lee but my arm and body simply wouldn't let me.

Perhaps the answer was in something Aloysius had just said. The 'glory' of this house? What was it? And would I discover it tonight?

CHAPTER THIRTY-SEVEN

Beer and Porridge

ALOYSIUS NOW CLAPPED those perfect hands of his together and everyone began to sit for dinner.

I was placed between Salton Manning and Gibble. Gibble gawped at his plate, whereas Salton stared only at the decorative tapestry hanging on the wall in front of us. I did want to say something, to break the silence, but then I remembered Granny's rule, 'Only speak when spoken to'. And perhaps that was for the best. I didn't want to give away too much about of my suspicions.

Allard served. I could see as he walked how he would be taller, were he not always bent over with eyes to the floor.

Dinner began with myrtle beer and porridge. Myrtle beer, I worked out from Meeler's words of praise, was the creation of Brewster Blaxton. It was green and thick, and made, apparently, not from hops but bog myrtle, caraway seeds, mugwort and gooseberry juice. It looked like tadpole soup, if there is such a thing. And it tasted much, much worse. Granny, when asked her opinion, said that she admired bog myrtle more for its insect repelling properties than its flavour.

Next course, a single herring. Bizarre.

Meat followed. Mutton, I heard somebody say. I discovered you don't really eat mutton, more chew it into submission. Not so bad you may think, but you should have seen what came with it. Pickles. Pickles, pickles and more pickles. Pickled beans, pickled parsnips, pickled mushrooms, pickled radish and, most disgusting of all, pickled prunes.

Meeler, it emerged, was the pickle man. Granny had once

observed, 'never trust a thin cook'. Never was a truer word spoken. Meeler offered me a shrivelled object floating in vinegar, claiming it to be a pickled turnip garnished with nettle leaves. Well, out of politeness, I thought, I should at least try a bit.

Urrrghh! It was like eating a surgically preserved toad. My grimace clearly gave me away.

'I believe,' grinned Meeler, 'Master William would prefer to sup with us with a longer spoon.'

No, Master William would prefer not to sup with you at all.

When asked for her opinion of these delicacies, Granny's only comment was, 'Pickles can be very bad for the complexion.'

Next Allard brought in a large colander, painted with red squirrels munching on hazelnuts. Lucky them, I thought. The bowl was passed round and eventually reached Salton Manning who stabbed at the contents with a knife and raised his quarry in the air.

'Would you like a potato?'

I realised it was the first time he had spoken to me. It was a muscular and military voice. And I noticed too how steady his hand was. Even with those welded bands across his fingers.

After what had gone before, a boiled potato had its attractions and I was about to say 'Yes', but before I even opened my mouth it had landed on my plate with a heavy thump. I jumped. It's not every day you get unnerved by a single spud.

I had to look away and take a breath, so I turned to Gummy Gibble, who, surprise, surprise, was still chewing on his mutton.

By now all the others had removed their hat pins and were using them as toothpicks. Then came the weird noises. Belches, burps and worse.

So that was supper. No one discussed their day, what they had done, who they had seen or where they had gone. The only talk was of the excellence of the myrtle, the merit of the herring and the wonder of the pickles. But I had survived it, I felt, without revealing too much of my unease.

That though all changed when Edwin turned to Elwin and observed, 'William Arthur does not speak.'

Elwin replied, 'Perhaps there is no kernel in the nut?'

'No slug in the shell.'

I lowered my head.

'Poor hurt fowl!'

'See how it creeps back into the hedges.'

Perhaps the Mead Twins had meant well. Or maybe not.

When I eventually raised my eyes again, I tried to feign interest in the tapestry on the wall. Woven in faded threads of red, black and green, it depicted an exotic woodland with mountains in the background. In the centre was a tree with a monkey in its branches and below, on the forest floor, was a boy in a loincloth with a python circling about his ankle.

Salton Manning noticed my apparent curiosity.

'It has a moral, as all art should.'

'A moral?' I replied.

'Its weave tells the story of the Boy, the Monkey and the Python. The boy and the monkey had been friends, spending their hours together climbing the banyan tree. Only one day the boy fell to the ground. And the monkey laughed. As monkeys often do. From under dead leaves a python heard the mocking and came to the boy, saying, "Feed me a mouse and I will be your friend instead." And that boy was good at catching mice –'

Salton stopped for a moment and looked over to Granny.

'Someone had been teaching him how to lay traps, so the young lad now had a new companion. The python seemed to grow fond of the boy, wrapping itself around his ankle. And as they played, the monkey watched from the top of the banyan tree. As monkeys often do.

'But one day, the snake refused even the fattest of mice, yet remained friendly with the boy, coiling itself about him. Observing this, the monkey came down from his banyan tree and said, "How is your new companion?" "I think my python is ill," said the boy, "for he says no to my mice, but I still love him and he loves me, for see how I am embraced." The monkey laughed. As monkeys often do. "Your python is not sick," it grinned, "and that is no embrace. The snake wraps himself around you to gauge how big you are. And he rejects your mice because he needs the space." "Space for what?" asked the boy. "Why," the monkey replied, "to eat you. Fool!"

From beside me came squealing, gibberish laughter.

'Aha-hha-ha-hahrr-ha-hahh!'

Gibble. His mouth, wide open with whooping, let slip some half-chewed mutton, which then dropped to the floor. His tongue, now free and unencumbered, joined in the merriment with a mad dance of its own.

No one else in the room laughed which made his all the more weird.

I clinched my hands together, so tight they hurt. How could laughter, I thought, cause so much pain?

Aloysius raised his thumb. The laughter stopped. Gibble's eyes looked to the ground. He must have spotted his mutton, for he picked it up from the floor, popped it back in his mouth and started chewing again.

Aloysius stood.

'Hesperus rises,' he intoned, 'and so must we as we welcome this collied eve.'

Everyone got to their feet.

Hesperus. Wasn't that the name of the evening star? As for 'collied eve', I had no idea. Perhaps he had used these weird old words to make me feel like an outsider.

Aloysius whispered something in Allard's ear and then turned to address the table.

'Gentlemen, there will be no sugared ginger –'

He stopped and again whispered to Allard, whose face immediately brightened.

'For tonight,' Aloysius went on, 'we shall have Pontefract

Cakes! It will be a treat Master William Arthur will never forget.'

Allard then lifted the corner of the tapestry to reveal a hidden doorway. Aloysius went through first and the rest of the party followed. Except Salton Manning.

'So, what was the moral? Of the story, I mean?' I asked.

'That is in the eye of the beholder. One moral for the teller, but many for those who listen.'

'Well, you told the tale, what's yours?'

'The python is cunning, the boy foolish and the monkey wise. Now you.'

'If someone too eagerly becomes your friend,' I replied, 'would it not be prudent to question their motives?'

'That's good. You are almost as smart as the monkey. But is there not also a warning for the python. Becoming too dependent against its nature?'

I never saw it like that.

'The monkey is wise, but cruel,' Salton Manning went on, 'for he knows the truth well before he tells it. But suppose the monkey had never said a word. Would his silence not be justified? A true friend abandoned for a false one.'

'He shouldn't have laughed at the boy!'

'Wrong! For only a true friend would laugh. Love and laughter. Do they not come from the same heart?'

Salton suddenly pushed me against the wall and barked, 'The boy was made to look a fool and tonight that too will be your fate! Let me tell you what he has ready for you –'

But before Salton could say more, Meeler's face appeared from behind the tapestry curtain.

'The Pontefract Cakes have arrived,' Meeler said, his eyes suspiciously looking at me then Salton. 'Come... both of you.'

I moved to the doorway and lifted up the woven picture that separated the two rooms, but as I looked down, I saw what I was holding in my hand.

The coiled python from the tapestry!

I instinctively jumped away. Just old threads, I knew that, but what came into my mind as I held them was that other snake, the one that attacked that Saturday morning on the High Street.

I would be safe here, Granny had said, yet I wasn't so sure – for the terror I felt as I stood in that doorway was as strong as the fear I had known that day...

CHAPTER THIRTY-EIGHT

Pontefract Cakes

THE DOORWAY LED to the second chamber, with a tapestry of its own hanging over the frame, needing to be raised to gain entry.

It was a smaller and more cramped room, but again wood panelled. Tatty armchairs were scattered round. On a table in the middle was a heap of Pontefract Cakes. Granny was saying to Brewster Blaxton, 'Magnesium limestone is what you need to grow liquorice. That's what Pontefract had in abundance. Not like the soil in our village. That was mainly rock and granite. So if we did any digging, all we would ever grow was worn and weary.'

The Pontefract Cakes were shiny black and stamped with that familiar Raven and Castle emblem. Aloysius then took one from the table, raised it high with a flourish, and held the pose as an actor might. Perhaps Allard thought this was his cue, for he now entered carrying an ornate silver dish covered by a lid with a solid gold raven on top.

'Boy will discover beneath his own embossed delights.'

I hadn't had any liquorice in ages. Not that the Pontefract Cakes on the table looked that appetising, but anything was better than tadpole soup.

So, I take the dish and I lift the lid.

What I see is certainly black and shiny, more oval though than those on the table. There's a pattern of sorts, but not a castle or a raven.

Wait! Did one just move? It couldn't have. Did one just grow legs? And another – and another? Impossible!

But yes, the Pontefract Cakes were alive. And running up my arm.

I scream.

'Ahhhh!'

Alive!

I drop the dish. Too late. They're on me. Everywhere. On my chest. Down my legs. Now in my hair. My ear. I push it off but as I do others run from my hands on to my face. No, no, please not my mouth. I spit. They're dashing across my eyes! I close them tight and instinctively my hand slaps my brow. I hit. I scratch. I claw at myself. And I cry out once more.

'Ahhhhhhhhhhhhhhhhhh!'

I am stone, unable to move. But still they crawl all over me.

And then it comes. The cruellest laughter ever heard. But familiar footsteps too. Though my eyes are shut, I sense a light shine across of my face. Dare I open them? No, not yet.

A familiar voice speaks, 'They don't like anything bright. Brush yourself down, William, they're gone now.'

Granny. Such a relief to hear her kind voice.

My body slowly comes to life. I stretch my fingers and touch my face. I shiver. Shudder. Even when gone, my skin still feels their presence.

At last I open my eyes and dare to look. Nothing on my hands. Or arms. Or chest. Not one. The light from Granny's flickering candle had frightened them away. Or so I thought. For just then, movement in the nape of my neck. One was still trying to escape? Would it fail?

Yes. I swung my arm behind me and splattered it. Whatever it was. I felt a sticky mess on my fingers and took from my neck a crushed black shell oozing with slime. More laughter. Though not from Salton Manning, who stood alone in a corner, in silence.

I heard what the twins were calling me as they whispered to each other.

'Poor Master Lackbeard.'

'Yes, the Dough Boy is not yet cooked.'

Aloysius then lifted his thumb and the laughter subsided.

'Enough, enough! A little harmless amusement on the occasion of the Boy's first supper.'

Yes, and last, if I have anything to do with it.

Aloysius examined the gooey innards on my fingers.

'Ah, I find eggs! A female in our midst. Even when crushed, her offspring live on. A hundred more will soon be hatched.'

'A hundred more what?' I asked.

'Cockroaches! Ha! Ha!'

The laughter that came next was the worst. Mean. Nasty. Spiteful. Vicious. Every word you can think of that enjoys making someone feel pain inside.

And in return I was angry. Hurt. Betrayed. Upset. Mad. Fuming. And every other word you can think of when you're wounded within. I wanted to cry but stopped myself.

What is wrong with these people? Why do they do this? They were boys like me once. How can lives become so wicked?

I would learn the answer to that question tonight. And that *would* make me cry.

CHAPTER THIRTY-NINE

As You Like It

THE LAUGHTER SLOWLY died down. Allard's was the last to stop and only then because of a sharp look from Aloysius. He gave out a short, phlegmy burst, 'Hrrgh-hrrgh-hrrgh!', dropped his head and put his eyes to the ground.

'Allard! A cloth for the Boy,' instructed Aloysius.

Allard grunted in disapproval, but a dirty dishcloth was eventually produced from one of his pockets.

'Lady will have a means, no doubt, of disposing of the runaways. Lady?'

Granny, as ever, was up to the challenge, but her voice had anger in it.

'I'll mix Plaster of Paris with some flour and rice to leave in piles next to bowls of water.'

Even in my shocked state I could see how this could work. I then spoke without thinking. Or being asked.

'After they've eaten they will grow thirsty, the plaster will set, hard, and then they will all be killed. From within.'

I said these words with a fixed defiant stare towards Aloysius. He glowered back, but gave no reply.

Missel Meeler broke the silence.

'Will you give us a recitation from the Bard, Aloysius?'

Aloysius thought over Meeler's suggestion and then said, 'Indeed, why not. *The Winter's Tale*, I think. Meeler shall play Autolycus. He does it so well and that speech is a favourite of mine.'

A stage of sorts was made ready by moving the armchairs into a half circle. And our backcloth would be the hanging tapestry covering the door. Another forest of sorts, but here, the trees were painted on scenery flats and the ground was a stage, for these woven threads depicted the setting of a play. A young actor, difficult to tell whether boy or girl, was sitting under one of the painted trees in Elizabethan dress. The inscription read: '*You should ask me what time o' day. There's no clock in the forest.*'

More Shakespeare, I supposed, but this time it was familiar. I read those words again. '*You should ask me what time o' day. There's no clock in the forest.*' Yes, I knew them from somewhere.

Brewster had been given one line as the Clown but he wanted to say it, as far as I could tell, from his chair, but Aloysius was insistent he make a proper entrance.

'Oh, I really don't think there's any need for that,' Meeler was arguing. 'The Clown does not require an entrance.'

The room went still. Aloysius glared at Meeler and then began to pull and squeeze his own plump fingers.

'Meeler, *I* say, you will *both* enter!'

Meeler nervously fiddled with his thin flute-like fingers and he bowed and said, 'Of course, your every wish, Aloysius.'

Meeler and Brewster took their places at the back of the tapestry but the only person who made an entrance, after a brief kerfuffle, was Allard, snorting.

Aloysius laughed loudly.

'Oh! Allard wishes to see the play from behind the arras! How fortunate we are not performing *Hamlet*!'

Much knowing laughter from the group. And Aloysius soaked it up.

'Oh, very well. Allard may watch. For a little while.'

Meeler and Brewster again took their positions and at last made their entrance. Brewster said his line – no idea what, as he was as incomprehensible as ever – and Missel Meeler began his speech.

'*He has a son, who shall be flayed alive; then 'nointed over with honey, set on the head of a wasp's nest; then stand till he be three quarters and a dram dead; then recovered again with*

*aqua-vitae or some other hot infusion; then, raw as he is, and
in the hottest day prognostication proclaims, shall be set against
a brick-wall, the sun looking with a southward eye upon him,
where he is to behold him with flies blown to death.'*

Was that really Shakespeare? Pretty nasty stuff if it was. But
my mind was elsewhere. That inscription on the tapestry. Yes, I
was pretty certain that was Shakespeare too. But I couldn't check
with Granny because she was so engrossed in her knitting.

'Again!' insisted Aloysius, before Meeler could even take the
briefest of bows.

And so we all had to listen to that horrible speech once more.
There sat Aloysius, savouring every tortuous word, with Beauty
on his lap, licking his master's neck with equal relish.

'Again! Again!' he cried.

Eight times Meeler was made to say those sinister and
menacing words and there would have been a ninth rendition
had not Marsden intervened and said, 'What role from the Bard
for the Boy?'

The twins were ready with suggestions.

'Arthur –'

'– in *King John* –'

'– when he's thrown from –'

'– the castle wall.'

'Or one of the princes –'

'– in the Tower –'

'– murdered!'

'No,' says Aloysius. 'Boy must choose for himself.'

The room looked at me, but obviously I couldn't think of
anything.

'Does Master William not know the Bard?' Aloysius went
on. 'We shall send to his room this very night every word, every
page, every book we possess.'

But I'm not as stupid as they think. For then it comes to me. That
line on the tapestry was from the play we had looked at in our English

class. The one I mentioned to Granny at the Parent Teacher Meeting.

As You Like It...

'*You should ask me what time o'day; there's no clock in the forest.*'

Then I realise, and everything fits into place. Of course, there are no clocks in the forest, just as there are no clocks in this house, not even, as Granny said, an egg-timer...

But that inscription gave only the reply. What was the question that came before it?

Think, William, think!

Then I had it! We Swidgers have a good memory and for that I was now grateful.

'Oh, but I do have a speech from the Bard,' I exclaim. 'Well, not a speech, just one line and more a question, really. *I pray you, what is't o'clock?*'

Silence.

'Oh,' I say, 'should I repeat it? Aloysius seems to like hearing things over and over – so let me say it again: *I pray you, what is't o'clock?*'

The silence goes on for every face remains frozen.

'I'll shout it, shall I? *I PRAY YOU, WHAT IS'T O'CLOCK.* But none of you know the answer for in this house there are no clocks because there is not Time!'

The silence continues but is then suddenly broken by laughter. Not Gibble's, but Rutley's. The innocent laughter that can only from a child.

'Ha! Ha! Ha! What-is-it-o-clock! What-is-it-o-clock! What-is-it-o-clock! What-is-it-o-clock! What-is-it-o-clock!'

The cat Beauty jumps from Aloysius's lap with a yelp, fixes his eyes on me, hisses and spits, then runs off.

'Oh dear,' Granny now says. 'I seem to have dropped a stitch.'

I then see Salton Manning. He has his pin in his hand only now it's not the spike he holds towards me but the decorative enamelled acorn. He points to the acorn and then towards the door, and then upwards. I think he's trying to tell me something.

The Tree! And Time! Were they somehow connected?

CHAPTER FORTY

The Shoebox

I RUN FROM the dining room.

Time! The Tree! Those together they make up the great secret of this house. But how are they linked?

My thoughts carry me up the stairs. *Clocks – hands – trees – wood.* So many thoughts at once that I again stumble on the knotted wood where I fell that first night, but I get up quickly and soon reach the top.

The landing is lit by an oil lamp hanging from a hook in the wood panelling. I see at the edges of the strips of wood long thin gaps that could be the outline of a door.

I wonder...

I hold my breath for a second and listen for movement from downstairs. Nothing.

Good. No one has followed me.

I remove the oil lamp from the hook and use it to find the hidden handle. Wrought iron, just like the others. I tease it up and, yes, it opens of its own accord.

But what will it reveal?

I raise the oil lamp up and peer in. Not so much a corridor more a tunnel. Then I hear a noise. Footsteps? No, too soft. I listen again. I'm sure there was something but all is now quiet and still.

I go through the entry and close it behind me. I tread carefully. Loose floorboards. Rickety beams. Cobwebs. On a shelf, an unlit oil lamp. I walk further to where the corridor divides into three, but two of the ways are blocked by boxes. Climb over them or take the easy option? I take the clearer path, but as I move along, the ceiling lowers and I'm forced to crouch and hobble, yet shuffle by shuffle, I make to where the passageway again reaches walking height. Yet here it ends. But then I see in the wooden wall another wrought iron handle and so I unlock it. The door opens onto the corridor where I found the soil on the floor. And where Edwin and Elwin found me. I begin to think if the twins have a purpose in this house it is to spy.

I try something. I put my oil lamp down on the floor, go back into the tunnel and close the door. All is dark – except for a light coming through a spyhole in the wood. So, they were spies.

Just then – footsteps. And through the spyhole I can make out flickering shadows. And voices follow. Oh no, I might have guessed: Edwin and Elwin.

'This lamp –'

'– left here –'

'The Boy –'

'– has been –'

'– snooping.'

They step closer to the door I'm hiding behind. I find the iron handle and feel it shifting on the other side but my grip is strong.

'The handle does not move,' says one twin.

'Let me try,' says the other.

'You will do no better.'

I tighten my hold.

'Do not force it!'

There's a sudden yank on the other side and the sound of something snapping.

'You've broken it! Clotpoll!'

'It was your idea! Cobloaf!'

'Shall we wait for the Boy's return?'

'No, but we will take his lamp.'

Footsteps walk away, then stop for a moment, only to move off again and fade.

There's silence now.

I attempt to tease up the handle. They weren't wrong. It's busted, all right. There's no longer an escape for me through this door so I turn to go back the way I came in complete darkness.

I bump and stagger to where the passageway divided. Wasn't there a shelf nearby with a full lamp? Sometimes I had seen matches placed on them. I begin to feel around the walls.

But then a noise. That hidden door on the landing is being opened, yet the other is dead-locked. I cannot go forward, I cannot go back. I then hear who it is. No surprise at all: Edwin and Elwin again.

My only means of escape is to climb over that pile of boxes that blocked the other passageways. And do it in darkness.

I try to picture in my mind what I had seen before. One large box, that I do remember. And several on top. I slowly extend my hands. Yes, found them. I lift one of the boxes and try to move it to one side. But those voices and flickering shadows are getting closer.

I must be still or they will hear me. But my hold on the box weakens and it falls on the floorboards. Not too much noise, but enough to alert Edwin and Elwin.

No time to waste. I squeeze round the box and make my way down this unknown passageway in the hope of finding another door. With no light to see by I'm forced to stretch out my hands, feeling along all the way along the side of the walls. But something's not right. My arms are being pushed closer to my body. This corridor is narrowing.

My nose suddenly scrapes against bricks and mortar. Another blind alley. Behind me, I can hear Edwin and Elwin are already where the corridor divided.

But did I sense a slight curve in the passageway as I made my way along just now? Maybe, if I press my body close into the wall I might not be seen. And yes, there is a bend, but no, it's not quite enough to hide me.

A light shines along the floorboards. Not reached my feet yet, but it's getting closer.

I hear a voice. Or rather two that speak together.

'We can see you!'

But then another voice. If a cat can be said to have a voice. Meeoow!

'Beauty, we've found you at last.'

'How did you get in here?'

'Silly puss-puss.'

'You come-ey here looky for spiders?'

'Aloysius has been worried about you.'

Of course, those soft footsteps from before. Beauty must have found a way in when I opened the door on the landing.

Edwin's voice now takes on that irritating sing-song rhythm people have when talking to cats. Or babies.

'Come to Aunty Edwin!'

'No, come to Aunty Elwin.'

I have no idea which of the twins that ugly mog preferred that night. All that mattered was that soon the three of them were gone and I was safe. Albeit in pitch black darkness.

I feel my way back to where the corridor divided and fumble for that shelf with the oil lamp. I accidentally knock it over but manage to save it from falling. My hand now discovers a match. No, several matches. I use the tips of my fingers to find rough plaster and strike the match. Light at last. And brighter still when I light the lamp.

Now I see it was a large leather trunk that blocked my way. I don't think Edwin or Elwin will be coming back for a while, so I take off the boxes on top, lift the lid and look inside.

It was a chest of curious treasures.

A battered toy train with a tatty string hanging from its front. A painted tin soldier with one arm missing. A drum with its skin split from one side to the other. An old and battered cricket ball. A small brass trumpet. Wooden bottles. No, not bottles. Skittles.

I see a square box patterned with purple-yellow triangles. I pick it up and undo the catch. The lid rises slowly and a ragged clown falteringly appears. A Jack-in-the-box. I begin to wonder what child first played with it. This toy would have been new then and the clown would have jumped out with surprise, making them laugh with joy. But that was long ago. That spring is now broken for the head offers no resistance as I push it back into its box. I pick up the toy train. Something scratched on the side. A name beginning with 'R' but the rest is lost to age and use.

I put the oil lamp down and as I do I notice a shoe box tied with string. I undo its binds and remove the lid.

A pile of old photographs. Very old. Not even black and white but that brown and pale cream from when photography was first invented. In one picture is a cross looking woman in wire glasses, dressed in a long white pinny. I slide it away and look at the one beneath. A bald man with great big sideburns that look more like overgrown hedges. He's sitting in a chair, a book upon his lap. A throne-like chair. The very same I have seen Aloysius sit in? Yes, it is.

I shuffle to the next photo. A group of young boys sat on long, low benches. A dozen or so, all in flat cloth caps. They stare gloomily at the camera. The thinnest catches my eye. There's something familiar about him. Then I see two boys together and a shiver runs down my spine, for what is familiar about these boys is each other. For they are twins. Edwin and Elwin!

Can it be?

Wait, I recognise another boy. That big sprout nose: unmistakable. Gibble. What age were they then, I wondered? Six, seven, eight? Standing behind the group, a round-faced child. Not looking into the camera but on those below him. Aloysius had mean eyes even then. But the others, they were just boys.

This place, a coaching inn once, but perhaps later, a school. I look again at the grim-faced woman in her long white pinny. A nurse, perhaps. Then I realise, perhaps this place wasn't a school, but an orphanage. I feel a tear fall on my cheek.

It must have been such a miserable and cruel world. No wonder it had created such miserable and cruel boys.

Well, I wasn't going to let it do the same to me.

CHAPTER FORTY-ONE

In the Moonlight

MUCH WAS FALLING into place, but there were still questions. How had Aloysius taken over the orphanage? And why did they stay here once he had?

Granny said on the day we met that we were all orphans in the storm. I could now see how lucky I was to have escaped that institution for abandoned children in Romania. Sad, though, the lady who brought me to England had died doing it. I never knew her but I quietly thanked her now for her kindness.

I put the yellowing photographs back in the shoe box as best I can. As I do, I glance down the passageway where I had scraped my nose against brick and mortar. A crack of light is coming through the wall.

I walk towards it and find a loose brick. The mortar crumbles as I pull the brick away and I can feel the air beyond is cold and fresh. My eyes adjust and I see the fractured light of a full moon. I break free another brick and I can see it better now. A huge tree and its roots run along the ground to this house.

No, the roots *are* this house, for the timbers and the wood of the tree are one and the same. The Tree has somehow become this house. And that must be its secret. But how is all this connected to Time?

I hear something outside. Howls of phantoms? Whatever they are they hang in the air and make painful cries.

I try to make out what is beyond the Tree but cannot. Even with a full moon, there's nothing but a void of blackness. Those strange cries float away and I replace the bricks and make my way towards the door to the landing. I feel for the frame, but as I do I catch myself on something sharp. A nail? Well whatever it was, I've discovered it before it can do me any harm.

As I opened the door, I half expected to find waiting behind it those boys from that photograph. Except, of course, much older now. But the landing was empty.

I returned to my room. A large trunk had been delivered and left on the floor with a book placed on top. *Cymbeline* by William Shakespeare. Never even heard of it, but every word of the Bard had been promised and no doubt, I thought, they'll all be in this trunk. I tried to open it. Locked. Fools, they hadn't even given me the key. It tried to lift it out the way, but it was too heavy. Well, I guess he did write a lot of plays.

But then I saw something unexpected in the corner of the room. A Grandfather Clock. Were they playing games with me? I hadn't been wrong. There were no clocks in this house. Until now. I listened, but no tick, no tock. What were they trying to tell me?

I was too tired to figure it out, but tonight I knew I had to protect myself and so I placed the chair and table against the door. Better still, I slid that heavy trunk across the floor to stand with them. No one was going to get in my room tonight.

A long eventful day. I readied myself for bed and no sooner had my head hit the pillow and I was asleep.

I had been warned that nightmares dance with your fears and appear as real as life itself. That's why, when I was woken by the chimes of the grandfather clock, I thought I was in a dream. Or rather nightmare.

DING-DONG-DING-DONG.

Impossible. The clock had been silent. And the dial hadn't moved. Yet now it was sounding its tune. I shut my eyes tightly.

It then strikes one.

BONG!

Silence. I wait. Another strike and a second follows.

BONG! BONG!

The hour of two has followed so quickly. No, that cannot be. It must be a dream. Silence again. Then the clock strikes once more.

BONG! BONG! BONG!

Three o'clock.

BONG!

No, four o'clock.

BONG! BONG! BONG! BONG! BONG!

What five? Six? Seven! This can't be real.

My eyes are still closed. If this is a dream the chimes will surely stop when I open them.

Can I? Yes!

My eyes are open and I'm awake. And yet the strokes go on. I count them in the darkness.

BONGGGG! BONGGGG! BONGGGG! BONGGGG! BONGGGG!

Eight. Nine. Ten. Eleven.

I suddenly feel a foul hot breath in my ear.

'Huuuhhhh…'

No! No! No! It can't be. Please say it isn't…

'The iron tongue is about to strike midnight, but not yet. It is not my will.'

Aloysius!

A match is struck. A candle lit.

I see his fat pink face. As close to me as I am to myself. This is no dream. I try to raise myself up, but I cannot. Am I dead? Poisoned?

He's so close that when he speaks, I can almost taste his rancid breath in my mouth.

'Do I see a quickening in your eye? You are thinking perhaps that by no assay of reason can this be real, but I assure you, it is. But how can I be here when you barricaded the door with the trunk? Because I was enclosed within the trunk. A devious ruse I stole from the play *Cymbeline*. Had you attended your bedtime reading you would have been forewarned.

'You have fled the world beyond – Lady does not say why and I do not ask – and I offer you sanctuary here. But it will be under my rules. Since you are now here to stay, let me tell you the secret of this house.

'You were right about the clocks. We have no need of them, for I, Aloysius Zachariah, am the Stopper of Time. Time here is frozen. As are you now. I kept the grandfather clock as a reminder that for those beyond these timbers Time and Life ticks away. Observe the hooded figure on the clock face, wielding a scythe? A grim joke to the Grim Reaper. But he cannot laugh at me, for I have beaten him and his deceitful cohort: Time.

'Time, you see, is a betrayer. You live in hope, then watch it slowly die. One day, they said, one day a new mother and father would take me from this place and learn to love me. Every hour I would sit by the window looking out into the world, waiting and longing for rescuers to come. Yet they never did. Never, never, never! And so I grew to loathe and hate a world where Time moves on. As for those who told me those lies, well, they became old and withered. And very soon after – dead. They now reside in the base of the Grandfather Clock. As dust in urns.

'I was about your age when I discovered how different I was. And with the endowment of the Tree, I found, if I embraced its bark tight with the Power of Hands, I could enhance and spread my gift. Mother Oak gave me this house, but I am its father and ruler. All who reside within share my gift of Timelessness and so will live forever!

'But there is a price and you shall be taught it. Feel these long fingernails of mine. So sharp they can even cut through the skin of your hands. I will weaken you with many cuts and slices. Of course, no Swidger can be violent to another but I have discovered that when Time has stopped, I can do as I please. So now... feel the hurt! For hurt will be the price you pay for your sanctum, as I was hurt by those who deceived me.

'When you wake you may think that none of this was real. But the truth you will feel in your scars. This flickering light tells me you have fear in your eyes, so I will close them for you, blow out the flame – *whhhuuhh* – and leave you with a lullaby to return you to your sleep.

'*Here comes the candle to light you to bed, Here comes the chopper to chop off your... head.*'

CHAPTER FORTY-TWO

The Gong Clangs

COCKROACHES! I FEEL them. Running across my chin. I awake slapping my face. I try opening my eyes but there's too much light. A figure stands over me. I cannot tell who, for the sun is coming through the window behind them. Aloysius? No, too tall. A head comes closer. Again, I feel a tickle on my chin. Only now I see what it really is. Long strands of bright copper hair.

'Entropy, I curse you!'

A familiar gloved hand sweeps up the tresses and puts them in their place. My eyes adjust.

Granny!

After the horrors of the night, it's good to see a comforting smile.

'Look what we have here on this chin of yours: whiskers! Well, more fluff than stubble, but the beginnings of something. No more Master Lackbeard for you.'

'How long have I been asleep?' I asked.

'Longer than a Polish winter. Look, I've even had the time to finish this.' Granny held up the woolly jumper she'd been knitting. It was huge. 'I hope it fits.'

I knew it wouldn't. And so did she.

'Perhaps you'll grow into it. I did warn you I was a very loose knitter. You can try it on when you get up. If you like.'

I didn't like. I knew that even with a shirt beneath it would scratch. But she'd put such effort into it and besides, her loving smile told me I had no choice.

I was now more awake with a mind filled once again with

thoughts of clocks, Time, the Tree, the Power of Hands, and Aloysius.

'I know why you brought me here.'

Granny heard what I said but she had her eyes fixed upon the open window.

'Cold winters are good for dormice,' she said, staring out into the cloudless day. 'They sleep till May. But if awoken too soon by an early spring, a sudden frost will kill them.'

Granny turned her head back to me.

'Readiness is all, William, and I worry sometimes you're still as green as leeks.'

Dormice? Leeks? What was she trying to tell me with these riddles? That I needed more time? But time for what?

I repeated what I had said.

'I know why you brought me here.'

'D'you, now?'

'Yes. Aloysius is the Stopper of Time. And the Tree by the Power of Hands extends that gift to the whole house. Here there is no Time, so whatever it is I'm running from cannot touch me.'

'Oh, Aloysius is an errant Fopdoodle! And if he was on the other side of the tunnel, I wouldn't give him the steam off my tea.'

I felt a pain in my hands, mainly scabs now, but those cuts into my flesh were still red.

'Don't say that!' I yelled. 'The house will hear. And we'll be punished!'

But Granny was in no mood to be told anything.

'Let it hear! And I hope that horrible little Fopdoodle is listening too.'

Granny spun her head and began yelling at the bare beams and wooden walls, 'Aloysius, you are a wicked soul with a verminous little mind! So there! Oh, even as a child he liked to squeeze a bruise.'

And she wasn't finished yet.

'Yes, you can hold back Time. Slow it down to the beat of a dying angel's wing. And yes,' she went on, shaking her fist at the floorboards, 'the Tree empowers you. But no! You cannot end Time, Aloysius Zachariah. No man or woman – or even a Swidger – can. Time may be snarled and bridled, trapped and locked, clasped and pinned, but no, not stopped. At least not forever.'

Granny now looked at me.

'Your body is young and wants to grow. Theirs did too, once. They were just boys, like you. But living in this house they grew up stunted. Not only in body, but mind and heart, too. But you're right, William, you are safer here, though I said there'd be a cost. What else could I do? Would it be this world of wounds or defeat on the other side of the tunnel by the Force that seeks you? There's little choice in rotten apples.'

I had never seen Granny like this. Rage almost, yet with it, a deep sense of regret. An uneasy silence followed. I knew that what she had said, she had wanted to say for a long time. And now it had been said I felt it was up to me to lighten the mood.

'When we first arrived,' I told her, 'do you know what I thought the men were?'

'What?'

'Vampires.'

Did I see a half smile? Yes, I think so.

'Vampires? Ye gods and little fishes! What made you think that?'

'Those gravestones. On the embankment. Then there was that funny ritual at the threshold. And in the kitchen, when you were busy with that blanket, I saw Gibble and Rutley moving a wooden trunk about. And some soil fell out.'

'Soil? That'll be for the Tree. It's a powerful tree but still a tree. But vampires? Fancy you coming up with that.'

But Granny's grinning face slowly turned more serious as she walked over to the window and pushed it wide open.

'Do you know, you can't help feeling sorry for them, because they are like vampires. They've survived, but never ever lived. All those empty years, what have they done with them?'

'But what made Aloysius so cruel?'

'The hurt born of being hurt that then wants to hurt others even at the cost to itself. Spite is the simple word for it. And that's a hurt that always needs feeding.'

'But I never hurt him.'

'No, but all his life he has carried a scar inside. The hurt of being discarded. He never forgave and he never forgot. And now he wants others to feel pain too. That is what spite can do to a person. Even a Swidger.'

'Why didn't you stop him?' I asked.

'Why didn't you?' she replied.

But I already knew the answer.

'Because I'm not ready.'

'No, you can't take a spoon to a knife fight. And Aloysius is nothing compared to what awaits you. But I was proud the way you stood up to him. Like Daniel in the lion's den. And the way you worked it all out. Oh yes, you've really started to think round corners.'

Granny closed the window, walked back to my bed and again began to stroke the hairs on my chin.

'But you're gonna need a lot more of that now these are sprouting out of you.'

I raise my hands to my chin. Stubble. Or something like it. Rough and soft at the same time. I feel one hair that's more wiry than the others. Like a tiny needle growing from my face. Weird. I touch my cheeks, but they're still smooth. The disappointment must have shown on my face because Granny laughs.

'Well, ha-ha,' she chuckles, 'it's not quite seeded there yet, but it will. Change is coming. You're young and your body wants to grow. Once you were the candle too easily blown out, but the wind that killed the flame may well now kindle the fire.'

Oh, not another riddle.

'But what is the change that's coming?' I ask, playing again with that wiry hair on my chin. 'And how will I know? Will I feel it or see it?'

Granny laughs again. 'Feel it, yes, see it, no.'

'Why?'

'You'll understand when it happens.'

That which she talked of would come to pass today. And no, I did not see it. No eye could. But again I jump ahead.

I always felt that morning that Granny had wanted to tell me more but suddenly from downstairs we heard a loud clanging of metal. The armoured boy. But this was no call to dinner. It was fast and urgent. And became more so with every strike.

The door flung open and two voices spoke at once.

'Aloysius –'

'– is distemperate.'

'He holds the parchment in his hand –'

'– it is as rare as the Phoenix!'

'– and he reads it as we speak.'

'You were right, Edwin –'

'– I know, the Boy should never have come here.'

Next, as ever with the twins, came a shared expression, but this was one I had never seen before: the face of fear.

'He commands you to come down –'

'– to listen to his pronouncement.'

'We gather now. Edwin!'

'I know, Elwin. I feel it too.'

They then ran from the room without even closing the door.

Granny pursed her lips and then said, quite casually, 'Listen to Mister Fopdoodle wittering on, I'd rather eat my own foot. But there'll be hell to pay if we don't, so I better go down and see what the big to-do is all about. You get dressed. It's a cold day so why not try on your new jumper.'

She then passed me the woollen heap and left me to get ready.

I was right, even with a shirt beneath, the coarseness scratched like crazy. And it was way too big. I looked like a sack full of nothing.

What good would I be against the power of Aloysius? And the loyalty of those who surround him?

CHAPTER FORTY-THREE

Cobwebs

BY NOW THE clanging of the armour coming from downstairs had stopped and all through the house there was a strange and empty silence. Even the staircase had given up its creaking.

Everyone was gathered in the dining chamber. At least I thought it was everyone. Missel Meeler was stood next to Aloysius, unmoving except for anxious eyes. Marsden was on his other side, his grey gloved hands nervously gripping at his even greyer robes.

As for Gibble and Rutley, they were sat cross-legged on the floor, with Rutley staring up in the air and making a curious blowing noise. I followed his gaze to the top of the tapestry. There I saw a floating feather. With each blow, Rutley was pretending to control its direction, though of course it was really only the draft that was coming in from under the window.

Salton Manning stood alone, running his swollen fingers along the wooden veins of the table. Those bands on his hands now looked heavier and tighter.

Two more had their back to me, but Brewster Blaxton was recognisable by his beard, which in the morning sunshine looked more like birch and bracken, and the other was Allard, who was easy to spot with that shaved head of his.

But someone was missing.

The Twins, who had been standing near the tapestry, now walked towards me and positioned themselves either side.

Were they now my guards?

I tried a polite nod but they just looked ahead at Aloysius, who began to speak.

'Make ready with the flint and taper,' he ordered. Marsden's hand dropped into the side pocket and Meeler lifted up a long thin taper with his equally long thin fingers.

'No more bed sheets for the Boy,' Aloysius bellowed. 'He shall have straw. And a wooden crate. If he should yammer let him remember Procrustes in the Greek myth, who, when his guest complained his bed was too short, had the protestor's feet chopped off to fit it.'

Allard added to this last remark a gleeful snort.

'Haghgahharrgh!'

'I am a facinorous spirit,' Aloysius went on, 'and have been from the hour of my nativity. *This* changes nothing.'

What 'this' was became clear when Aloysius raised high a piece of linen-like parchment, which, until then, had been hidden behind his back.

What I heard next is difficult to describe. A breathless gasp, a wheezing whine, more like an animal in distress than words. 'Ahhssrhhaasshaha!' And it came from everyone in the room and wouldn't stop until Aloysius put a fist above his head and pressed his thumb against the air.

'Oppose me and you will weep seas! By a rope you will hang high – and your feet shall swing at my head.'

I tried to catch Granny's eye but found only Aloysius's intent stare.

'Lady is wise but not even Solomon could help you now. I say once more,' Aloysius barked, 'nothing shall change. *Nothing!*'

As he spoke these words, all heads turned. Someone had just entered. I spun round.

Of course, that's who was missing: blind Zavier.

The room stilled to hear what he had to say.

'There is a raven at the threshold and it has cried three times!'

The name of the bird echoed about the room. In shock. In wonderment. In disbelief. In panic. But most of all in dread.

'Raven?'

'Raven!'

'*Raven.*'

'Raven –'

'RAVEN!'

'Rav... en.'

Aloysius stamped his foot in fury.

'The flint! The taper!' Aloysius demanded, but he had to say it three times more before it was even heard.

At last the room quietened, but only to a whispering discontent. The taper was lit and passed to Aloysius who thrust it in the air with such vigour that the flame almost went out. His hands shook as he put the linen parchment to it. Even so, the document, whatever it was, took light and soon burned fiercely.

'See how easily its words catch fire and die. I tell you, nothing will change! *Nothing! Nothing!*'

And yet everything already had.

No one ever knew for sure what the parchment had said. Or how it had arrived. Perhaps, I thought later, it had always been there. Waiting for me. But whatever its origins, the dwellers of that house knew that to destroy it was to deny Destiny itself. And for Swidgers, that is the act of a fool. And no one wants to be ruled by a fool.

Aloysius tried raising the burning parchment even higher, but no one took any heed, for all eyes now ignored those flames and looked to me. But it was far more than that: they were turning against Aloysius. Who made the first move I could not say, but it was as if they were as one. United in treachery.

Even Gibble was on his feet. I hadn't noticed him get up but there he was, standing stiff and tense. Rutley was the only one not standing, he was still on the floor. Gibble tapped at his shoulder, but Rutley's mind seemed elsewhere. Once more I followed the line of his gaze. That feather again. Still high in the air. But now something had joined it. A floating fragment of burning parchment had separated itself from the rest.

Suddenly I felt that sharp pain across my forehead. More penetrating than before. Without thinking I closed my eyes and let out a cry.

'Ahhhhhh!'

Whatever the men saw when I opened them again took a moment for them fully comprehend, yet when they had, they gasped. And I did too, for now they were all bowing before me. What had they seen? I knew not.

What happened next all occurred in what seemed like an instant, but there were three distinct parts. First, the cry.

When Aloysius saw the bowing, his pink face became blood red with anger. Thinking of it now, I'm not sure he ever fully understood why his authority was disappearing. Nevertheless, he was Aloysius and he wasn't finished yet.

'You fools,' he yelled. 'I shall go to the Tree! The Tree is mine and mine alone! Mine! Mine!! Arrrhhhhrrrh!'

That was the cry. Now I shall tell you of the cat and the twins.

Beauty had been lying at Aloysius's feet but felines have sharp senses and he must have known what was to come. And so that cat scarpered quick and somehow disappeared. Where Beauty had fled, I could not tell but Elwin saw and now ran after it, with Edwin following.

And finally, and fatally, part the third: the cobwebs.

If people tell you that cobwebs do not burn, they are, of course, correct. But cobwebs by their very nature are traps, capturing and holding whatever comes their way. Not just flies but fluff and hair, feathers and moths, even cat fur and decomposing mice. Such were the cobwebs behind that floor-length tapestry. Perfect kindle for fire. And what set them aflame was that floating piece of burning parchment that only Rutley and I had seen.

The shock of the blaze was immediate. At first just a firecracker of sparks, but the frail cords that held the tapestry aloft soon took light. The threads were old and dry and showed no resistance.

Down the tapestry fell.

The cobwebs behind the arras now had air and the flames seized on it. In a flash, scorched and burning debris took flight in all directions.

Gibble panicked. The door to the chamber where the boy's armour was kept was the easiest means of escape but fear does strange things to people and Gibble rushed to the window and tried to open it. A struggle at first, as the catch was rusty, but at last he managed to lift it.

Was that the moment I knew the true danger of what was happening? Maybe. For the wind that blew, to borrow Granny's riddle, now gave life to the fire and the flames it bred spread all about.

This fire was now taking hold.

CHAPTER FORTY-FOUR

Edwin and Elwin

AS THE TAPESTRY lay in a burning mass against the skirting boards, Granny shouted to me, 'The timbers –'

But I finished her sentence for her, '– are soaked in paraffin!' No Solomon was needed to know this house would burn. And quickly, too.

Aloysius must have seen enough of the flames to recognise the growing threat, but even so, he disavowed what was now all around him.

'The Tree! The Tree will save us!' he cried, as he raced through the door into the room where cockroaches had been my torment.

Now everywhere the wood was afire and already that tart smell of burning paraffin pervaded the air. But could Aloysius be right? Could the Tree save the Old Coach Inn? Granny's thoughts and mine were one. She shook her head.

'Not even living wood could survive this. And much of the timber in this house has been dead for years. It is ending, William Arthur, it is ending!'

'Edwin!' Elwin was shouting. 'We must find Beauty. I will not let him die. Come! We must.'

If I had to choose between the two, I would say it was Elwin who was the slight subordinate of his brother. And so it was here, for Edwin was against the rescue. And forceful with it.

'No, Elwin, we must save ourselves.'

But Elwin had already disappeared through an open panel in the wall that, with a push of his hand, had somehow become a door. And next to it I saw a small hole in the skirting. Just large enough for a fleeing cat. So that's how Beauty had escaped.

Edwin called after his brother, but it was too late. Elwin was gone and, without hesitation, Edwin, brushing aside the burning debris, followed.

I looked to Granny. She knew what I was thinking.

'Don't! Don't!' she urged. 'Leave them to their fate.'

By now the flames were everywhere. They had taken control and the house would soon be theirs.

'I must –' I cried, only this time it was Granny who finished my sentence.

'– not let them perish. I know. But be careful, William.'

In that briefest of moments, Granny's eyes told me so much. I believed she wanted me to defy her.

She clasped at her blouse and hollered, 'Remember, you will be protected.'

Of course! The alum rinse. In the yarn of my jumper. 'Protects against fire,' she had said.

'Go!'

I rushed towards the hidden panel door, flames all about me. But even as I ran, I was thinking that blasted cat could be anywhere.

Where did it like to hide? Yes, that corridor where I had found the boxes and the twins knew that too.

That open panel of theirs led into a long passageway and at the end of it I found myself climbing through another secret door and into the entrance hallway.

And there was the door to the house with its stone threshold. A way in but also a way out.

I could just leave and be safe. I owe these people nothing, for they have shown me little but cruelty.

I begin to cough. That biting acrid smoke is everywhere, including on my lungs. I look to the staircase and then back to the stone threshold. Two paths lay before me, but which to take?

My mind goes back to where my story began, on that High

Street in north London. It was the same question: should I follow or not? We are who we are, but we always have choices in what we become. Did I want to be the Swidger who, when he could have saved others, only saved himself?

Again, there was no choice all at. And so I take those stairs. Two at a time.

When I reach the top, I see that the secret panel door in the wall is already open. Yes, the Mead Twins must have had the same idea as I have, that Beauty has run off to somewhere in that maze of corridors.

Peering inside I see the flickering light of a lamp. Who's holding it, Edwin or Elwin? I can't tell. Then I hear a voice call out, 'Help me! Help me!'

CHAPTER FORTY-FIVE

The House Cries

'HELP ME!'

The voice of one of the twins, but which? Edwin or Elwin?

I peer along that secret corridor on the landing and see the flickering light of a lamp and that voice shouts out again.

'Help me!'

'Elwin! Elwin!' comes the reply. 'Where are you? I'm in the corridor.'

'Edwin! I've found Beauty. I hold him now.'

'Then bring him to me, Elwin.'

'I cannot.'

'Why?'

'I fell. I thought I knew my way but in the dark I tripped over the boxes.'

'Are you hurt?'

'My leg is caught in the floorboards. I cannot free it. Oh Edwin, help me! Help me!'

The glow of what must have been Edwin's lantern suddenly disappears.

'It's William,' I cry. 'Keep calling out. I'll follow your voice. I'll help you find Elwin and together we can carry him out.'

As I go through that secret door I feel a slight tug, as if something is pulling on me, but there's no time to look back. The dark of the passageway is somehow different from what I remember. As I make my way along, I then realise the corridor is getting warmer. There's little smoke in here, and no flames, but there's heat coming from somewhere. Again, no time to think on that, and yet I must not rush. I don't want to trip and fall as Elwin has.

Carefully I follow the trail of that calling voice.

'Edwin! Edwin! I'm here! I'm here!'

Soon I see them. Edwin with his lamp and Elwin lying prostrate on his back, his foot trapped under a rotten floorboard and the cat Beauty grasped tightly in his arms.

'Why didn't you free yourself?' Edwin is asking.

'Because if I did, I would have had to let Beauty go.'

'Give him to me,' demands Edwin, putting down his lamp, but as soon as Elwin lets Beauty go, he flees them both and makes his escape.

'That stupid, stupid animal!' I exclaim. But no, that feline isn't stupid. It can smell the danger.

Elwin and Edwin turn and see me.

'Let me help,' I say to them.

I squeeze past Edwin and then climb over Elwin. I tell Edwin that I will lift his brother up by the shoulders so he can release the bleeding leg. My plan works but when the foot is freed more floorboards fall away around it and the flames beneath have new air to breathe and shoot up into Elwin's face.

'Ahhhh!' he cries.

'Come on, we better get out of here!' I tell them.

But Elwin's leg is so badly injured, he can only crawl. Yet somehow he manages to get past his brother. It was just a matter of inches but it made all the difference.

How suddenly it happened. And how easily it could have been me. Or the clambering Elwin. Who knew how rotten the floorboards were? Or how strong the fire below.

Edwin watched his brother drag himself to safety. He then turned round, perhaps to thank me. I like to think it was that. But I would never know. Because he just went. All of him. Through the floor. Not even a moment to cry out. Edwin just disappeared into the raging flames beneath.

CRASH!!!

In a way I'm glad Elwin didn't see it. Or was just hearing the noise of the drop worse?

'What's happened?' cried Elwin. 'Tell me! Tell me!'

But how could I? What was there to say?

'Edwin's fallen,' I tell him.

'Edwin! Get up! We must leave now. Get up, Edwin. Edwin! Why does he not reply?'

I think he knew. He was his twin, after all.

'He's gone, Elwin. He's gone.'

As I think on it now, it was almost like a magic trick. Edwin was there. And then he wasn't.

'You must save yourself, Elwin!'

'How can I? I cannot see! The flames, they've burnt my eyes.'

The gap in the floor was now so wide it would be difficult for me to cross it. And even if I managed to jump to where Elwin was, the floorboards could have easily collapse and taken us both with it.

Then I spotted something. And I let out a thankful sigh.

'Elwin!'

'What is it?'

'Elwin,' I said again. 'Move your hand six inches forward.'

'Why?'

'Just do it! Do as I say.'

He did.

'I've found something. String.'

No, not string. Yarn. Granny always said she was a loose knitter. That is what tugged me at the door. My jumper had snagged on that nail in the doorframe. But the thread would lead Elwin to safety.

'Follow it along, it will take you to the landing.'

'I want Edwin! I need Edwin!'

'I know you do. But your brother is gone. There's just you now. There's no time, Elwin. You must go.'

The flames were rising and getting closer. Almost at Elwin's feet. He must have felt the pain. He cried out, and then slowly, desperate and despairing, crawled away.

Flames! Flames! Flames!

Now was my moment to follow him. I knew if I was careful and kept my body close to the wall, I could maybe creep around on what little floor remained. Granny's knitted jumper, or what was left of it, would protect me. I had to believe it.

But that is something else I would never know, for just at that second, two timber joists fell across my path. And more rotten floorboards were fed to the fire beneath. I was cut off. No means of escape that way.

I must find another.

CHAPTER FORTY-SIX

The Seagull Cries

BUT I HAD lost my bearings. The smoke, it was all over the place, but I knew I was somewhere near where the corridors divided. I put out my hand into empty space. Please, I thought, let this not be the narrowing corridor.

With my arms stretched out to my sides, I touched my way along. But were they already being pushed in towards my body?

Yes.

And soon my nose scraped against that brick wall.

But wait, those loose bricks I removed that night to see the Tree outside, where are they?

I feel around. The wall is firm and solid. Has it been repaired? Not that it matters. The smoke grows thicker and the fire, ever closer.

No! I will not give up.

I spread my arms to explore all round the wall's edge. Is that a timber frame I've found? Perhaps where the bricks are now there was once a door. Yes, there's a gap between the wood and the mortar. And it's loose. Someone may have patched up those bricks but they haven't bothered round the edges.

I pull away at the mortar where the join is, tearing my skin as I do. It's working. The binding sand is old and it crumbles like broken biscuits. I can even see the daylight.

I don't want to turn around, but I must. I need to know how long I have left, but whatever time that is, it won't be enough, for everywhere the wood burns.

I keep pushing my shoulder against those bricks. Oh, if only it would loosen more, but it's a gainless task.

BOOOOOMMMMMMHHM!!!

A huge explosion rent the air. Powerful. Deafening. But what was it? And where did it come from? My feet begin to shake. Then I realise, no, it's not my feet, it's the floor itself. Beams all around me start to collapse and fall into the room below.

Then it happens. It was as if the whole house somehow twisted itself round to adjust to the jolt it had just received. I turn back to the bricks. My fingers feel around the frame. Yes, the blast has moved the timbers. Not much but part of the doorframe has come away.

Thank you, timbers! Thank you, wood! And thank you house!

The smoke is as dense as the fumes of hell. I must close my eyes. I don't need to see. I need to push. One more heave on this door-of-brick.

Yes, it's shifting, it's opening, but what will I find on the other side? The Tree, yes, but what else? I know I'm at least a storey high, I may be about to fall to my death.

I'm still pushing with eyes closed when the whole brick structure suddenly breaks free of its frame, falls forward and takes me with it. But into what? The empty air?

No, the slab and I are now sliding down what feels like a hill of rubble. I hold on tight and a few moments later we come to a bumpy stop. At last I can rub away the dirt and open my eyes. I see exactly what has happened. What I thought was a hill of rubble was a mound of loose soil piled up against the house.

Well, at least I'm safe. Only then I heard that voice.

'Boy! You shall not destroy my world. I will not let you.'

Aloysius!

There he was with his back to the Oak, his arms behind him, gripping its bark so very, very tightly. But was Aloysius protecting the Tree? Or was the Tree protecting Aloysius?

I heard cries in the air. I raised my head. So that is what those ghostly yowls had been when I saw the Tree in the moonlight.

Not phantoms or vampires but simply the squawks of seagulls.

My eyes were still watery but I could now see around me. That night when I peered through the loosened bricks, I'd not been able to make out what was beyond the Tree, except of course the moon, but now I could. It was the sea. And the Oak was dangerously near the cliff's edge.

Aloysius spoke again.

'Master William! The Destiny Parchment cannot lie. It foretold many things. Strangely, it said your future would be the past, but what else can that mean except you belong here in this house? Yes, yes, yes, you must stay. Touch my hand and together we will share the Tree and its strength.'

Aloysius reached out one arm, with his other still forcefully gripping the bark.

'The Tree will give us its wood and together, you and I, will rebuild the house with new timbers.'

Yet there was something about what I was seeing that wasn't right. I stepped to one side and now saw that the angle had been deceptive. The Tree was leaning away, attempting, I think, to distance itself from the burning house. Or maybe even its ruler himself.

'Take my hand, Boy! Take it, take it!'

As he said this, Aloysius smiled a smile of sneering smugness. Was he seeing something I was not? His eyes now became a vivid emerald green and they were staring at my feet.

I looked down, but hardly believed what I saw.

My legs were somehow moving forwards towards the Tree and now my arms were rising up and stretching out, reaching for the Tree and Aloysius. I tried to pull them back, I tried to stop my steps, but could not.

Suddenly what seemed like dark shadows surrounded me and a voice from nowhere cried out, 'Go no further, William Arthur!'

Zavier! Blind Zavier.

I spun my head. Yes, here he was behind me, his long black

cloak spread high in the air like a giant bat. His reddened hands took me by the shoulders.

That voice, though scratched and blistered, roared. And so loudly that it must have caused him pain, 'Aloysius! *Illi autem non habent*! You shall not have him!'

'Traitor!' yelled Aloysius. 'You will burn again, as you did before.'

Zavier held me back but my legs still wanted to move forward.

Aloysius stretched out his hand further.

'Let go of the Boy! Let him choose for himself,' he entreated. 'It is his life, not yours.'

Slowly Zavier's hold lessened and my legs, once more, began taking me to towards the Tree.

'Give in to its pull. It wants you. It knows your gift. It will help you enhance your power, as it did with me when I was "the Boy". Touch my hand, Child! Flesh on flesh. Give me your palm and know the Power of Hands and the Gain of the Tree!'

It was as if I was in a trance. I tried to resist, defy it, yet something inside kept drawing me towards them both.

I twisted my neck round to appeal to Zavier. Then I saw something behind Zavier's cloak? A steel head? The helmet on the armoured figure they used as a gong?

Yes! And it was moving. Was it alive? Must be, for now the helmet was trying to speak. Yet I couldn't make out the words as the visor was down.

Oh, but the pull of the Tree and Aloysius were too strong. I couldn't stop myself, and now my fingers and those of Aloysius were almost touching. But then, from behind Zavier's long black robe, I heard the sharp clang of metal on metal followed by a familiar voice.

'No, you don't, you nasty little Fopdoodle!'

A dainty gloved hand then pushed mine out of reach of Aloysius's grasping touch. I turned round. What a bizarre sight! Clothes badly burnt and wearing the armour boy's helmet, but still unmistakeably Granny.

She'd pushed the visor up so she could be understood, only now it's dropped down again with a clank. As it did, the hand that had saved mine was suddenly grabbed by the madman at the Tree. Aloysius pulled at Granny's glove until it loosened and fell to the ground. He then snatched her hand, it was now flesh on flesh and his grip was unyielding.

As Granny and Aloysius tussled and pulled, the Tree lurched back, bending itself closer to the cliff's edge. And it appeared to be gathering in its branches, as if holding itself in fear. And those branches soon wrapped themselves around Aloysius, as well.

'The Tree wants me!' he yelled, insanely. 'It needs me! It needs me! We will fall together!'

Clasping. Clinching. Clenching.

Those branches had now completely enveloped Aloysius. Yet Aloysius still had Granny in a knuckle-white grip.

'Well, if I cannot have the Boy, I will take Lady. Together we shall share our end.'

I grabbed Granny's other hand.

The Tree swayed once more and Granny was tugged away and all I had now was an empty glove. The Tree was teetering on the cliff's edge and would fall at any second – and take Granny with it.

CHAPTER FORTY-SEVEN

Sir Isaac Newton

I THREW GRANNY'S glove to the ground and grabbed her free hand once more. And there we were: the Tree and its branches holding Aloysius, Aloysius grasping Granny tight, and me trying to pull her away from it all.

Granny was shouting something. But the helmet visor across her face muffled her words. Again she shouted, but the more she yelled, the more muffled she sounded.

I turned to Zavier.

'Help us!'

Zavier did his best to pull me back but the palms of his hands were so scolded and blistered that the red skin flaked off and his grip was lost.

'I cannot!' he cried in despair.

'Boy!' shrieked Aloysius. 'Alone you will be. The prophecy said: the past will be your future and there you will willingly choose death.'

The Tree shook. Granny was still shouting something from behind the visor. If only I could tell what it was...

Of course!

With my free hand I pulled the shiny metal off her head. Now I could hear what she was saying, but I had already worked it out.

'Throw the bloody helmet at him!'

Even if Aloysius heard what she said, he never saw the helmet coming. My aim was good, right in the middle of his fat bald head.

The shock loosened his grip and I tore Granny away. Aloysius's body went back, then jerked forward. It was enough.

The Tree faltered for the last time and shuddering and trembling, it fell. So anchored to the rock were the deep roots, it took with it into the sea much of the cliff's edge. And, of course, Aloysius as well, trapped in its branches.

Granny cautiously looked down as he disappeared into the watery depths.

'Well, thank you, Sir Isaac,' said Granny, casually, 'and his Third Law of Motion.'

If I understood what she meant, I would tell you, but I didn't. And still don't.

The new cliff's edge was close to our feet, and loose rocks were still falling, so I seized hold of Granny's arm and pulled her to safety. I was worried too for Zavier, for where he stood was even closer to the new precipice.

'He's blind,' I said, moving towards him. 'He might fall.'

But Granny stopped me and went over to Zavier herself. She then took him by the hand and gripped it tight. All of a sudden, her green eyes brightened and dazzled. As they did, Zavier's own eyes came to life. No longer black and dead but a strange sparkling blue.

Granny let go of his hands and came back over to me.

'Don't look!' she begged. 'Please, don't look.'

I wanted to go to him, but she wouldn't let me. Instead, she gripped my arm tighter than anyone could have believed.

'No, William, no,' she said, tearfully. 'Look away.'

But I wouldn't. Zavier, with arms raised high in the salty breeze, was now weeping.

'Take it from me! I beg you, take it from me!' he howled, raising his blistered reddened hands high in the salty breeze.

'What's he doing? Who's he talking to?' I cried.

Clouds parted and the sun blinded in my eyes. When they adjusted to the light, Zavier was no longer there and in his place stood a boy. A boy even younger than me. And this blue-eyed child could see, because he smiled and waved and called me 'William Arthur'.

When the cliff took him, as he knew it would, Zavier's now young face told me he was content to let it. The wind blew wildly, and then waned and as it did an empty black cloak fell at my feet.

'What just happened?' I asked, but another falling tear was Granny's only reply.

The inn was still ablaze. We stood and watched for what seemed a lifetime and then Granny began to answer what questions she could.

It seemed that Zavier, who knew his way round the house with no eyes, had guided Granny through the smoke-filled corridors. His long black cloak was thick enough to resist the flames and Granny's many layers had guarded her. Plus she had taken the metal helmet in order to stop her long unruly hair from burning.

When the two saw me by the Tree with Aloysius, Granny hid behind Zavier's robe in order to make Aloysius think he had come alone.

'What about the explosion that rocked the house?' I asked.

'That came from the kitchen. Ammonia, hydrogen peroxide, as I told you when we were doing all that cleaning, is very unstable at high temperatures. And then there was the paraffin and the lime they kept nearby.'

'How did everyone escape?'

'Mainly through the window, but poor Allard knew he'd be the last, so he ran away. In the summer he'd hide himself in the pantry, the coolest part of the house. Perhaps that's where he went. Thinking he'd be safe. Oh, he was never the sharpest knife in the box.'

The timbers of the inn went on burning.

'Hundreds of years ago an acorn grew a tree. The energy that helped it thrive, the sunshine, became caught in the wood, but now the wood burns that sunshine escapes as flames.'

I thought for a moment.

'Coming here. Being safe. It wasn't just about Time, was it? It's about our energy, as well.'

'Story books will tell you Life is created of fire and clay.

Power and substance. Energy and being. But there is pure energy too. And that is something different, even in the science of the Commonality. My friend Albert explained it all.'

'Is your friend Albert the one I think he is?'

'Yes, Professor Einstein. A lovely man, though I never could get him to cut his hair. Albert put it like this: the hydrogen atom, bless it, is a humble little fella with only one proton. Despite protons being shy and not liking company, they will fuse if you push them together hard enough. And when you do, one of them will chuck away a positron and a neutrino thereby becoming a neutron. It's those bits which are pure energy.'

'But what do protons and neutrons have to do with being a Swidger?'

'To Albert, energy is about what's positive and what's negative, plus, I suppose, them poor neutrons that haven't made up their mind yet. But for us Swidgers, energy is more about what is good and what is bad.'

'When Aloysius was with the Tree, and reached out his hand to me,' I said, 'it was like I was in a trance. As if I wasn't in control of what I was doing.'

'We Swidgers are not angels. We are here for what is good, yet we can be drawn towards a darker energy. The path Aloysius chose when he was young took him to a shadowy place.'

'You once said, "Time is out of joint", and that we were "born to set it right."'

'An old sin casts a long shadow. But that's why we are here: to bring light to the darkness. Oh, but you'll understand it all soon enough,' she said, running her fingers across my stubbly cheek.

But I wanted to understand it then and there. And I half believed I did.

This Swidger energy Granny talked of, well, I was sure it was somehow connected to Albert's energy, too. The static from the train, the ECG unit at the hospital, the electrical cables on the High Street. Then there were those lightning flowers I'd seen on

Jayden's and Granny's hands. The link was electricity – the one energy the Old Coach Inn did not have. That's why I was safe here. Yet I still felt there was a piece missing in this jigsaw.

The house burned still. Sparks cracked and flew up from the timbers, the sea breeze raised them high, only to then release them and so now they floated upon us both as ash.

'Odd place to build an inn,' I said, rubbing my curls to get rid of it all.

'Well, the cliff edge wasn't here then, the sea was miles off. And it stopped being an inn when the railway came.'

'Is that when it became an orphanage?'

'Yes, but that cliff edge was always getting closer, with power of the waves forever crashing against it.'

'So the Tree would have eventually fallen into the sea, taking the inn with it,' I said.

'It would,' Granny replied. 'Time can be stilled, but never stopped. As I've said before, the future is always waiting.'

'Aloysius told me the parchment said my future would also be the past. What did he mean?'

'I don't really know. How very curious.'

'And there I would willingly choose death.'

Granny now looked to me.

'Don't worry yourself too much over what Aloysius said, for words can have many meanings.'

That black cloak of Zavier's still flapped against my feet in the wind and I thought again about what he'd said: 'Take it from me.'

In that moment I understood the enormity of what had happened. And my thoughts spoke for me without me even knowing.

'Zavier was giving back his Swidger energy. He wanted to die as – as –'

But Granny finished the sentence for me.

'As a *human* boy. We are like the Commonality in many ways. The only real difference between us and humans is our Swidger energy.'

'But if Zavier could give that back, that means *I* must be able to give it back as well. And then the gift I have – or would have had – will never even happen. And that means I'd be safe.'

Granny didn't answer but simply said, 'Come, time now to join the others.'

As Granny walked away, I began to see a different future for myself. The Dark Force wants my gift, but if I no longer had it, why would it seek me? I'd be human. And with a future free from danger.

What would be so wrong with that?

CHAPTER FORTY-EIGHT

The Seagull Cries Again

WHILE I HAD lived inside the wood of the Old Coach Inn, there was day and there was night, but I had never really seen the passing of time. Yet now the sun falling slowly into the horizon and as dusk came, only the stone walls of the kitchen and tall brick chimneys were left, each standing proud and defiant among the ashes.

The survivors had gathered at the entrance of the inn. Well, the stone threshold that remained. Meeler was being argumentative about something.

'I will not turn husband and sigh away my Sundays. I tell you, I will not be wenched. Exchange me for a bat if ever I were to do such a thing.'

Marsden saw our arrival and called over to Granny.

'There is talk of going to London,' he told her.

'London! A dog-hole that merits not the tread of a man's foot,' insisted a clearly distressed Meeler.

I looked about me. Odd what can survive a fire for there in amongst the debris was Granny's carpet bag. Perhaps someone had rescued it for her. But what caught my eye was a half-burnt piece of the tapestry and on it that coiled snake. Inside I suddenly felt a fearful shiver.

'Come hither, Boy,' a voice beckoned.

It was Salton Manning. I hardly recognised him for he had taken off his tunic and put on what looked like an army uniform. As ever, he was standing some distance from the others. Salton called me over again but, once more, I ignored him. I would not answer to that name.

The would-be soldier then came over. As he got closer, I saw the army uniform was in fact made from an old brown blanket. Salton put his hand on my shoulder. The copper rings that had bound his hand were gone but they'd left his fingers dark and green.

'I'm sorry, I should have called you William. If you are willing to listen, I have a final tale to tell,' he said. 'No monkey, just a boy and a snake. And this time, a viper.'

'Go on,' I replied.

'The viper's poison was deadly, but, unknown to him, the boy had developed a poison of his own, so when the attack came, the snake it was that died.'

Salton's manner as ever was brusque, but as he walked away, he added in a quieter tone, 'Find that poison, William, for it's all that can save you.'

I wanted to ask what he meant but Gibble had started crying noisily and Granny beckoned me over.

'Come with me and William to London,' Granny was saying to him, her arms round his shoulders trying to offer some comfort. 'There we'll find some bark of a birch. Cures warts, does birch bark.'

'No, Madam,' interrupted by Marsden. 'We have been tortive and erring in our path of life. When the moment comes, I know which train tunnel I will choose.'

Faltering footsteps could now be heard behind us, and I turned to see a limping Elwin aided by Brewster Blaxton. No need to ask if Elwin was blind for his head was unmoving and he saw not a soul. As his feet met the stone threshold, he stopped, as if waiting for someone to open the door. He did not yet know it was no longer there. Never had I seen anyone so alone.

Brewster left him to himself and went over to join Rutley, who was now excitedly running around shouting, 'Train-Tunnel-Train-Tunnel-Train-Tunnel!!!'

Weakened by the fire, the tallest of the brick chimneys all of a sudden collapsed and smouldering ashes rose into the air.

'Our consanguinity, gone,' whimpered Meeler.

Granny came over to me and said softly, 'Just think what good those Swidgers could have done had they lived in our world but that is the time that never was. Instead, they chose a long dead winter with no hope of spring. Oh, the poor little woodcocks. What are we to do with them?'

Again, that sharp pain came across my forehead.

'Ahhh!' I cried. 'What's happening to me?'

Gibble, still tearful, took from his tunic his looking glass, the one I had seen on the day of my arrival and put it to my face. I stared at myself. No difference, I thought.

Granny smiled.

'You don't look in a mirror that often, do you, William?'

'No,' I replied.

'Try again. Learn not just to look but to see.'

Yes, this time I did.

My eyes. No longer hazel but green. Not as bright as Granny's, but definitely green.

'We saw them begin to turn,' said Marsden, 'as Aloysius burnt the parchment letter. You have truly come of age, Master William Arthur.'

So that's why they all bowed.

From nowhere came a plaintive, 'Meow!' and then out from the rubble emerged a furry grey beast. It shook itself of ash and Beauty began to look more like himself. It ran straight to Elwin, brushing round his feet for attention. But none was given.

'Oh! That cat has had many lives, but I don't envy its new one,' said Granny. 'They had a dog here once. Savage thing, it was. Turned up out of nowhere. Oh, but it was no match for Beauty. Buried somewhere, it is. Not that any of that matters now.'

The sky was turning from gold to red.

'We ought to make a move,' announced Granny.

Brewster bent his head towards Granny's shoulder. I didn't

hear what was said but as we began to move away from the ruins, the grieving brother was left behind at the threshold, with blind a man's stare.

Greeting us at the top of the railway embankment, that seagull. Our last meeting seemed an age away. Perhaps it was.

We all climbed down the gravestone steps, me, Granny, Meeler, Gibble, Rutley, Marsden, Brewster and, at the rear, Salton Manning. There in front of us was the railway tunnel, no longer just an entrance but an escape. Though not, it seemed, for Marsden and Meeler.

'You're going the wrong way,' I shouted, as they began to walk along the track in the opposite direction.

'No, Master William, there is another tunnel beyond the bend,' replied Marsden, 'and that will take us to where we must go.'

'So, who's coming with me to London?' asked Granny, cheerfully. Rutley's hand went straight up and Gibble's reluctantly followed. Brewster then stepped forward to join us, as did Salton Manning.

'We wish you well,' said Marsden, moving away, 'but our tunnel will take us to a different land.'

'And you must come with us, Gibble,' added Meeler.

A disappointed Gibble lowered his arm, took hold of Rutley and began to pull him in their direction. But Rutley was having none of it and grabbed hold of Granny's scorched apron and refused to budge. Gibble saw it was no use, let go and ran off to join Marsden and Meeler. I don't think he knew what that final destination would be, but the others did, for there was deep sadness in their eyes.

So, it would be Granny, Rutley, Brewster, Salton Manning and me who would go to London. But as we entered the railway tunnel, Granny said we could not be sure.

'A Swidger tunnel will only ever take us where it believes we should go. But I do hope it is London because, in all my years, I've never been to St Paul's. But it's never our decision, only the tunnel's.'

Perhaps so. But by now I had made a choice of my own.

If Zavier could become a human boy again then why not me?

Of course I didn't understand how, but I knew it was possible because I'd seen it with my own eyes. Yes, I knew who and what I was but now I simply didn't want to be it. And that is what that wicked world of the Old Coach Inn had done to me.

As we walked along, the dying light of the day faded and the cold darkness of the railway tunnel soon took its place. The tunnel, unlike before, seemed to go on for miles and miles, but appeared straight enough. Even so, to avoid walking into the brick walls, we kept our steps to the old wooden sleepers that ran down the middle. And it was decided as well that it was probably best if we didn't speak, as the echo was very distracting.

At first, we kept together as much as we could, but then Salton Manning quickened his pace and the noise of his marching footsteps soon disappeared.

'Oh, he's an oyster, that one,' Granny whispered. 'Prefers his own shell.'

I was now leading the way, with Granny and Rutley close by, and Brewster a few steps behind carrying Granny's carpet bag.

As I walked, I thought more and more about my time in the house. And it's cruelty. These thoughts made me firmer in my belief that I no longer wanted any part of the Swidger world. And if trees could hear, then maybe tunnels too, so I whispered to the sooty brick, 'I don't want to be who I am, so take me where I will become what I need to be.'

Rutley all of a sudden interrupted these thoughts, shouting excitedly, 'Train coming! Train coming! Train coming!' We all stopped for a moment to listen, but the tunnel was deathly silent. No sign of movement at all.

Granny started jabbering away nineteen to the dozen, and that seemed to settle Rutley. Plus the promise of a toy train when we reached our destination.

We seemed to walk for hours and hours. There was still no hint of light, but was we walked I had the feeling that what we were stepping on had changed from wooden sleepers to something more like concrete. It was then I began to see sort of light ahead. Green, I think.

Where had the tunnel brought us?

I began to make out metal tracks on the ground and to the side there was some sort of tin box. As we passed it, I could just about make out impressed lettering down the side: LONDON UNDERGROUND. On the wall there was some sort of yellow marker, with letters and numbers and below it some words I now read aloud, 'CHARING CROSS STATION.'

Then I saw that the green light was on a signal box. Suddenly there was a rumbling sound and I could feel the air hitting our faces like a wind.

'Train here! Train here! Train here!' Rutley was shouting, excitedly.

He was right, there was a train. And it was coming straight towards us.

William and Granny to return in
The Time They Saved Tomorrow

The Time That Never Was

Thought Notes for book clubs and reading groups

William is an orphan. There are many stories which feature a girl or boy who has no mother or father. Why do you think this is?

The book is called *The Time That Never Was*. Why do you think it's called that? And what does the word 'Time' mean to you?

People have said that they really, really love Granny because she's so funny. What is it about her, do you think, which makes people like her so much? And why do people laugh at the things she says?

William Arthur describes the colour of Granny's hair as ginger and the clothes she wears as having lots of flower patterns, but what do you think her face looks like? If you have an image of Granny in your head, why not draw it or paint it. And if you have Twitter you can even tweet it to @SwidgerBooks.

William doesn't really talk about what he looks like, but what is the picture you have of William in your own mind as you read? And again, if you'd like to draw it, why not Tweet it to @SwidgerBooks.

If you could ask the writer of this story one question what would it be?

When Granny took William Arthur to the Old Coach Inn, what did you think he would find there? And when its secret was finally revealed, were you surprised?

Which character in the story would you most like to meet?

Granny says that Echo is a 'Hopeful Monster' because he has a Swidger 'gift' that allows him to hear almost everything. But if you were able to hear everything that everybody says, do you think that would be a good thing or a bad thing?

In book two, *The Time They Saved Tomorrow*, there are several characters that come back into the story. Obviously William and Granny return, but which other folk would you most like to meet again? And which characters would give you the biggest surprise if they did come back?

Not everything in the book is explained because there are still two more books to come, but what is the one thing that you weren't told in *The Time That Never Was* that you would most like to know right now?

The writer has said that he based Granny on his two grandmothers and his many aunties. Who in your family would make a great character in a story?

Without giving too much away, in the next book, *The Time They Saved Tomorrow*, William and Granny do a bit of time travelling. If you could travel in time, where in history would you most like to go? And where wouldn't you like to end up!

Acknowledgements

Advice and encouragement. Guidance and suggestions. Ideas and changes. Corrections and warnings. Contacts and emails. Recommendations and endorsements. Concepts and plans. Images and covers. Promotion and marketing. Put all these together and eventually a book is born. But each step along the way is only possible with the help of colleagues, friends and neighbours. And *Swidgers* has been no different and so now I would like to acknowledge the contributions and assistance made by Rachel Adams, Dhanil Ali, Ali Belbin, Ninia Benjamin, Jindi Banwait, Matthew Barnbrook, Mandy Bateman, Sonia Beldom, Matthew Bielby-Nichols, Ian Billings, Jack Bowman, Neil Binley, Jon Bradshaw, Rory Bremner, Steve Britton, Gaynor Conner, Tim Cherry-Jones, Ed Clarke, Sercha Cronin, George Dyer, Phil Eason, Kathryn Ellinas, Simon Ellinas, Joseph Elliott, Jane Harrison, Steve Holyland, Dick Fiddy, Kevin Flynn, Robin Kingsland, Bradley Foster, Barry Gurney, Clare Knowles, Joshua Knowles, Oliver Knowles, Justin Johnson, Jenny Lecoat, Kate Lennard, David Lodge, Helena Maitland, Jonathan Maitland, Mark Mander, Sue McGorrigan, Alistair McGowan, Kyl Messios, Collette Nicolle, David Nicolle, Geoff Norcott, Sam Page, William Palmer, Nathan Pattison, Dane Preece, Marcus Prince, Lesley Richardson, Jenny Slater, Carolyn Scott-Jeffs, Sam Supple, Paul Smith, Kate Somerby, Paul Sullivan, Nodari Tamarashvili, Julia Tarnoky, Adam Trembath, Giles Usher, Jim Waites, Johnny Walker, Tim Wallers, Jean Woods, Eddie Woods, Clair Woodward, Sue Yates and Zeb Soanes. A special thanks to Chris Davis at CDM for his faith and persistence and to Gavin MacDougall and his brilliant team at Luath Press for their hard work and creativity, plus my editor Alice Latchford for her many improvements and amendments.

Then, of course, there's family. Those who came before, who inspired the book, and those who come after, for whom it is written. 'Granny', you see, is both my grandmas and every auntie I ever knew when I was growing up. They're all in her somewhere! And my biggest joy in writing *Swidgers* has been to pass 'Granny' on to my family today, especially my niece Jordan and my nephew Scott. They tell me that in reading the book they've learnt a few things about me too. Yes, I think they worked out who William really is…

Resources

The *Swidgers* official website – www.swidgers.com – offers some fascinating extras for readers of all ages. There's *Orphans and their Mentors* which looks at the history of lost children and orphans in stories ranging from Moses in the Bible to the Australian soap opera *Home and Away*. There's also a FREE ONLINE BOOK on Time Travel called *Telling the Tales of Time*. It's a brilliant read that's available to all and it explores the history of many famous time travel stories, including favourites such as *Doctor Who* and *Back to the Future*. It's a scientific book as well because it asks the question 'Is time travel really possible?' – and the answer may well surprise you! There's another section on the website called *Curiosities and Trivia* and that looks at the influences behind *Swidgers*, including where the name came from, the writer's own school days and favourite stories that helped shape and inspire the book. Happy reading!